THE HONEYMOON MURDERS

*Louise Brindley titles available from
Severn House Large Print*

I Remember You
A Presence in Her Life
Time Remembered
View from a Balcony

THE HONEYMOON MURDERS

Louise Brindley

Severn House Large Print
London & New York

This first large print edition published in Great Britain 2006 by
SEVERN HOUSE LARGE PRINT BOOKS LTD of
9-15 High Street, Sutton, Surrey, SM1 1DF.
First world regular print edition published 2005 by
Severn House Publishers, London and New York.
This first large print edition published in the USA 2006 by
SEVERN HOUSE PUBLISHERS INC., of
595 Madison Avenue, New York, NY 10022.

British Library Cataloguing in Publication Data

Brindley,   Louise
     The honeymoon murders - Large print ed.
     1.   Honeymoons - Scotland - Lewis with Harris Island - Fiction
     2.   Serial murders - Scotland - Lewis with Harris Island - Fiction
     3.   Detective and mystery stories
     4.   Large type books
     I.   Title
     823.9'14 [F]

     ISBN-13:   9780727875297
     ISBN-10:   0727875299

Printed and bound in Great Britain by
MPG Books Ltd, Bodmin, Cornwall.

PART ONE

PART ONE

One

It had been an emotional goodbye. As Bill's hatchback drew away from the kerb, hands were raised in farewell, kisses blown, and a drift of confetti, thrown by Bill's mischievous sister Rio, had landed on the bonnet of the car.

'Trust Rio,' Bill chuckled, 'I wouldn't put it past her to have bunged a potato in the exhaust.' He spoke lightly to minimize the pain of departure from the group of close friends and family gathered together on the pavement to speed the newly-weds on the first stage of their belated honeymoon in Bonnie Scotland.

'You OK, love?' he asked his bride concernedly, noticing the tears in her eyes.

'Yeah, I guess so,' Gerry Bentine, née Mudd, replied uncertainly, waving back at the people on the pavement until the car turned a corner and they were out of sight. 'Oh Bill, what a marvellous send off! What ever put the idea of a farewell party into your head?'

'Oh, *that*?' A stickler for the truth, 'It

wasn't my idea,' he admitted. 'Ma, Rio and Maggie Bowler cooked it up between them. Maggie did the catering while Ma and Rio rounded up the guests. *I* simply acted under orders.'

Bill was rather good at that, Gerry thought, remembering that acting under her own orders he had gladly agreed to a week long postponement of their honeymoon to spend more time with his family – his mother, whom he fondly referred to as 'Ma', his sister Rio and their menfolk who had flown respectively from San Francisco and the south of France, to attend the wedding.

Liking her 'in laws' enormously, it had seemed a crying shame to Gerry to rob Bill of their company straight after the wedding reception. Come to think of it for her too, when they could have a whale of a time showing them the sights of London. Visiting the Tower of London, Westminster Abbey, St Paul's Cathedral, and so on. Not to mention treating them to afternoon tea at the Ritz and dinner at the Savoy followed by visits to the West End theatres to see *Mamma Mia* and *The Mousetrap*. In short, to give them the holiday of a lifetime – in Bill's company. After all, who knew when they would all be together again? His beloved 'Ma' was now happily married to a jovial American lawyer, Martin Broomfield and his sister Rio was engaged to a handsome young Frenchman,

Henri Ducroix.

It had certainly been a week to remember, Gerry thought happily, despite having put her and Bill's honeymoon back a week. But here they were, alone together at last, on the first stage of their journey to wedded bliss.

Leaning her head against Bill's shoulder, Gerry said mistily, 'Promise me one thing, darling. When we get to where we're going, let *me* sign the register. Where *are* we going to, by the way?'

Frankly, Bill hadn't the faintest idea. Hopefully to a decent hotel, en-route to the Outer Hebrides which Gerry had chosen as their ultimate destination. Far removed from the rush and bustle of city life he hoped they could spend time together in blessed seclusion, listening to the sound of lake water lapping the shore, holed up in some kind of shepherd's bothy with Gerry cooking fish over an open fire. Fish caught by himself, perhaps? But he'd never caught a fish in his life. As for building a fire, his mind boggled at the thought.

Tired of driving, with rain beginning to fall like stair-rods from a leaden sky, all Bill wanted right now was a king-size bed, a decent meal, a hot bath, a close shave, and a good night's kip with his beloved beside him. A sleeping arrangement devoutly wished for since he'd spent the first week of married life beneath an eiderdown on a couch in Gerry's studio on the top floor of her Hampstead eyrie. Whilst she had occupied a single bed near the fire-escape door, falling fast asleep as soon as her head touched the pillow.

Cheered by street lights shining through the rain of what appeared to be the outskirts of a sizeable town with neon signs penetrating the gloom, Bill said, placatingly, 'Don't worry, darling, we'll soon be home and dry.' While he nosed the bonnet of the hatchback into the driveway of a brightly lit hotel with a Vacancy notice in its downstairs window.

'You go on ahead, darling,' he insisted, 'get indoors out of the rain, I'll bring in the luggage.' He added, tongue-in-cheek. 'A penthouse suite would be nice, with room service, champagne and caviar. Let's make this a night to remember.'

'Sorry, Miss,' the receptionist said apologetically when Gerry waltzed up to the desk to book a double room, dinner, and a full English breakfast for the morning. 'All we have left is singles. Two nice little en-suite rooms on the top landing. Ever so comfy. I'd take them if I was you. Folk have been flocking in since the rain started. The way of the world, ain't it? Half an hour earlier and you'd have struck lucky.'

The way of the world indeed, Gerry thought wryly, wondering what the hell her bridegroom would say faced with another night of solitary confinement. On the other hand, any port in a storm. At least the rooms were 'en-suite' and, with a modicum of luck, if they were adjoining rooms, they'd be able to tap out Morse messages to one another on the partition.

Bill had figured out beforehand that marriage to an unorthodox best-selling crime novelist would never be easy, predictable or boring, and had learned to 'roll with the punches'. Nothing that Gerry said or did really surprised him. The girl was prone to incidents, and often accident prone, with a genius for landing herself in hot water. In recent months she had become deeply embroiled in two murder investigations; had been abducted, shot at, very nearly smothered to death, and damn near strangled. She had taken it all in her stride, and had emerged as ebullient and good natured as she had been when they had first met for lunch in a Greek restaurant in Red Lion Square, with a view to establishing their author/agent relationship.

Love at first sight? Far from it. Initially, Gerry hadn't seemed his type at all. Hitherto, his preference had lain in slender women, not heavyweights with dietary problems, Cockney accents, a penchant for calling a spade a spade and a curious propensity for coming across corpses in unlikely places. It was when he'd come close to losing her in

11

the final stages of what the press had called the Antiques Murders, that he had realized how much she meant to him, that his life would seem empty without her, his brave, wonderful, resourceful, one and only Gerry Mudd.

Entering the lift together, en-route to the top floor landing, 'I'm sorry about the penthouse, Bill,' she said dejectedly. 'I just figured we'd better stay put than venture out in the rain again. This way, at least we'll have dinner, bed and breakfast to look forward to. Are you cross with me?' Sighing deeply, aware of her shortcomings, 'No matter how hard I try, I never seem to get things quite right somehow. Well, go on, Bill, admit it. Tell me exactly what you think of me?'

Bill chuckled. 'As if you didn't know! At least you got one thing right. You *married* me, didn't you? So let's stop pining the loss of the penthouse, champagne and caviar served in our double room. How about cocoa and cheese and pickle sandwiches as an alternative?'

'I don't deserve you, Bill,' Gerry said softly as the lift doors opened on a long corridor, of which Gerry's room was at one end and Bill's at the other. Suddenly, they fell about laughing, safe in the knowledge of their absolute rightness for one another, with the best yet to come. Not tonight, but tomorrow night, in the honeymoon suite Bill had booked for them at the Cockburn Hotel in Edinburgh.

The rain had stopped, the sun was shining early next morning when Bill and Gerry emerged from the Cumberland Hotel on the outskirts of Rotherham to continue their journey to Bonnie Scotland. They had dined reasonably well the night before, on tomato soup, grilled steak and chips, apple pie and custard. Adequate if not world shaking cuisine. Breakfast was bacon, eggs, sausages, toast and marmalade. Now they were eagerly anticipating the open road before them on a clear, bright October morning aglow with happiness and well being.

Seated at the wheel of the car, Bill sang lustily, '"It was a lover and his lass, with a hey and a ho and a hey nonny nonny no".'

Gerry grimaced painfully, 'Don't ring us. We'll ring you.'

Bill continued, unabashed, '"In springtime, in springtime, the only pretty ring time, when birds do sing hey ding a ding a ding, sweet lovers love the spring".'

'OK, Pavarotti, you win.' Gerry laughed. 'Now how about something more in keeping? "Loch Lomond" or "I Love a Lassie"? On second thought, don't bother?' She continued happily, 'Oh, Bill, isn't this feeling of freedom simply wonderful? Just to think that we have a whole fortnight of freedom ahead of us. No strings, no connections, no phone-calls, no deadlines to meet. No plots to thicken in my case, no clients with writers' blocks in yours. Just peace, perfect peace.'

'Yeah, sure,' Bill enthused. And yet, for no apparent reason whatever, he felt suddenly uneasy, apprehensive, wishing that they had brought mobile phones with them – just in case. In case of what? Darned if he knew. Just a vague premonition of danger?

Bill headed the car north east towards the Yorkshire Wolds, a quieter more scenic route, to Gerry's delight. Revelling in her new found feeling of freedom, she expressed her appreciation of uncluttered skylines, rolling acres of farmland, tucked away hamlets with cobbled streets, greystone churches and picturesque pubs with tempting 'Food Available' signs in pebble-dashed forecourts.

They had lunched on roast beef sandwiches and blackberry and apple pie at the Bluebell Inn, near Driffield. As she ate Gerry had pushed to the back of her mind a former visit to Yorkshire one snowy day in the not too distant past, to attend the funeral of a murder victim called Annie Scott. The memory still haunted her – an innocent girl who hadn't deserved to end up strangled to death in a women's lavatory at King's Cross Station, at the hands of a crazed killer, now detained at Her Majesty's pleasure, in the security wing of a prison for the protection of the criminally insane.

Bill said understandingly, 'If you're thinking what I think you're thinking, Gerry love, forget about the past. All that matters now is the future. *Our* future. OK?'

Gerry smiled wistfully. 'Yeah, Bill,' she said. 'You're perfectly right, as usual. Thanks, love. So let's crack on to Edinburgh, shall we? What time shall we arrive there, by the way?'

Bill laughed. 'At the rate we're going, around midnight at a rough guess!'

In the event, they arrived at the Cockburn Hotel in time for dinner. It was preambled by a quick visit to their honeymoon suite to glory in the sight of a four-poster bed, a luxuriously appointed en-suite bathroom, and a flower filled sitting room with sprawling settees, a wide screen television and a plethora of pink shaded lamps to provide a romantic atmosphere after the velvet curtains had been drawn to exclude the shining neon lamps tracing the outline of Princes Street in the busy thoroughfare below.

But Gerry didn't want the curtains drawn. She did, however, want her dinner – and what a dinner. Mouth-watering slices of Aberdeen Angus beef served with light-as-air Yorkshire puddings, slightly al-dente green vegetables, crisply roasted potatoes and a wine-enhanced gravy.

Extravagantly, Bill ordered a bottle of Bordeaux to complement the main course, a lighter white wine to accompany the raspberry pavlova. A grave mistake on his part, he realized, when Gerry started to giggle and to mispronounce her syllables. 'Ishn't thish delishous?' she said owlishly. 'I adore rash-perries, don't you?'

'Yes, darling.' Tenderly yet firmly, taking her hands in his, Bill helped her to her feet. 'Time for bed, love,' he murmured, escorting her from the dining room to the lift.

'Oh Bill,' she giggled, 'thish is so shudden. Hic. Pardon. Shorry, I burped.'

'Not to worry, love. It happens in the best of circles. Not feeling sick, are you?'

'No, I feel wunnerful!'

Steering her from the lift to their suite and propping her up against the wall while he unlocked the door, he switched on the lights and led her into the bedroom, where he lowered her on to the four-poster, took off her shoes, plumped up the pillows, covered her with the duvet, removed her glasses, kissed her forehead, and whispered, 'I'll be in the other room if you need me.'

Looking up at him, she murmured, 'I need you *now*, Bill.'

When, next morning, Gerry expressed a

16

wish to remain in Edinburgh a while longer, Bill had a word with the manager who assured him that the bridal suite would be available for a further twenty-four hours. He added, 'Am I right in thinking that your wife is the well-known crime novelist, Geraldine Frayling? She *is*?' The manager glowed. 'I've read all her books, and I do so admire her super-sleuth detective, Virginia Vale. A wonderful creation. Your wife must have a lively imagination, Mr Bentine.'

'That she has,' Bill concurred. 'Very lively indeed.'

'Does she have much trouble with her plots? Does she plan every detail beforehand?'

'No, she just makes them up as she goes along. That way, she keeps the readers – and herself – in suspense.' He was speaking the truth. Gerry often had trouble with her endings. In her own words, 'I start out with a rough idea who dun what. It's *why* they dun what they did that beats me.'

Later, imparting to Gerry the glad tidings that the bridal suite was available until the next day, she said soulfully, 'About last night. I behaved badly, didn't I?'

'Did you? I hadn't noticed.'

She blushed becomingly. 'I didn't mean *that*. I meant beforehand, in the dining room. I seemed to be talking tosh, as if I had a toffee stuck to the roof of my mouth. I must have had too much to drink. What do you think? All I remember drinking is one glass of Bordeaux and two glasses of mineral water with the pudd'n.'

'Ah, well then,' Bill said solemnly, 'it must have been the gravy.'

They had a marvellous day exploring Princes Street, visiting the Castle, the art galleries and Arthur's Seat. A lover and his lass, caught up in the magic of bagpipe music as a Scottish regimental band marched along Princes Street, kilts swirling and Glengarry ribbons flying in the breeze.

On their way back to the Cockburn, they bought postcards to send to friends and relations. His Ma and Martin would be back home in San Francisco now, Bill reckoned, Rio and Henri in the south of France. Their friends, Maggie and Barney Bowler, working at their hamburger joint and DCI Brambell and Bert Briggs up to their eyes in police work.

Not that Bill had a wish to draw Gerry's attention to Hampstead right now, considering the sinister events which had taken place there in the far from dim and distant past; the discovery of a dead body in a spinney on Hampstead Heath, for instance, and her abduction from a Hampstead supermarket car park by a psychopathic killer with yet another murder in mind. Her own.

Thank God, he thought fervently, that Gerry's bravery, resourcefulness and Cockney common sense, had brought her through that ordeal unscathed. So what if she couldn't tell the difference between wine and mineral water? He had scarcely known, or cared, if it was Christmas or Easter, on their wedding day when, floating down the aisle towards him, a vision of loveliness in her rose pink wedding dress and rose embellished straw hat, he had known, beyond a shadow of doubt, that she was the only woman in the world for him.

Now, here they were, together, in their bridal suite, planning the next stage of their journey to the Outer Hebrides. Bill's heart sinking at the thought of exchanging the four-poster for a palliasse. Inured to his creature comforts, the prospect of drying his socks at a campfire, in October, sent a chill down his spine.

He said hesitantly, 'Look, Gerry love, have you thought this through? Wouldn't we be better off in a warm little pub on the mainland? Inverness has a nice ring to it.' He added feverishly, 'We could take long walks in the fresh air, make sandwiches, have open air picnics; commune with nature, hire a rowing boat, go to the pictures if the weather turns nasty. Think about it, Gerry. What do you say?'

'Well, if you really don't want us to be

alone together,' Gerry demurred, 'I mean *really* alone together, away from civilization, sharing a sense of adventure, being close to nature, fending for ourselves for a change, we might just as well go back home and have done with it. Is that what you want?'

'No, of course not. It's just that I'm not cut out as a boy-scout. I haven't a clue about campfires and catching fish. Have you?'

'No, but I'm willing to give it a try. You see, this has to do with making a fresh start, putting the past behind me. A new challenge, if you like. You were away most of the time during the Aubrey Sandys case. First in America, then in Stuttgart, later in Wiltshire. Oh Bill, darling, I'm not blaming you, it's just that I felt vulnerable all of a sudden.

'No, please hear me out. Let me explain. I felt lost, at times, trying hard not to show it. Annie Scott's murder upset me far more than I let on. When DCI Brambell asked me to help the police with their enquiries, I was only too willing. I would have done anything to help bring her killer to justice. Even so, I felt the need to toughen up, so to speak, to prove that I was capable of standing on my own two feet once more. It scared me to think how close I had come to losing my nerve that day Aubrey Sandys stuck a knife in my ribs and threatened to kill me if I didn't do as I was told.'

'Oh God, Gerry love, I'm so sorry. I should

have known, I should have guessed,' Bill said tenderly, holding her in his arms. 'Then of course we shall go to the Outer Hebrides, build fires, catch fish, if that's what it takes to make you happy. I'll probably make a bloody fool of myself, but I could probably do with a few lessons in self sufficiency an' all, come to think of it. I'm soft, that's my trouble. All flab and no fibre,' he added laughing, 'Not to worry, I'll make you proud of me yet, just you wait and see!'

The next morning, as they had bade a fond, lingering farewell to their honeymoon suite, Bill suggested a return visit on their way back from the Outer Hebrides, as a kind of softening up process en-route to the flesh-pots of London.

Fleshpots, Bill thought ruefully, blowing out his cheeks. A few pots of flesh wouldn't come amiss after a fortnight's diet of fish and porridge. More porridge than fish, he shouldn't wonder. In any case, what kind of fish? And how would he catch it? With a bent pin on the end of a piece of string? And had the agent he'd contacted earlier really understood his request for solidly built accommodation with a few, if not all, mod cons? A proper fireplace, for instance, a sink, a cooker and a lavatory? Not to mention a bed.

'Oh aye, sur,' the agent had replied, 'leave

it to me, ye'll be well suited.' Bill wasn't so sure, but what could he do about it? Nothing at all, he would just have to wait and see.

They had put up for the night before the crossing, at a bed and breakfast cottage whose windows overlooked the heaving waste of grey, wave-capped water.

'Ye'll be in for a rough crossing, the morn, I'm thinkin',' the landlady said dourly, serving up two dollops of stew on lukewarm plates. 'A pity about the weather. It were main fair earlier on, ye ken. Now look at it.'

Bill looked, didn't like what he saw, and looked down at his plate, not liking what he saw there, either. The landlady said, 'Ye'll no be wantin' much breakfast, the morn, I'm thinkin', if this keeps up. Why waste good vittals tae feed the fishes?' She added, 'Is yer lady wife nae very weel? She looks kinda peaky tae me.'

'I'm fine,' Gerry responded. 'Just not very hungry, that's all.' Catching Bill's eye across the table, she smiled weakly, dangling a piece of fatty lamb on her fork as she did so, before laying down the fork and its lukewarm appendage, and sticking out her tongue at him when the landlady's back was turned.

'That was the worst meal I've never eaten,' Gerry said when she and Bill were in bed, huddled close together for warmth. 'The ferry crossing will be a doddle after this.

Huh, talk about wasting good vittals on feeding fishes. I wonder there are any fish left if all they have to feed on is fatty lamb stew.'

The ferry steamer was anchored near the jetty when Gerry and Bill set off after breakfast next morning. 'Ye'll nae be wantin' bacon an' fried eggs. I ken?' Mrs MacNab, the landlady, enquired.

'No, indeed,' Bill replied heartily. 'Just toast and marmalade,' swallowing hard at the very mention of fried eggs.

Awaiting the stowing away of the hatch-back, Gerry stared anxiously at the turbulent waste of wind-whipped water ahead of them, wondering how the fish would react to two rounds of toast and a cup of tea. A dozen or so other passengers had gathered on the quay to face the trial by water. Mainlanders as opposed to tourists, Gerry figured, hud-dling into her anorak, beginning to wish herself and Bill safely back in Hampstead.

Too late to change her mind now, she realized. The hatchback was already in the belly of the ferry, alongside other vehicles, including a vintage Bugatti owned, if she was not mistaken, by a tall gentleman, dressed all in black, standing apart from the rest of the travellers. His arms folded and his face half hidden by a black homburg and a pair of dark spectacles perched on a hawk-like nose above a flourishing black moustache. More than likely a false moustache, Gerry surmised. So why the disguise?

Her writer's instincts fully aroused, she stepped across the gangplank to the upper deck of the ferry steamer, forgetful of the heaving waves beneath her. Gerry fully intended to discover the identity of the sinister looking stranger standing aloof from his fellow passengers, reminiscent of Count Dracula in an old black and white movie.

'What's up, Gerry?' Bill asked, recognizing the writer's glint in her eye.

'That *man*,' she hissed. 'What's he up to, I wonder? Why the black cloak, the shades and the false moustache?' She added fearfully, 'He could be a foreign agent, an escaped convict, a terrorist.'

'He could be, but he isn't,' Bill assured her. 'How do I know? Because I asked one of the deck-hands. Apparently he's just an eccentric old johnny – a laird, no less – with a taste for the dramatic, who owns a castle, of sorts, in which he chooses to spend the winter months in solitary confinement, writing books on folklore, witchcraft, old murder mysteries, and the like. So now you know. His handle's Glencochlin, by the way. The Laird of Glencochlin.'

Gerry said artlessly, 'A writer, you say? Hmmm, then chances are he's in need of an agent?'

'Uh-huh. No way!' Bill said decisively. 'We're on honeymoon, remember? I don't intend mixing business with pleasure. Take my advice, forget about Glencochlin, just concentrate on Bill Bentine. OK?'

Two

Disembarking at the ferry-landing on Lewis, Gerry was congratulating herself at having retained her toast and cuppa, yet still seriously hungry, when the hatchback emerged from the steamer and she noticed a sizeable hotel near the jetty. 'I could murder a bacon butty,' she said wistfully.

Bill grinned. 'So could I. So what's stopping us? We're not due to meet the agent till eleven. Let's have a good tuck in – a full Scottish breakfast – shall we?'

'Oh yes, let's,' Gerry complied happily, linking Bill's arm as they made their way to the hotel dining room.

Later, her hunger pains appeased, 'What's the name of the agent, by the way?' Gerry asked. 'How come you got in touch with him?'

'Oh, that? I answered an advert in *The*

Times,' Bill replied, 'and his name's Mac-Nally. He sounded a bit dim when I spoke to him on the phone, but he appeared to get the message when I explained to him that we wanted a modicum of creature comforts; a decent bed, a proper lavvy and so forth. What I mean to say is, there is no way I could cope with an earth closet and a straw mattress. Could you?'

'I guess not,' Gerry conceded, recalling the four-poster bed in their honeymoon suite, and the lavish bathroom, 'just as long as we can be alone together Far from the Madding Crowd as it were, dependent on one another for our survival without the aid of all mod cons.'

They met up with MacNally later, in the centre of Stornoway. He was a lanky individual, wearing corduroy trousers, a waxed anorak, wellingtons and a deerstalker hat. As he alighted from a mud-spattered landrover, he said laconically, 'Name of Bentine? How do, sur, you too, missis. A rough crossin', were it?'

'You could say that,' Bill commented cheerfully. 'Well now, what's on the agenda?'

MacNally looked mystified.

Gerry said, 'About the cottage. We're dying to see it, to get settled in. Is it far from here?'

'Nae, lassie,' MacNally assured her, 'four miles, as the crow flies, an' ye'll nae be disappointed, I'm thinkin'.' He grinned widely, displaying a row of tobacco-stained teeth. 'Now, if you an' your man'll foller me, I'll lead the way.'

He climbed into the driving seat of his landrover, engaged gear, and nosed his vehicle from the environs of Stornoway, a bustling little town with a thriving fish market as its centrepiece, onto a bumpy road leading north towards their honeymoon destination.

Bill said, 'I should have left the car in Stornoway, hitched a lift from MacNally. Wish I'd thought of it sooner. I'm worried about the tyres' suitability on rough terrain. I should have asked Mac's advice. I meant to, hence my mention of an agenda. I could see he hadn't a clue what I was on about, and frankly, neither had I. I kind of lost the thread of the conversation seeing that look of blank amazement on his face.'

'Not to worry, darling,' Gerry advised him, 'you could always nip back to Stornoway; hire a jeep or a Sherman tank. But hi-up. Mac's braking! No, he's stopping. He must have run out of petrol.'

Gazing askance at a modern bungalow set back from the road, she added, 'Surely, this can't be *it*. Our stone built cottage miles away from civilization? There must be some mistake!'

'I'll have a word,' Bill said, getting out of

the car to confront MacNally, closely followed by Gerry, anxious to put in her two cents' worth.

'Now see here, Mr MacNally,' she said crossly, 'this just isn't good enough. I'd set my heart on a broken down bothy, not a bungalow.'

MacNally looked pained, hurt and confused. Pushing back his deerstalker, he scratched his head bemusedly, 'But he zed tae mek sure of mod cons, which I has done. There ain't nae mod cons in bothys: leastways none as I'se heard tell on. Ah thowt as 'ow yer'd be best pleased with a canny wee dwelling like this 'un. Ony road there's naething ah can do about it at this time o' day.'

'This time of day? It's only twelve o'clock, for Pete's sake,' Gerry reminded him.

'Aye, but there's a storm brewin',' MacNally uttered fearfully, glancing up at the cloud embellished sky. 'Best tek my advice, missis, get indoors while t' goin's good, otherwise ye'll end up soaked tae'd skin.'

After handing Bill the keys, MacNally got into his landrover and drove back in the direction of Stornoway. As he did so, the sky opened and so did the front door of the bungalow.

Rain hammered down on the roof and lashed against the windows as Bill and Gerry struggled to close the door against the rising wind which had sprung up as suddenly as the rain had descended.

'Phew,' Gerry uttered, blowing out her cheeks with exertion. 'Well, since we're here, we'd best take a look round, hadn't we?'

'Hmm, shouldn't take long,' Bill commented drily. 'No upstairs to worry about! Come on, love, let's find the kitchen and make ourselves a cup of tea.'

'The tea bags are in the car,' Gerry reminded him, 'along with the rest of the groceries – and our cases.'

'Oh *hell*,' Bill muttered savagely, re-opening the door and dashing out in the teeth of the gale to empty the car of their belongings, with only one cheerful thought in mind. At least they weren't stuck in a bothy, miles from anywhere with rain dripping through the roof and a straw mattress to look forward to.

With a modicum of luck, he considered, all mod cons would include an electric cooker, an immersion heater, a decently sprung bed, adequate kitchen equipment and, hopefully, a microwave oven in which Gerry would soon rustle up a mid-afternoon snack. Later, a roast beef dinner, washed down with a couple of glasses of wine. Never, in all his life, had he been so wet, so cold before. He hadn't known the half of it, then. Had he done so, he'd have headed straight back to the mainland before their troubles really began.

In the early hours of next morning, a persistent knocking on the door aroused Bill from his sleep. He shrugged on his dressing gown and slippers and opened the door to find a couple of uniformed policemen on the doorstep, a weatherbeaten sergeant and a fresh-faced constable. He had stared at them uncomprehendingly, wondering what the hell they wanted.

'Name of Bentine, sir?' the sergeant asked brusquely, producing his badge. 'My name is Kirk, my colleague's name is Mitchell. We'd like a word with you.'

'You'd better come in, then,' Bill said surprised, leading the way. 'So what's the problem, sergeant? Is my tax disc out of date?'

'It's more serious than that,' Kirk informed him. 'We are inquiring into the death of Mr Samuel MacNally, an acquaintance of yours if I'm not mistaken. You are more than likely, according to information received, the last person to see him alive.'

Deeply shocked at Kirk's · dramatic announcement, Bill asked disbelievingly, 'MacNally? Dead? But how? He was as right as rain when he left here yesterday afternoon. What happened? A stroke? A heart attack?'

'No, sir. MacNally's body was discovered on the back seat of his landrover. There were signs of a struggle. A post-mortem examination revealed the cause of death as a blow from a blunt instrument to the back of the head. In short, Mr Bentine, Sam MacNally was brutally murdered.'

Gerry appeared on the scene at that moment. Hearing voices, she had got up, dressed hastily in the nearest garments to hand, slacks and a thick-knit sweater, and arrived at the kitchen door to hear, with a feeling of horror, Sergeant Kirk's grimly uttered words.

Entering the arena, Gerry exclaimed, 'Surely you don't think we had anything to do with poor Mr MacNally's demise, do you? We scarcely knew the man. Why on earth should we have wanted him out of the way? I know a thing or two about murder, and there has to be a motive. In this case, there isn't one.'

Throwing Gerry an anguished look, 'My wife's a crime novelist,' Bill offered by way of an explanation to the craggy-faced Kirk, 'well known to Scotland Yard – in a consultant capacity, of course.'

'Oh, stop waffling, Bill. I've been up to my neck in murder before now, as the sergeant's bound to find out sooner or later.' She added thoughtfully, 'Mind you, the last thing I expected was to come across a murder in this neck of the woods. London, fair enough, but not in the Outer Hebrides.'

Brightening a little, she added, 'Not to

31

worry, Sergeant, we'll have this cleared up in a jiffy now you know that we had nothing to do with it. Find the motive and you'll find the killer, is my motto.'

Kirk said stonily, 'I have it, on good authority, that you and your husband appeared to be in confrontation with the deceased, prior to his demise. I want to know the reason for that argument. Well, I'm waiting.'

'It wasn't a confrontation, just a misunderstanding, that's all,' Gerry explained. 'I'd set my heart on a bothy near a burn, catching fish and cooking them over a campfire, living close to nature not in a bungalow near a main road. Where's the fun in that?

'We're on honeymoon, you see, and wanted to get away from it all.'

'All – *what?*' Kirk asked dourly, reminding Gerry of her old protagonist, dull-witted Detective Inspector Clooney, formerly in charge of the Hampstead cop-shop – Gerry's local nick.

'*What?* Well, dead bodies for one thing. There's lots of 'em knocking about in the London area, and *I* should know, having discovered my fair share of them. Deadlines, for another. If there's anything I hate, apart from dead bodies, it's deadlines.'

Bill groaned inwardly. He said placatingly, 'You must forgive my wife. Being a writer, she has a vivid imagination. But she's right in saying that there was no confrontation, as such, with Samuel MacNally, simply an exchange of views. After which he handed me the keys of the bungalow, warned us that a storm was brewing and we'd best get indoors before the downpour started, which we did. The last we saw of the deceased, he was in the driving seat of his landrover, heading towards Stornoway. That's it in a nutshell.'

Kirk said doggedly, 'I shall require statements of your testimonies. I'll be in my office at two o'clock sharp. Don't keep me waiting.'

What puzzled Gerry most was, why should anyone have wanted to bump off old Sam MacNally? There had to be a reason, be it jealousy, revenge, financial gain or mental instability. Picturing Sam in her mind's eye, she couldn't imagine him as the seducer of another man's wife who, out for revenge, had attacked him in broad daylight. Except, of course, that the attack had taken place during a deluge, beneath a leaden sky, a stygian gloom scarcely describable as broad daylight.

Had the murderer, taking advantage of the inclement weather conditions and an empty country road, mounted his attack secure in the knowledge that he wouldn't be seen on a lonely road in the middle of nowhere? If so, he must be a local man, au fait with the territory, Gerry figured, sitting at the kitchen table, making notes, while Bill, swearing softly under his breath, was desperately involved in stoking the belly of the Rayburn, with knobs of damp anthracite lugged indoors from a leaking lean-to near the back door.

Some fine honeymoon this was turning out to be, he thought despondently, with a defunct agent on one hand, a near defunct source of warmth on the other, and a murder-rap hanging over him, not to mention the two o'clock appointment with Sergeant Kirk. And what was Gerry doing? Writing letters home? Beginning a new novel?

'Look, love,' he said patiently, 'I could do with a bit of help here. A cup of coffee and a sandwich wouldn't come amiss. Frankly, my stomach feels like a flag at half mast.'

'Oh, Bill darling, I'm sorry. I was just trying to figure out who murdered Sam MacNally, and why. Making a list of questions to put to Sergeant Kirk to determine the identity of the killer, such as, were the lights of the landrover on or off when the body was discovered? Ditto his deerstalker. Had he been robbed? Who were his employers? Had he a criminal record? Was he in debt? Was he married or single? *Who*, in essence, was Samuel MacNally? *What* was he? A bona-fide agent or a con-man? We took him at face value as a bit of a bumbling idiot, but suppose that he was nothing of the kind?

'Don't worry, Bill, no way can Sergeant Kirk pin the murder of a complete stranger on us, and he'd better believe it.'

'But will he?' Bill demurred uneasily.

'He will when *I'm* through with him,' Gerry said grimly. 'Now, about that Rayburn. Have you tried drawing out the dampers?'

Later that afternoon, their interview with Sergeant Kirk over and done with, as to Bill's infinite relief the police had seemed to believe their innocence over the murder of Samuel MacNally, he said gruffly, 'Thanks, darling, you were simply magnificent drawing Kirk's attention away from ourselves. The fact remains that I hate this bloody bungalow, so why don't we head back to civilization first thing tomorrow morning? Leave the Rayburn to its own devices, pack our belongings and get the hell out of here?'

'Fair enough, Bill,' Gerry conceded, albeit reluctantly, 'I just wish that things had worked out differently, that's all. The last thing I'd envisaged was another murder to mess things up. I was really looking forward to spending our honeymoon in peace and quiet, in romantic surroundings. But you're right about this bungalow. I can't wait to see the back of it, though I'd rather not head back to civilization just yet. Couldn't we just tour around for a while, staying at out of the way places? I'd really like that.'

'All right, Gerry, you win.' He could think of far worse things than staying at out of the way places, preferably nice little pubs, with warm fires, decent beds and good wholesome grub to sustain himself and his beloved.

'Oh thanks, Bill. I knew you'd understand.' Gerry sighed blissfully.

Early next morning, having tidied up the bungalow, the keys to which they had secreted beneath a plantpot near the front door, they set off on their tour of Lewis. Not that Harris and Lewis were separate islands, but conjoined, a bit like Siamese twins, both of which were interspersed with clusters of black roofed houses, unsmiling women wearing black skirts, black woollen stockings, black shoes, and head-shawls, clustered together in groups, impervious to Gerry's merrily called out greetings from the passenger seat of the hatchback.

There were occasional village stores to be seen, manifold places of worship, no jolly little pubs or cafes. When land ran out and they were faced with a grey, swirling sea beyond a stone built jetty, Bill stopped the car near a cluster of sheds in which fisher-men were stacking wooden boxes containing the early morning landing of herring, cod, haddock and woof, brought up from various cobles anchored alongside the jetty.

Gerry's heart sank. A steely rain had begun to fall. 'Wait here,' Bill said. 'I'm going for a look. Shan't be a jiffy!'

A look at what? Gerry wondered. There wasn't much to look at apart from a heaving mass of water and wet cobblestones – grow-ing wetter by the minute as the downpour of rain increased in intensity to stair-rod pro-portions. Right now, even lukewarm lamb stew seemed appealing, having missed breakfast.

Bill returned hefting a bass bag.

'Wotcha got there?' Gerry asked. 'Apart from the bag.'

'Fish,' he said. 'Dabs, flounders, plaice, herring. You name it. A stone of it, all bright-eyed and bushy-scaled.'

'Huh?' Gerry stared at him bemusedly. 'So what, in heaven's name, are we supposed to do with it?'

'Cook it,' he said. 'What else? We can scarcely eat it raw.'

'Cook it *where*?' Gerry responded.

'The only place we *can* cook it,' he remind-ed her, 'in that blasted Rayburn.'

'Go back to the bungalow, you mean?'

'Unless you have a better idea,' he said

grimly. 'Think about it, darling. The keys will still be under the plant-pot, possession is nine-tenths of the law, and I'll make that bloody Rayburn work if I have to strangle it with my bare hands.'

Switching on the ignition, 'Look, love. Let's head for Stornoway, shall we? At least there are shops there. I'll buy dry kindling and coal: a sack of spuds, what ever else is necessary for our survival. Frankly, darling, I'm so hungry I could eat a horse!'

In view of the inhospitable weather, her own need of a dry roof over her head – albeit in that wretched bungalow – Gerry croaked dejectedly, 'Yes, let's go back there. Why not. Before we catch pneumonia.'

The Rayburn was roaring following Bill's administration of dry fuel. Soon, supper would be ready, fried fillets of fish accompanied with mounds of mashed potatoes, frozen peas and cauliflower florets – the latter purchased from a Stornoway minimarket, along with tins of Heinz tomato soup and treacle pudding and custard.

The fish had needed gutting and filleting, and there was a great deal of it. They'd be living on fish for the forseeable future, Bill reckoned, plopping chunks of it into a pan of water for his version of bouillabaisse, a hearty fish stew, and stowing the herring in the fridge for next morning's breakfast, thinking he quite fancied oat-rolled herring.

The chilly atmosphere of the bungalow was soon dispelled, the Rayburn ensuring a plentiful supply of hot water for bedtime baths. Bill had also lit a fire in the sitting room, to Gerry's relief, who had spread out their damp clothing to dry.

They had eaten hungrily, not to say wolfishly. Everything had gone down a treat especially the treacle pudding and custard. Afterwards, they went in the other room to relax. 'I wonder if Sergeant Kirk is any closer to finding Sam MacNally's killer?' Bill mused.

'We could always ask him, I suppose. Pay him a return visit tomorrow,' Gerry suggested.

'Why not? We could always have another wander round Stornoway. I could do with some bay leaves for my bouillabaisse, a few shrimps, a small squid.'

'Now see here, Bill Bentine, bring an octopus into my kitchen and I'll scream blue murder. Ugh! If there's anything I can't stand it's fish with legs.'

Bill smiled at Gerry's nonsense, as she had meant him to, but something was missing. Deeply intuitive, she said, 'This secluded honeymoon idea of mine isn't working out very well, is it? A bit of a disaster to put it mildly.

'I can see now that I was wrong in wanting

to do something different for a change, something new, exciting, adventurous. I'd imagined that being alone together in idyllic surroundings would bring us even closer together. The last thing I'd envisaged was ending up in a four-roomed bungalow with a view of a dusty road. Frankly, love, I'm bored stiff, and so are you. So let's call it a day, shall we, go back to the mainland, and head for home?'

'Amen to that, but what about the fish? We can't leave it here to rot,' Bill said, his sense of humour coming uppermost once more, to Gerry's relief. 'What I'm saying, Gerry love, let's not be too hasty about leaving here. After all, who knows, tomorrow the sun could be shining, something exciting may turn up?' Loving her so much, the last thing Bill wanted was to burden her with a sense of guilt that her dream honeymoon had failed to live up to expectation, through no fault of her own.

After all, he considered carefully, the girl was scarcely responsible for the lousy weather, or the murder enquiry which had dogged their footsteps so far, not to mention his own lack of enthusiasm for the venture. Bill felt badly about that, his lack of encouragement when Gerry had needed a reliable, comforting presence in her life, not someone to depress her flagging spirits over what she now as regarded, not as a happy, carefree honeymoon, but a disaster. His fault entirely, Bill reckoned, now desperately anxious to end their stay in the Outer Hebrides on a high note. Even to the extent of delaying their departure to the mainland in order to find her a bothy by a burn if necessary – anything to prove his love for her.

Later that evening came an insistent knocking at the front door. 'Who on earth can that be?' Bill frowned, getting up to find out.

On the doorstep stood a tall man, dressed in black. The man Gerry had noticed on the quayside the day of their departure from Mrs MacNab's boarding house. The man who had reminded her, fearfully, of Count Dracula.

Three

'Forgive my intrusion,' the man said pleasantly, in an accent which Gerry couldn't quite figure out – predominantly Australian with an underlying Scottish burr. 'I called earlier on today but there was no sign of life, and your car was missing. My name is Glencochlin, by the way. Fergus Glencochlin.'

'Won't you come in, sir?' Stepping aside to admit the bizarrely dressed stranger, 'I am Bill Bentine, and this is my wife, Gerry,' Bill said courteously, wondering what the hell the man wanted at this time of night, not entirely sure that he wanted to find out. Leading the way, he added, 'My wife and I have just finished supper, but there's plenty left over if you would care for a bite to eat.'

Bill cast a puzzled glance in Gerry's direction as Glencochlin entered the room to stand with his back to the fire: bestriding the hearthrug like a colossus, as if he owned the place, not even bothering to remove his wide-brimmed hat.

Gerry said pointedly, 'Make yourself at home, Mr Glencochlin. Mind you don't scorch the back of your cloak.'

Fergus said, not one whit abashed, 'Not to worry, I'm not stopping. I came to proffer an invitation to a house party, this weekend. At my ancestral home, Glencochlin Castle. Please say you'll come. Just a small get-together of close friends of mine to welcome my return to the islands. Allow me to explain. I have reason to believe that your holiday so far has not quite lived up to your expectations, for which I hold myself partly, if not entirely responsible.'

'How come?' Gerry asked uncompromisingly, remembering the old adage, 'Beware of Greeks bearing gifts'.

'Because the late lamented Samuel Mac-Nally, who had the misfortune to meet his Maker so abruptly, happened to be an employee of mine, commissioned to ensure that you found the kind of accommodation you were seeking. A secluded stone built cottage near a burn, if I'm not mistaken, not a modern bungalow such as this, which I happen to own, by the way. Why he did so is past my comprehension, especially since I also own a cottage ideally suited to your requirements, should you decide to spend the remainder of your holiday there, following a stay at Glencochlin Castle for my house party.' The laird paused dramatically, 'But that, of course, is entirely up to you.'

'You're on!' Gerry assured him thinking quickly, the murder of Sam NacNally uppermost in her mind. Despite her reservations regarding Glencochlin, she needed to find out what he was up to. Why the invitation to join his house party? What role he had played in MacNally's murder, if any? There must be some link, she realized, and it was up to her to discover that link.

'Great! That's settled then. I'll look forward to seeing you on Saturday at around noon, in time for lunch and to meet your fellow guests. I can promise you excellent food and wine, stimulating conversation, indoor or outdoor recreation, depending on the weather. Are you fond of fish, by the way?'

'Fish?' Gerry smiled weakly. 'Fine, as long as it hasn't got legs. We could bring our own, if you like.'

'Well, what did you think of that?' Bill closed the door behind the Laird of Glencochlin with a feeling of relief. 'A queer cove and no mistake. Is he eccentric, barmy or as clever as a waggon load of monkeys?'

'Clever,' Gerry nodded sagely. 'Devious into the bargain, I shouldn't wonder. All that jazz about his house party and that holiday cottage he was on about. What's he after, I wonder?'

'I thought you'd be pleased,' Bill commented drily, 'so what's bugging you? Perhaps he's had an attack of conscience over old Sam MacNally's failure to follow instructions? Hmm, I wonder. Sam must have known that cottage was available, so why bring us here?'

'*That's* what's bugging me,' Gerry said, frowning. 'It seems a bit fishy to me. I wonder if he's scared that Sam MacNally told us something he shouldn't have?'

Bill pulled a face. 'Do you mind not harping on about fish, darling? Have you thought how much we have to get through before Saturday? Two herring breakfasts, a sodding great pot of bouillabaisse! Bouillabaisse for lunch, tea and supper! In short, fish stew. No bay leaves, no white wine to enhance it. No

44

Mediterranean herbs or spices, just great slabs of fish.'

He added darkly, 'And I'll bet any money that's what we'll be given for lunch, come Saturday. If so, I'll probably start swimming for the shore.'

'Or drinking like a fish?' Gerry suggested, tongue-in-cheek. 'Not to worry, love, they say fish is good for the brain. So how about a nice hot bath, Einstein?'

They had trouble finding Glencochlin's castle. When they finally located a creeper clad, turreted building poised on a spit of land jutting into a slate grey sea, 'Blimey, is *that* it?' Gerry exclaimed, staring fearfully at the crumbling stonework, cracked mullioned windows, worn steps leading to an ancient oak door beside which hung a massive iron bell pull. 'Gawd's truth, it looks like a film set for a Gothic horror movie.'

Imagination getting the better of her, she added, 'Suppose it's a trap? What if there aren't any other guests, just us? What if we've been brought here to be grilled?'

'Calm down, love,' Bill advised her. 'In case you hadn't noticed, there are cars parked in the forecourt. I daresay we're the last to arrive, what with losing our way, damping down the Rayburn and burying the left over bouillabaisse in the back garden. Huh, and to think I paid lots of squid for it.'

'That isn't remotely funny,' Gerry said huffily.

'Then why are you laughing?'

'I'm not, just exercising my lips. Oh come on! Let's get inside and get it over with. Will you ring the doorbell, or shall I?'

A gaunt, cadaverous looking man ushered them into an imposingly large hall with an uncarpeted oak staircase leading to the upper landings. From the hall they were led to a ground-floor room with a brightly burning log fire, in which were gathered the laird and his guests, partaking of liquid refreshment from a well stocked sideboard on which stood bottles of gin, whisky, rum, brandy, cut glass decanters of sherry, Madeira, port; ice-coolers, nibbles in silver dishes, sliced lemons and soft drinks galore.

'Ah, here you are at last,' Glencochlin greeted them warmly. 'Allow me to introduce you. Not that you'll remember everyone at first. That will come later.'

He was right about that, Gerry thought. Not that there were many names to remember. Six in all, four men and two women. 'Now, what'll you have to drink?' the laird asked. 'You, Gerry? Gin and tonic with ice and lemon? And you, Bill? Whisky and soda? Coming up. Well, cheers. Here's to a happy weekend.'

Meeting Glencochlin's eyes, Gerry recoiled suddenly. The laird's lips were drawn back in a false smile, his eyes were as cold as the ice cubes in her gin and tonic.

The dining room was far less welcoming than the drawing room had been – decidedly chilly. The table was presided over by Glencochlin, wearing a black polo-neck sweater, black gaucho-style ankle boots, and a black, quilted body-warmer but thankfully, no hat.

Regarding him suspiciously from her end of the table, Gerry wondered if she had imagined the diabolical expression on his face back there in the drawing room. But she knew she had not, despite his apparently animated conversation with a physically well endowed, casually yet expensively dressed middle-aged woman seated next to him.

The first course, served by the cadaverous manservant who had shown them to the drawing room, just *had* to be fish, Gerry thought darkly. Not that she actually disliked prawns served in melba glasses with shredded lettuce, mayonnaise and tabasco sauce, just as long as she didn't have to cope with their legs, shells or feelers.

Meanwhile, Bill appeared to be getting along just fine with his table companion; a skinny-ribbed redhead with too many teeth, wearing a figure revealing black cashmere sweater hung about with numerous gold chains. An ornate gold cross nestled seductively between the cleavage of her Wonderbra. It had to be a Wonderbra, Gerry figured – to make the best of a bad job.

The laird's guests were a mixed bag, she considered, glancing about her as the cadaver cleared away the glasses and brought in the main course, thankfully not fish but creamed chicken in a mushroom sauce.

Wonderbra, she decided, belonged to a fair-haired young man wearing a blazer and an old school tie, though which old school, she hadn't a clue. The middle-aged woman was with a thickset, prosperous looking gent, as bald as a coot, seated on the host's left hand side. Next to him, on Wonderbra's right hand, sat a lean, olive-skinned man with an Italian sounding name which Gerry tried to recall. Spaghetti? was that it? No, it couldn't be Spaghetti. Ravioli? Macaroni? No! Cannelloni? Getting warmer. Ah yes, Cannelli, that was it. Tony Cannelli.

Then there were her own table companions, Bill presently delving into a bowl of savoury rice to supplement his creamed chicken and mushrooms, and a wizened, very old man wearing a hearing aid. He had not so far uttered a word of conversation. Perhaps the hearing aid was switched off? Just as well, Gerry thought, vaguely recalling that he was a professor of some kind, with another odd-sounding name. Telemann.

What was this house party, she wondered,

a kind of League of Nations convention? Or a dress rehearsal for a Pirandello play – *Six Characters in Search of an Author*? The author they were in search of being herself, perhaps? But no, surely not? If so, *why*, for God's sake?

Wonderbra, she realized, possessed a marked American accent. With names such as Cannelli and Telemann, Tony and the Professor had to be, respectively, Italian and German, and she'd bet a hundred pounds that the buxom, middle-aged woman and her bald-headed husband were not British. So what had this lot in common with Glencochlin, a Scotsman by birth, a Queenslander by adoption? It didn't make sense to Gerry's way of thinking, and Gerry needed things to make sense, otherwise she might just as well stop writing crime novels and start writing fairy tales.

The first glimpse of the drawing room with its glowing log fire had convinced Gerry she had been mistaken in her assessment of Glencochlin Castle as a background for a Gothic horror movie. Now she was not so sure. The building reeked of dampness and decay, the interior resembled a rabbit warren of long, chilly criss-crossing corridors leading to the guest-rooms. Gerry and Bill's bedroom was situated on the top floor, a poorly furnished apartment overlooking the grey waste of water crumping in on the rocks beneath its windows.

The laird's dour manservant had shown them upstairs, after lunch, had switched on a two-bar electric fire and explained dinner would be served at seven o'clock sharp, preceded by drinks in the drawing room an hour beforehand.

When the man had gone, 'Ye gods, Bill,' Gerry said disbelievingly, 'this is appalling. A two-bar fire to heat a room this size? Chances are we'll freeze to death before dinner. Well, if this is old Cogwheel's idea of hospitality, it certainly isn't mine.'

In full spate, letting rip, she continued, 'Ancestral home indeed. A death-trap more like. I'll bet the beds haven't been slept in since Robert the Bruce was a lad. And just take a gander at those tapestries, hand-knitted in Bayeux, I shouldn't wonder.' Suddenly she burst out laughing, 'Not to worry, darling, I always talk nonsense when I'm scared stiff.' She added more seriously, 'And I *am* scared, Bill. There's something strange going on here. I don't know what, but I don't like it.'

Bill said, 'Look, darling, let's talk about it, shall we? You've been through a rough patch lately; with the Aubrey Sandys affair, your abduction, the murder of Annie Scott. Sorry to remind you of all that, but you coped magnificently at the time, and I was so proud of you. Then came the wedding, all the planning and preparation beforehand, the hard work entailed in giving Ma and Martin, Rio and Henri, the time of their lives.'

'Hard work? But Bill, I loved every minute.'

'I know, darling. So did I, and I can't thank you enough, but I couldn't help noticing how tired you were, and no wonder. You gave so much, expended so much energy in making other people happy. Myself above all.'

'So what you're really saying is you think I'm over reacting? Imagining things? But I didn't imagine the murder of Samuel MacNally, and I'm certain that something sinister is going on here.'

'In which case, love, we'll leave first thing tomorrow morning. Right now, if you like. I'm game if you are. I'll make our excuses and apologies, then we'll leave Glencochlin to his own peculiar devices, bung our belongings in the car, and catch the early morning ferry to the mainland. OK?'

'No, Bill. I'm sorry. I just can't do that. If something sinister *is* going on here, I need to find out what it is. After all,' she managed a smile, 'I *am* a Scotland Yard consultant.'

This was the old indomitable Gerry speaking, Bill thought proudly, and she was right. There was something odd about the set-up.

Why, for instance, had Glencochlin taken the trouble to invite them to the castle, to fob them off with a damp, plug-ugly room such as this? Surely, a man of means, the owner of a vintage Bugatti no less, should have had central heating installed years ago?

According to the deck-hand Bill had spoken to, awaiting the departure of the ferry from the mainland to Lewis, the Laird of Glencochlin was an an eccentric old johnny who chose to spend the winter months in solitary confinement; writing books on folklore, witchcraft and old murder mysteries. Fair enough. But surely not with the wind whistling about his ears and his fingers numb with cold? And why would the reclusive old laird hold a house party, inclusive of such an eclectic assortment of guests?

Frankly, Bill had felt overwhelmed by his table companion, Penny Douglas's strident American accent and her name dropping of Bergdorf and Tiffany as her favourite New York shopping venues, in the latter of which she had picked up the cross she was wearing for a mere twenty thousand dollars, at which point Bill's eyes had glazed over with boredom.

Recounting that one-sided conversation to Gerry in the privacy of their room, after lunch, she said, 'Doesn't it strike you as odd that Mrs Douglas and that "old school tie" husband of hers should have jetted in from New York to attend Glencochlin's home-coming party? *Why*, for Pete's sake?

'Come to think of it, why on earth should old Professor Telemann and Tony Macaroni have flown from, presumably, Germany and Italy, to join the celebration? For the pleasure of his company? For the sake of a few drinks, indifferent grub, to run the risk of hypothermia away from the drawing-room fire? I don't think so.

'Another thing that bothers me, the day we went to visit Sergeant Kirk at the Stornoway nick, one minute we were suspects in the MacNally murder inquiry, next minute, we were let go with no further questions asked, thank God. But *why*? Had Kirk been advised, by a higher authority, not to press charges against us? Could that directive have come from the Laird of Glencochlin? If so, *why*? Because he knew the identity of the real murderer?'

She added perplexedly, 'In short, Bill, is Glencochlin the eccentric he purports to be, or something far more sinister?'

Sensing danger, Bill said, 'Gerry, darling, do you really need to find out? You're a crime novelist, not a detective, for heaven's sake.'

'Yes, Bill,' Gerry replied thoughtfully, 'I do need to find out what's going on. You see, love, I have a gut feeling that something unpleasant is about to happen.'

Penny Douglas had been missing from the pre-dinner drinks party in the drawing room, to her husband's distress. He claimed that she had left the castle at four o'clock that afternoon, to take a stroll along the beach, from which she had failed to return in time to dress for the evening festivities.

Immediately, Glencochlin had instigated a search party to look for the missing woman, who may well have been cut off by the tide on the rock-littered crescent of sand beneath the castle promontory.

'Not to worry, Brian, old chap,' the laird assured the distraught husband. 'We'll soon have Penny back with us, safe and well, in time for a drink before dinner.'

But Penny Douglas was destined never to grace the dining-table at Glencochlin Castle ever again. Her lifeless body having been discovered, face down, in a pool of seawater, her neck firmly pinioned to a jagged spur of rock by the twenty thousand dollar cross she was wearing at the time of her death.

Four

Sergeant Kirk had arrived to survey the scene of the accident. Obviously the victim had lost her footing and fallen, face down, in the pool of water. There she had lain tethered by the restraining bond of the cross she was wearing which had somehow become entangled with a jutting piece of rock and which, despite her struggles to free herself, had made it impossible for her to raise her head above water level.

Deep cuts and bruises on the dead woman's neck bore witness to her struggle for survival, Kirk pronounced solemnly. Apparently, the more she had struggled, the deeper the heavy gold chain had gouged into her flesh. He had then authorized the removal of the body to a boathouse further along the beach, in view of the worsening weather conditions which precluded a more detailed examination of the deceased until the following morning.

Gerry went along with that and stood quietly beside Bill, two of the silent, shocked gathering of onlookers who had discovered the body. No way could the poor lady's lifeless remains stay where they were, in the open air, at the mercy of the rapidly incoming tide, she realized, clinging to Bill's hand for comfort. Lifting up his wife's body from the pool of water, the bereaved husband, Brian Douglas, bore it tenderly towards the boathouse, tears streaming down his face as he did so.

Yet, somehow, Gerry could not bring herself to believe that Penny Douglas's death had been accidental. Why, for instance, had she gone out alone, that afternoon? To meet someone? As an attractive, sexy young woman, had she arranged an assignation with a secret admirer? If so, had a violent quarrel led to her death? Had that admirer deliberately attached that heavy gold cross and chain of hers to a rock to ensure her silence over a clandestine love affair, the discovery of which might well have placed his own future in jeopardy? Therefore, she reasoned, maybe a married man of some substance and importance in the community, who had lost his head in a fling with a much younger woman? That made sense, Gerry thought. But who was that man? A member of Glencochlin's house party?

Of the guests present it was more than likely the thickset, prosperous looking gent she had noticed, at lunch; seated opposite the well endowed woman, seemingly engaged in intimate conversation with Glen-cochlin. But no, surely not? So who else was likely to have engaged in a secret liaison with Penny Douglas? One name stuck firmly in Gerry's mind, that of Tony Cannelli.

The more she thought about it, the more certain Gerry became that Penny Douglas's death had been no accident, that she had been deliberately and brutally murdered. And the murderer was almost certainly a guest at the laird's house party.

The tragedy had obviously overshadowed the festivities, but the guests had fore-gathered in the drawing room as if in need of human warmth and companionship to dispel the horror of what had happened. Speaking in hushed voices they crowded near the fire to discuss the ghastly turn of events which had effectively put paid to the laughter and bonhomie of the pre-luncheon get together.

Glencochlin was fulfilling his role as host to perfection, Gerry thought, striking exactly the right note in announcing quietly that dinner would be served, as planned, accurately assessing his guests' need of sustenance following the trauma of the past few hours and, when the dinner gong sounded, leading the way to the dining room unawkwardly. As if to reassure his guests that there was no shame in the enjoyment of good food and drink, even under the direst of circumstances.

And the food, to Gerry's surprise and relief, was extremely good – a heart-warming cock-a-leekie soup followed by roast pheasant, apple pie and cream. The meal over, the host announced that coffee would be served in the drawing room. At dinner, Gerry had noticed the skilful rearrangement of the chairs to cover the absence of two members of the party from the table, Brian Douglas having elected to stay in the boathouse with the body of his wife. Not that Glencochlin had insulted his guests' intelligence in supposing they hadn't noticed the absence of Penny and her husband. Indeed he had raised a toast to 'absent friends'. All told, a faultless performance by a consummate actor, Gerry reckoned, suppressing a strong urge to give him a slow hand clap. Either that or a Bafta award.

In the drawing room, she kept her mouth closed and her eyes open, observing her fellow guests, listening to conversations. She was watching Glencochlin like a hawk, mistrusting the man intensely, remembering that malevolent expression in his eyes when he had handed her that gin and tonic.

The well endowed lady and her prosperous looking husband were Gloria and Arnold Crowther, she discovered, eavesdropping on their conversation; mill-owners from West

Yorkshire, which figured. Textile manufacturers were not short of a bob or two, and the Crowthers were obviously inured to rich living. Gerry imagined a purpose-built stone bungalow in an exclusive residential area on the outskirts of Bradford: state of the art fitted kitchen and bathroom, split-level cookers, wide screen TVs, gold plated bathroom taps, picture windows overlooking a golf-links, a double garage with his and her Mercedes, entertaining on a lavish scale, holidays in the Bahamas. So why had they chosen to spend a chilly weekend in a crumbling castle in the Outer Hebrides? Was this a business meeting of some kind? Gerry pondered.

If so, why had she and Bill been invited? Darned if she knew, unless Glencochlin had felt it necessary to keep them under close surveillance.

Professor Telemann had gone to his room directly after dinner, and who could blame him? The poor old man must feel worn out following his long journey to Glencochlin Castle, scarcely au fait with events concerning the death of Penny Douglas, since he alone had not been involved in the search party instigated by Glencochlin. How could he have been? A man of his age, as deaf as a post, had been excluded from the search.

Even so, there must be a valid reason for

his being here, Gerry thought. If so – *what*?

Bill was talking to Tony Cannelli, an introvert, Gerry suspected. Unusual in a man as good looking as he was: slenderly built yet muscular, olive skinned, with dark hair and eyes, regular, well defined features, strong white teeth, mobile lips, a straight nose, not a fraction of an inch too long or too short. A deep, well modulated voice demonstrated a faultless command of the English language while an aura about him was suggestive of quiet self containment – and extreme wealth, betrayed by his impeccably cut clothes, well manicured hands, gold Rolex watch and the heavy gold signet ring on his wedding ring finger. The hands of a murderer? Gerry wondered.

Meanwhile, the cadaver had brought in and later removed the coffee cups and saucers, and Glencochlin had served drinks from the numerous bottles and decanters on the sideboard, playing to perfection his role as host. And yet Gerry had discerned a kind of edginess about him, as though he wanted this charade over and done with as soon as possible, as if his store of charm was wearing thin, and he had other, more important things on his mind.

So had Gerry, come to think of it. Waylaying him at the sideboard, she said, in her usual forthright fashion, 'I realize, of course, that Bill and I were afterthoughts to your guest list, but the room we've been given is rather cold and damp. Somewhat isolated too, and well, I am of a slightly nervous disposition, especially so at the moment, in view of – well, you know what.'

Regarding her balefully, yet knowing when he had met his match, the laird said grudgingly, 'Really? I had no idea. But of course, if you are dissatisfied with your present accommodation, I'll instruct my manservant to remove your belongings to another room.'

'No need,' Gerry responded cheerfully, 'just get your manservant to point us in the right direction, and Bill and I will hump our own belongings, ta very much.'

Having settled that to her satisfaction, tugging Bill's sleeve, 'Come on, love,' she hissed. 'We're on the move.' On the threshold of the drawing room, she called out, 'Goodnight, everyone. See you in the morning.'

The manservant led the way to a room on the first landing – a twin-bedded apartment, reasonably well furnished, with an adjoining bathroom, mullioned windows overlooking the forecourt, so far as Gerry could discern by starlight, on which was parked a police car. Beside it stood two men, deep in conversation, one of whom was Glencochlin, the other Sergeant Kirk.

'That's odd,' she said, 'I thought Kirk had left here ages ago, after the removal of Penny

Douglas's body to the boathouse. So where's he been? What's he been doing all this time? Why didn't Glencochlin invite him to dinner?'

'Perhaps there wasn't enough pheasant to go round?' Bill suggested. 'Perhaps old Cock-a-leekie felt it expedient not to have a uniformed law enforcement officer at the dining table? Why ask me? In any case, perhaps he hasn't been here all the time. Perhaps he nipped back for his gloves? Look, darling, it's been a long day, so why don't you take a shower while I nip up to the turret to fetch our belongings? I shan't be a tick.'

Half an hour later, when Bill had failed to return, worried sick, Gerry went in search of him and found him on the stairs to the turret room, doubled up with pain, nursing his ankle.

'Ye gods! What happened?' Gerry hurried to his side. 'I'd better get help.'

'No, don't do that. Just give me a hand up. Help me back to our room. I'll be fine once my shoes and socks are off. I don't think my ankle's broken, just sprained. Please, Gerry love, the last thing I want is a crowd of spectators.' Gritting his teeth, 'All I really need is a crutch and a parrot.'

'OK, Long John Silver, you win.' Supporting Bill as best she could, Gerry helped him back to their room, dumped him on the nearest bed, and eased off his right shoe. The sock, she reckoned, would need cutting off to spare him the pain of its removal. Delving into the contents of her shoulder bag – which Bill had often jokingly referred to as a cross between a mobile office and a chemist's shop – she came across a small pair of scissors, with which to do the removal.

Bill's ankle had ballooned to twice its normal size. Immediately, Gerry hurried to the bathroom to soak guest towels in ice cold water to use as compresses to reduce the swelling. Next, searching through the contents of her trusty shoulder bag, she came across a packet of paracetamol to act as painkillers, to ensure a decent night's sleep for her wounded hero.

Gerry had switched on the lamp between the beds – a low watt bulb beneath a yellowish parchment shade. Lying on the other bed, she realized that their overnight bags containing their night clothes were still on the stairs of the turret room, where Bill had dropped them when he'd slipped and injured his ankle.

Desperately in need of her night clothes and toothbrush, just as Bill, come the morning, would be in need of his shaving gear, clean shirts and socks – well, maybe just one sock – she silently quit the room to return to the turret room stairs to retrieve their belongings.

To her amazement she heard voices coming from the turret room: a heated argument between a man and a woman. The man's voice was instantly recognizable as that of Glencochlin. Listening intently, she heard him telling the woman that unless she trusted him completely, the deal was off, and heard the unknown woman's reply: 'Trust *you*? My dear Fergus, I wouldn't trust you if you swore on a stack of bibles.'

The woman was certainly not Mrs Crowther, who possessed a distinctive Yorkshire accent. The woman in conversation with the laird had a foreign accent. But who was she? Where had she sprung from? And what was the nature of the deal under discussion?

Not waiting to hear more, grabbing the overnight bags, Gerry pussyfooted back to Bill and his balloon-sized ankle. He would need medical attention if his ankle was broken, not sprained: X-rays, a plaster cast, crutches. Gerry's heart sank. Of all the diabolical situations. A house party from hell, a dead body in the boathouse, a murderer on the loose, an eccentric host to contend with and, presumably, a mysterious woman with foreign accent secreted in the turret room?

Ye gods, Gerry thought darkly, if only she'd taken Bill's advice to stay on the mainland. But no, she'd been far too pig-headed to relinquish her notion of a more adventurous honeymoon. So serve her darn well right. The last thing she'd envisaged was landing up in a crummy old castle, up to her neck in murder once more, with no easy means of escape – especially if Bill's ankle was broken.

'I'm sorry, darling,' he murmured apologetically, 'what a damn silly thing to have happened. I slipped and fell. My hands were full at the time. I couldn't save myself. I must have blacked out momentarily when I banged my head on the stairs. When I came to, I knew that I'd twisted my ankle. But not to worry, I'll be fine, just fine, come the morning.'

That remained to be seen, Gerry thought, applying another cold compress to his foot.

Not bothering to undress fully, Gerry lay on top of her bed, the light on, watching Bill sleep, getting up at intervals, padding through to the bathroom to soak more towels in cold water, aware of the silence of this ghastly, crumbling castle, apart from the sound of rain beating against the windows, and a rising wind rattling the strands of ivy on its creeper clad walls.

Seldom, if ever before, had Gerry felt so isolated, so helpless, so physically exhausted, but thankfully Bill's ankle appeared less swollen than before, and when he awoke at three o'clock in the morning, she was at hand to slip him more painkillers and a glass of water to wash them down.

'What time is it?' he asked bemusedly. 'Why is the light still on? Why are you still awake? Still dressed?'

'Well, you know me, Bill. I never settle down properly till midnight,' she lied convincingly.

'Then am I allowed to kiss you goodnight?'

'Oh yes, Bill. Please do.' Tenderly their lips met. 'Now, go back to sleep, love, and let me do the same.'

Yawning drowsily, Bill said, 'Sod this single bed lark for a game of darts.'

Gerry could not have agreed more. Throughout the night, she remained wide awake to tend Bill's ankle, finally falling asleep when it was time to get up.

'Darling,' he murmured, bending over to plant a kiss on her forehead, 'sorry to disturb you, but I need a hand with my sock.'

Opening her eyes with a start, 'You're up and dressed. How did you manage that?'

'With considerable difficulty.' He chuckled, well pleased with himself. 'I hopped to the bathroom, showered and shaved, hopped back, found some clean clothes in my overnight bag – shirt, underpants and so on – but darned if I can manage my right foot sock and shoe.'

Scrambling inelegantly out of bed, 'You mean to say you're about to hop downstairs to breakfast?' Gerry uttered bemusedly. 'But are you sure that's wise?'

'Put it this way, love,' Bill replied, 'I'd hop from here to the Mull of Kintyre for a bowl of porridge, bacon and eggs, toast and marmalade and a cup of coffee. Frankly, darling, I'm famished. How about you?'

'Yeah, me too,' Gerry confessed. 'What shall we tell Glencochlin to account for your lameness?'

'Huh?' Bill frowned concernedly. 'Why not tell him the truth, that his turret stairs need fixing? Or is there something you're not telling me?'

'I'd rather not draw attention to the turret room, that's all,' Gerry said reluctantly, 'you see, love, there's something fishy going on up there!'

'*Fishy?* How fishy?' Bill demanded.

'I'm not sure, but when I went to retrieve our belongings from the turret room stairs, I heard voices: Glencochlin and a woman having a bust up over some kind of deal as far as I could make out. It wasn't a friendly discussion, I can tell you, and well – he must have seen our luggage when he went up the stairs, and noticed it was missing when he came down, in which case, putting two and two together, he must have realized their conversation had been overheard – and who by.'

'Oh, lord,' Bill groaned. 'But what, if anything, can he do about it? A woman, you say? The fair Gloria?'

'No, not Gloria, a foreigner with a peculiar, guttural kind of accent I couldn't quite place.'

'Flemish?' Bill suggested drily. 'Oh, come on love, stop worrying. Chances are we'll find out at breakfast. She's probably an auntie of his with a nasty head cold, here to add lustre to this joyous occasion.'

He was probably right, Gerry thought, helping him on with his sock. She was probably making a mountain from a molehill – not unusual in her case. At least his sock was safely in place, his ankle swelling reduced, and his dry sense of humour fully restored.

But what of herself? Lord, what a fright she must look following her night long vigil. 'Shan't be a sec, Bill,' she said, heading for the bathroom to shower, wash her hair, clean her teeth and apply her makeup, in readiness for breakfast and to assist 'Long John Silver' to the dining room.

Thankfully, Bill hadn't noticed that she was still fully dressed beneath her camel hair dressing gown, nor had he recoiled when he'd planted that good morning kiss on her forehead – he must never know that she had spent the entire night wide awake doing her 'in sickness and in health' routine.

She might have known she couldn't pull

the wool over Bill's eyes. When she emerged from the bathroom, holding out his arms to her, he said huskily, 'Thank you for last night, my darling girl. Now, come here, let me kiss you as you deserve to be kissed!'

'Oh that? T'weren't nothing,' Gerry said airily, happily accepting his invitation.

Later, entering the dining room together to the welcome scent of hot coffee and the mouthwatering smell of bacon and eggs, sausages, kippers and kedgeree from the hot-plate on the sideboard, they glanced around the table at the assembled house party guests. Their host was not present. 'Good morning everyone,' Gerry said brightly. 'Lovely weather for ducks.'

No-one smiled. The Crowthers nodded briefly, Cannelli and the professor kept their eyes on their plates of eggs and bacon, the silence was broken only by the beating of torrential rain against the windows, the howling of a gale force wind prowling the perimeters of Glencochlin Castle, as if anxious to gain entry through its crumbling façade.

So where were Glencochlin and his 'Flemish' auntie? Gerry wondered, helping Bill and herself lavishly to breakfast, at the same time sparing a thought for the lifeless body of Penny Douglas within the confines of a cold and lonely boathouse, remembering that, very soon now, police officials would arrive at the castle forecourt to conduct further enquiries into the manner of her death, whether by accident or deliberately, by means of foul play. The latter of which Gerry strongly suspected and, given the chance, would say so, in no uncertain terms.

If only her dear friend and colleague, Detective Chief Inspector Brambell of Scotland Yard was here with her now, Gerry thought wistfully, to take command of the situation in his inimitable laid back manner reminiscent of a kindly country doctor. But, ah, the intellect beneath that battered felt hat of his.

Glencochlin put in an appearance at that moment, apologizing profusely for his tardiness, explaining that he'd had matters of importance to attend to and had breakfasted earlier on. So where was his nasally challenged 'auntie'? Lying in a damp bed? Surveying the Bayeux tapestries? Watching the flickering of the two-bar electric fire on the damp-spotted ceiling of the turret room? Gerry wondered.

Glencochlin said tautly, 'Please listen, everyone. The police will be here directly. An unavoidable intrusion, I'm afraid. But questions into the death of Mrs Douglas must be asked, and answered. Hopefully, their enquiries will not take long.'

Suddenly the doorbell rang.

Five

From the bedroom window, Gerry saw that two police vehicles were parked on the forecourt. Minutes later, a small procession emerged from the front door, a team comprising two constables, a WPC and presumably a medical officer judging by the instrument bag he was carrying. The group were led by Sergeant Kirk, which figured. No show without Punch, she thought darkly, disliking the man intensely, certain that he would forcibly express his accidental death theory to the detriment of any other possibility – murder for instance.

At least they wouldn't have an easy passage to the boathouse, Gerry surmised, with a gale force wind to contend with, slippery paths and a rock-strewn beach, and with heavy rain falling from a pewter grey sky. At which point, she shuddered involuntarily, thinking of the lifeless body of Penny Douglas contained within that boathouse, beyond human aid.

Bill said compassionately, placing a comforting arm about his wife's shoulders, 'Try not to worry unduly, darling. I'm feeling pretty rotten myself, truth to tell, wishing I'd been more tolerant of the poor girl yesterday, at lunch.'

'But you seemed to be getting on well together,' Gerry reminded him. 'Very well indeed, from where I was sitting, smiling at her and hanging on her every word.'

'I couldn't get a word in edgeways. The woman never stopped talking. All I could possibly do was to smile and nod as she went on and on about herself, her clothes and jewellery, her husband's business success, their new apartment overlooking Central Park.'

'Go on, Bill,' Gerry said hoarsely, 'tell me exactly what Penny told you. It could be important!'

'Huh?' Bill frowned. 'Oh come on, Gerry love, I can scarcely remember. It was all so trivial. I was glazing over with boredom half the time.'

'But doesn't it strike you as odd that an old school tie Englishman should have done so well in the USA?' Gerry mused. 'And so early in life.'

'Not really. Depends on his line of business. Could be computers, fast food outlets, fancy restaurants, casinos, dating agencies, antiques. Your guess is as good as mine. That cross and chain she was wearing cost a mere twenty thousand dollars, she informed me.'

He shivered slightly. 'The wonder is she could bear the weight of it. It gave me a hell of a shock to discover she'd been strangled by the damned thing.'

At that moment, another car drew up in the forecourt and two men got out. Her heart rejoiced. If the two men heading towards the entrance of Glencochlin Castle were, as she suspected, detectives, not rank and file policemen, Sergeant Kirk would find himself well and truly outranked. Hallelujah to that.

The laird had made the drawing room available for the police interviews. When Bill and Gerry went downstairs, an hour later, to await their summons, they were regaled by coffee and biscuits served in the dining room, in the company of their fellow inter-viewees, Gloria and Arnold Crowther, Tony Cannelli and Professor Telemann. All of whom appeared to be gloomy and with-drawn, none of whom engaged in conver-sation with one another. Why the veil of silence? Gerry wondered. Guilty consciences perhaps? She, for one, could scarcely wait to have a word with a policeman far outranking the wooden-headed Sergeant Kirk.

The DCI's name was Moncrieff, his sidekick was DS Murdoch. Rising to his feet when Bill and Gerry entered the drawing room,

'Please, do sit down,' Moncrieff said pleasantly. 'As you know, we are here to investigate the untimely death of your fellow guest, Mrs Penelope Douglas. Now, I need to know what you were doing prior to the discovery of her body yesterday afternoon.'

'My husband and I were upstairs in our room,' Gerry explained eagerly, 'enjoying each other's company. We're on honeymoon, you see? We had thought of going out for a breath of fresh air, but decided not to, because of the weather. It was raining, and the wind was rising, and so we decided to stay put until dinner time.'

'Then what happened?' Moncrieff asked mildly.

'Well, then we came down here to the drawing room for pre-dinner drinks when suddenly Brian Douglas burst into the room to say that his wife had not returned from an afternoon walk along the beach. Immediately our host, Laird Glencochlin, organized a search party to look for her.

'No need to tell you that we came across her lying face down in a pool of seawater, her neck tethered to a spur of rock by a gold chain and cross she was wearing. An accidental drowning on the face of it. But I couldn't help wondering if the attachment of the cross and chain to the rock had been deliberate, not accidental.'

'An interesting theory, Mrs Bentine,'

Moncrieff remarked drily. 'Any reason for that supposition?'

'Well yes. I noticed that the spur of rock was higher than the pool of water. The cross and chain were quite heavy. When Penny fell forward, the cross and chain would have stayed in place. Put it this way, Chief Inspector, have you ever tried your hand at Hoopla? If so, you'll realize the near impossibility of hitting a fixed target with a Hoopla ring. It occurred to me to question the likelihood of a weighty object, trapped beneath Mrs Douglas's body when she fell down, becoming entangled with a jutting spur of rock, higher than her head. It doesn't make sense. Well, not to my way of thinking, at any rate.'

'So how do you account for the fact that the chain Mrs Douglas was wearing *was* attached to that spur of rock?' Moncrieff asked intently.

'Because it was put there deliberately by someone who wanted her dead. Perhaps her fall was accidental, but her death certainly was not. My belief is that Penny Douglas was murdered.'

Oh God, Bill thought bleakly, Gerry had fairly put the cat among the pigeons now. Knowing her as well as he did, next thing she'd be harping on about the murder of old Sam MacNally. And he was right. Well, Gerry never did things by halves, as he knew to his cost. But what if, this time, the cost was too high? What if, by speaking out so frankly, she had placed her own life in jeopardy? It wouldn't be the first time nor probably the last.

Aware of sounding fraught, he said apologetically, 'My wife has a lively imagination, Chief Inspector, due to her profession as a writer of crime fiction, which has landed her in trouble on more than one occasion.'

'And you are especially concerned for her safety on this occasion, is that it?' Moncrieff enquired mildly. 'May I ask why?'

Drawing in a deep breath, Bill said levelly, 'For the simple reason, if there is a killer in our midst who believes that he has got away with murder, he might feel compelled to silence someone who believed otherwise.'

Moncrieff sighed deeply. 'Quite so, Mr Bentine, and your concern for your wife's safety does you credit. I should make it clear, however, that we came here with open minds concerning the death of Mrs Douglas and the murder of Mr MacNally.' He added ruefully, 'Unfortunately, there's a world of difference between suspicion and the proof of murder. But it's early days yet, and we shall arrive at the truth sooner or later, believe me.'

Glencochlin's manservant knocked, and entered the room at that moment. 'The master wishes to remind you that luncheon is ready in the dining room,' he said impassively, 'if you would care to come this way.'

'Thanks, Harker,' Moncrieff said briskly, glancing at his watch and getting up from his chair. 'How quickly time flies. One o'clock already.'

So the cadaver's name was Harker, Gerry thought, wondering if he and the rest of the domestic staff had already been interviewed. Not that she had been aware of the presence of other staff members so far, but surely one elderly manservant, and presumably a cook, could not be expected to look after a house of this size – to make beds, dust, light fires, set tables, wash and iron clothes and linen – without the aid of at least a couple of ancillary helpers? The mystery of Glencochlin deepened in Gerry's mind as she, Bill, Moncrieff and Murdoch entered the dining room to find the rest of the house party guests assembled there, along with their host, who rose to his feet to welcome them charmingly.

Taking her seat next to Bill, and glancing round the table at their fellow diners, Gerry noticed that Brian Douglas was missing from the assembly. There was also no sign of the uniformed members of the police force who were, presumably, being fed elsewhere. Sergeant Kirk wouldn't like that one little bit, Gerry thought happily, tucking hungrily into a portion of shepherd's pie and chips.

A feeling of unreality suddenly struck

Gerry. Her appetite appeased, what the hell were she and Bill doing here in this crumbling ruin with its meandering passages, wonky stairs, rattling windows and draughty rooms, she asked herself, a dead body in the boathouse, and a missing 'auntie' to boot?

Common sense told her that Penny Douglas's body would have been removed from the boathouse to a mortuary following the Medical Officer's examination of the poor woman's remains. That more than likely the distraught husband would have accompanied his wife's body to its resting place in a police station morgue, hence his non appearance at lunch.

The thought also occurred that the house party guests, herself and Bill included, would be required to stay on at the castle until Moncrieff and Murdoch had concluded their enquiries into the death of Penny Douglas.

Gerry's heart sank at the prospect of remaining a moment longer than necessary in this Gothic horror of a house with, in all probability, a mentally deranged killer stalking the corridors, by night, intent on finding and silencing the next victim on his list.

Returning to their room after lunch, she noticed that the official police cars were missing from the forecourt. Having completed his examination of the body, the MO would have authorized its removal to a mortuary van, Gerry surmised correctly, thankful that she had not witnessed the arrival and departure of that particular vehicle.

Sick at heart, she imagined the mortuary van attendants' grim task of lumbering a stretcher up the steep, slippery paths from the boathouse, faced with the inhospitable conditions. 'Oh Bill,' she said bleakly, 'that poor girl. What a horrible way to die.'

'I know, love,' he said compassionately. 'But what's done is done. If only she hadn't gone out alone. I can't figure out why she did that. She was scarcely the outdoor type, quite the reverse, I'd say.' He winced suddenly from the pain of his injured ankle.

Oh lord, Gerry thought, there she was – staring into the past – when she'd be better employed tending Bill's ankle. Helping him to his bed, removing his shoe and sock, she hurried to the bathroom to prepare more cold compresses to ease the pain of his badly bruised right foot, the swollen toes of which were huddled together like orphans in a storm, as if the swelling from his ankle had moved down a peg to inhabit his digits.

'Look, Bill,' she said firmly, giving him more painkillers and a glass of water, 'you've got to rest that foot. If it's no better by morning, I'm sending for a doctor, and that's that.'

'No, Gerry. Please don't! I'll be fine, just fine!' He smiled bravely. 'Sorry, darling, not much of a bridegroom, am I?'

'Oh, I wouldn't say that,' Gerry assured him. 'You haven't done too badly, so far!'

An hour later, when her beloved bridegroom was sleeping soundly beneath his duvet, her mind in a turmoil – in dire need of action, of fresh air and exercise – she donned her anorak and a stout pair of shoes and quitted Glencochlin Castle to take a solitary walk down the slippery paths to the boathouse.

Scarcely able to stand upright against the force of the gale, barely able to see the path ahead for the rain running in rivulets down her face, she asked herself severely, what on earth had possessed her to leave the comparative safety of the castle, to run the risk of running headlong into a murderer. There appeared to be no satisfactory answer.

So what the hell was she doing here? Acting on impulse, as usual, came the immediate mental response. Or was she simply being ghoulish in wanting to see the boathouse for herself? And there it was. Wiping the rain from her glasses, she beheld a sizeable wooden structure with double doors, apparently padlocked, towards which she hurried for shelter.

Breathlessly she leaned against the doors, psyching herself for the return journey to the castle, when to her amazement the padlock fell away from its rusted hinges, and she had to prevent herself from falling backward into the boathouse. How she had managed to maintain her balance, she would never know and once inside its dim and dusty interior, she could not have cared less.

Accustoming her eyes to the gloom, all she could hear was the racketing of the wind, the drumming of rain on the galvanized iron roof of the boathouse and the hiss of the sea crashing in on the rocks beyond this temporary refuge she had entered so abruptly.

The last thing she'd expected to see was a motor launch mounted on rollers, a dynamo, a winch, a pulley, in short, state of the art launching and landing gear, decidedly at odds with the crummy building in which they were housed, secured – scarcely that – by a useless padlock now dangling pathetically from its rotten, rusted hinges.

So what was the answer? Gerry pondered. Was the motor launch a rescue vessel of some kind? Or was it used for more sinister purposes? Smuggling, for instance? The landing of hard drugs, ecstasy, cocaine, and so on, worth millions to a cartel masterminding the sale of such horrors both here and abroad by cold blooded dealers. Could this be the underlying motive for Glencochlin's house party? A meeting of his cartel of drug smugglers to determine their future courses of action? And yes, Gerry thought, that was not only possible, but probable.

About to quit the boathouse, to return to the castle as quickly as possible, she turned suddenly at the sound of woman's voice calling out to her for help, uttered in a foreign accent which Gerry recognized immediately as that of the occupant of the turret room. The woman that she and Bill had jokingly referred to as Glencochlin's 'auntie'.

But this was no laughing matter, Gerry realized, as she saw a distraught elderly woman, her grey, shoulder-length hair in disarray; with dark, frightened eyes in the pale oval of her still beautiful face, clutching an ankle-length sable coat about her slender, attenuated body. The woman uttered hoarsely, 'Please, I beg of you, help me, before it is too late.'

But seemingly it was already too late, Gerry deduced, when a large, overbearing lady, with a marked Scottish accent, appeared on the scene to take charge of the woman in the sable fur coat.

'Och, there ye are, Countess,' she uttered clearly relieved, 'I've been searching high and low for ye. Now, stop all this foolish nonsense an' come back to bed where ye belong.'

Then, turning her attention to Gerry, the woman said apologetically, 'She's nae weel, at the moment, as ye can see for yerself. How she came to be wandering abroad in this weather, I canna think. I just pray the Lord she hasna caught her death of cold.' She added, 'The puir wumman's no reet in the head, ye ken?'

To argue with the Scotswoman or to attempt to help the countess, as she had called her, would prove both useless and dangerous, Gerry realized. The best she could do was to act daft – as she had done often before, when to play the fool had seemed a better option than ending up dead. Fortunately, for this, nature had endowed her with a plump, pleasant face, a ready smile, and her owlish horn-rimmed glasses enhanced the illusion of simple mindedness, and so, edging her way towards the doors of the boathouse, she said nonchalantly, 'Well, I'd best be on my way. By the way, the padlock's broken, I wouldn't be here otherwise. I quite literally dropped in. Backwards, as it happens. Well, toodleoo.'

Never would she forget the stricken look on the countess's face as she left the poor lady at the mercy of her brawny Scottish captor. Not for one moment had Gerry believed the tissue of lies she'd been fed about the countess's state of mind, or the tale of her 'wandering abroad' in this weather. The countess's sable coat was as dry as a bone, and so was the Scotswoman's clothing, leading to the supposition that they had reached the boathouse by means of stairs and passages linked internally to Glencochlin Castle.

So all was not lost. If such a labyrinth existed, and could be found, Gerry determined that she would not let the countess's cry for help go unheeded.

Six

'Gerry. Where the hell have you been? I've been going crazy with worry.'

Bill was sitting on the edge of his bed, trying in vain to stuff his right foot into its sock when she entered the room. Looking all hot and bothered and sounding decidedly irritable, 'Oh, damn and blast this bloody sock,' he muttered, 'it must have shrunk in the wash. Well don't just stand there. *Do* something. *Say* something. Tell me where you've been for starters!'

'Out,' Gerry said mildly, 'for a breath of fresh air.'

'Yeah, well that much is obvious! I didn't figure you were sitting in the shower fully clothed. When I realized you were missing, I

panicked, to put it mildly. You might have left me a note, but oh no. I guess it never occurred to you that I'd be out of my skull, thinking the worst. Worried that you'd been abducted, kidnapped, made off with by some maniacal killer or other? Then, to make matters worse – about to go in search of you – I couldn't get my bloody sock on.'

'I'm sorry, Bill,' Gerry said contritely, 'but you were sleeping peacefully when I went out, and I only intended to go as far as the boathouse and back, which I did.'

'Then what took you so long? You've been gone almost two hours. And look at the state of you. Did you stop to take a mud-bath, en-route?'

'Not exactly, though the path was very slippery and I did land flat on my back a couple of times. Then I sheltered for a while in the boathouse.'

'The *boathouse*?' Bill frowned. 'How the heck did you land up in there?'

'The padlock was bust,' Gerry explained, deciding to say nothing about her meeting with the countess and her keeper for the time being, not wanting to add to Bill's distress. 'I'll tell you all about it later. Now, just lie down, stop fretting and fuming and let me see to your foot.'

Shedding her muddy anorak and walking shoes, she went through to the bathroom to soak more towels in cold water. Catching sight of herself in the mirror over the basin, she shuddered slightly at her dishevelled appearance; her wind-reddened nose, mud-spattered cheeks and spaniel ears coiffure.

Had the Bride of Frankenstein looked like this on her honeymoon? Gerry wondered. Stepping into the shower to repair the damage before dinner, she worried about Bill's foot with its bunched up toes, wishing the dining room was not so far away.

'Bill,' she said, emerging from the bathroom with her newly washed hair wrapped in a towel-turban. 'About dinner. I've been thinking...'

'The answer's no,' he said stubbornly, knowing exactly what she was thinking before she'd had time to tell him. 'No way am I prepared to have my grub sent up to me. From now on, where you go, *I* go. I'll go down to dinner sockless, wearing carpet slippers, if necessary. And if Glencochlin wants to know why I'm limping, I'll tell him the truth, that I damn near broke my neck on his lousy, rotten stairs.'

'No, Bill! Don't do that,' Gerry beseeched him, aware of the danger of crossing swords with the laird. 'I have a much better idea. Just tell him you have a touch of gout, that it runs in the family.'

Bill laughed. 'Gerry, you're priceless. Why didn't I think of that?'

And so, when the dinner gong sounded,

they went downstairs together, Bill's right foot encased in a camel-hair slipper. They were chuckling like a couple of schoolchildren about to pull the wool over the headmaster's eyes until Gerry saw the woman she thought of as 'The Wardress', coming towards her. Not that the woman gave the slightest sign of recognition as she headed towards what Gerry imagined to be a passage leading to the kitchen quarters.

Dinner was plentiful and well cooked; hot vegetable soup, a lamb casserole, savoury baked dumplings, mashed potatoes and swede, followed by a steamed ginger pudding and custard. Glancing round the table at her fellow diners between courses, Gerry noticed that Brian Douglas had joined the assemblage of guests. A sad, somewhat remote figure, a far cry from the bright-eyed, bushy-tailed young executive he had been prior to his wife's death.

Gerry's tender heart went out to him, recalling the tears which had streamed down his face when he had carried Penny's lifeless body to the boathouse. Impossible to believe that such a happy young couple had become involved in drug smuggling – or whatever. Were they aware of the goings on at Glencochlin Castle when they had accepted the laird's invitation to the house party.

Conversation was desultory, practically

non-existent under the circumstances. The bereaved husband was obviously still in a state of shock over his tragic loss – barely touching a morsel of food.

Scarcely anyone spoke at all, not knowing what to say, as if fearful that even a chance remark about the weather might trigger a chain of thought too painful for him to bear. Surely someone must break the silence, Gerry reckoned, and so she said impulsively, 'Speaking on my own and my husband's behalf, I want you to know that you are not alone – in grieving the loss of your wife. Forgive me if I'm speaking out of turn – a habit of mine, I'm afraid, rushing in where angels might fear to tread, but silence is not always golden, in my experience. So now, Mr Douglas, with your permission. I'd like to raise a toast to Penny. God bless her.'

She raised aloft the so far untasted glass of wine that Harker had poured for her. The rest of the guests followed suit. 'To Penny, God bless her,' they declaimed solemnly.

Brian Douglas's eyes brimmed with tears. 'Thank you, thank you all so much,' he uttered briefly. 'Now, if you'll excuse me—' Hurriedly he left the dining table, a man about to grieve the death of his wife in the privacy of his own room.

Meanwhile, Moncrieff and Murdoch were dining in a small hotel near Stornoway, comparing notes as they did so. They had crossed over from the mainland on the early morning ferry, a journey which they were unlikely to forget in a hurry, given the shocking weather conditions, as they headed towards Glencochlin Castle to begin their enquiries into the deaths of Samuel Mac-Nally and Penelope Douglas, by order of Superintendent Crossley. The man in charge of operations at Police Headquarters, Glasgow, was an irascible individual who felt strongly that the Stornoway constabulary were incapable of investigating a murder and a suspicious death by drowning.

'Well, Ted, what do you make of it so far?' Moncrieff asked his good looking, intelligent young colleague, valuing his opinion.

'Dodgy,' Murdoch said succinctly, finishing his portion of apple crumble. 'There's something fishy going on yonder. Talk about a weird set-up. That laird gave me the creeps, poncing about in his black Russian boots and polo-neck sweater, with his black hair slicked back from that death's head face of his.

'Sorry, sir, I shouldn't let prejudice stand in the way, but the whole thing smacked of a – charade, a staged performance for our benefit. As if those house guests of his had been primed beforehand to keep their mouths shut – apart from the Bentines, especially Mrs Bentine, who certainly wasn't afraid to speak her mind. Her opinion about the death of Penelope Douglas being deliberate, not accidental is interesting.' He paused, then, 'What did the MO have to say about it, by the way?'

Moncrieff sighed deeply, 'Nothing specific so far. A full scale post-mortem will be necessary to determine the true cause of death. Whether by drowning or strangulation, dependent on the state of the lungs. If seawater is found there, death by drowning will be proved conclusively. If not, death by strangulation is more than a likelihood, though we'll have the devil of a job proving that the chain she was wearing was tethered to that spur of rock deliberately by someone who wanted her out of the way.'

'So what's our next move, sir?' Murdoch asked respectfully.

Moncrieff smiled grimly, 'As I see it, in-depth research into the backgrounds and credentials of every member of Glencochlin's house party, including the man himself and his servants; who they are, where they came from, and why. Also, we'll need to delve into the background of Samuel Mac-Nally, to discover why he was killed, and by whom. I have the gut feeling that the two murders are linked, in some way, to Glencochlin Castle.'

'*Two* murders!' Murdoch exclaimed. 'So you believe Mrs Douglas's death was not accidental?'

'I'd stake my life on it,' Moncrieff replied. 'She was murdered, right enough.'

Next morning, after breakfast, the detectives paid a visit to Sergeant Kirk, to find out more about the murder of Sam MacNally. Moncrieff, who had no great opinion of Kirk, and was in no mood for prevarication, asked to see the murder file. Expecting to be handed a dossier of neatly typed notes, he stared disgustedly at the folder he was handed. It contained a series of hand-written pages, paper clipped together in no particular order, torn, he suspected, from Constable Mitchell's note-pad.

'This is totally unacceptable,' Moncrieff said angrily. 'What excuse have you to offer?'

'Pressure of work, sir,' Kirk spoke dourly, 'and shortage of staff. The typist is on sick leave. It was a case of improvisation. The notes will be typed up when she returns. The salient facts relating to the murder of Sam MacNally are, however, all present and correct.'

'Precious few facts, in my opinion,' Moncrieff uttered coldly. 'Nothing at all about the man's background, his lifestyle, his friends, his habits. This is a close-knit community for heaven's sake, he must have been well known. He's described here as an agent. What kind of an agent? Not a secret agent by any chance?'

Murdoch smothered a smile. Moncrieff could be unintentionally funny at times, and the DS loved it when the DCI went into action against slackness and inefficiency. Little wonder that the MacNally murder inquiry had not reached a solution if the case notes were anything to go by.

Ignoring the 'secret agent' jibe, Kirk said frostily, 'MacNally was an estate agent by profession.'

'I see. And is business brisk in this neck of the woods?'

'You'd be surprised, sir.'

'Go on then, Sergeant, surprise me.'

'Well, just prior to his murder, MacNally had left the keys to a bungalow with a honeymoon couple called Bentine who were seen to be in confrontation with him before he got into his landrover and drove off along the road back to town. There was an eye-witness to the confrontation, and so I called upon the Bentines early the next morning to request statements from them here in the office.'

'And what was the confrontation about?' Moncrieff asked intently.

'They had requested a stone built cottage in a remote area, not a modern bungalow,' Kirk said. 'Naturally, Mrs Bentine was a bit upset, but since they had never met Mac-Nally before he gave them the keys to the property, it seemed unlikely they were involved in his murder. I gave them the all clear: told them they were free to go.'

'Rightly so,' Moncrieff nodded. 'Now I want to know the name of MacNally's employer.'

'Glencochlin,' Kirk said stiffly. 'The Laird of Glencochlin.'

Moncrieff and Murdoch exchanged glances. His superior officer had been right in thinking that Glencochlin was linked in some way to the murders of MacNally and Penelope Douglas, Murdoch thought elatedly. Now the game, in his schoolboy hero, Sherlock Holmes' language, really was afoot.

When Moncrieff and Murdoch had departed, taking with them the case-notes, Kirk dialled a number and awaited a reply, albeit impatiently, although he knew from experience that the call was unlikely to be answered quickly. Glencochlin Castle was a big place, and the telephone was situated in the laird's private sanctum in the east wing; his office-cum-studio workroom, kept under lock and key, a no-go area to all save the laird's trusted manservant Jock Harker and his wife, the cook, who possessed keys and acted as caretakers of the property when their master was away during the summer months.

Suddenly a voice came on the line. 'Glencochlin here ... Ah, it's you. Kirk. This had better be important ... I see ... Not to worry, I'll handle it.'

And that was it. End of conversation. Reluctantly. Kirk hung up the receiver. His hands were shaking slightly as he did so. He felt suddenly afraid.

Murdoch had expected Moncrieff to request an immediate return to Glencochlin Castle, instead of which the DCI asked him to pull into a lay-by on the road out of town. The wind had dropped but rain was still bucketing down, and the sea, flanking the spit of land on which they were travelling towards Tiumpan Head, was angry looking; white-capped, churned by the recent downpour to a seething cauldron, emiting a continuous dull roaring as it lashed against the coastline.

Anticipating action, primed and ready for it, Murdoch asked, 'What now, sir? Why have we stopped?'

'To *think*, laddie. To plan our course of action. What is it we need most, right now?'

'A strong, hot cup of coffee wouldn't go amiss,' Murdoch ventured. 'Sorry, sir. I was being facetious.'

'Oh, is that what it was? Well stop being facetious and start being realistic. Where would we be most likely to find strong, hot coffee?'

'In a cafe? A snack bar? An hotel?'

94

Murdoch frowned. 'I doubt we'll find any-where open at this time of year.' Suddenly, latching on to Moncrieff's train of thought, 'Oh, I get it. You mean an incident room? Of course. With access to a telephone, recourse to research material? Chairs, tables – a kettle, milk, sugar and a jar of Nescafe?'

Moncrieff smiled. 'Precisely.' He added astutely, 'No way can we make headway without back-up from headquarters. We haven't the facilities. Now, before we tackle Glencochlin Castle, we'd best find ourselves accommodation closed for the winter, the owner willing to aid the police in their enquiries. Well, what do you think?'

Restarting the engine, ready and eager for action, 'Leave it to me, sir,' Murdoch said, 'I'll find an hotel, if I have to traipse the streets of every village between here and Tiumpan Head.'

'You'll be lucky.' Moncrieff chuckled. 'Bed and breakfast places more likely, I shouldn't wonder. But you go ahead, laddie. Turn on the charm. In any case, your legs are younger than mine, so I'll wait in the car.'

'Sir,' Murdoch responded smartly, getting out of the car to begin his search for an incident room. Now, he thought wryly, the game really was – afoot.

Seven

Reclining on his bed, Bill thought longingly of his busy, cheerful suite of offices in Red Lion Square, wishing he was back there awaiting the arrival of the morning crop of letters and manuscripts, hearing the ringing phone in the outer office, anticipating his first cup of coffee, brought in to him by his super efficient secretary Janet Crosby. It was always delivered exactly ten minutes after she'd heard his footsteps on the stairs and bidden him good morning when he'd appeared to begin his day's work at what he jokingly referred to as 'the salt mine'.

Now, bored rigid with inactivity, and with his right toes resembling a pack of sausages, he wished to heaven that he and Gerry were well away from this god-awful house and Glencochlin's weird assortment of house party guests. House parties were meant to be fun occasions. Fat chance of that in view of Penny Douglas's death, he realized. Even so, before the tradegy, he'd been aware of a strange undercurrent of unrest, a lack of conviviality and warmth, despite the drawing room fire and the cornucopia of booze on the laird's sideboard. Then had come the upset of the ghastly turret room which Gerry had flatly refused to occupy, and their removal to this equally depressing apartment.

Meanwhile, after exerting his charm and flashing his badge to establish his credentials, as a last resort, Murdoch had managed to winkle his way into the good graces of a Mrs Grace Cameron, an elderly yet feisty widow who, having given him the 'glad eye' through her pince-nez spectacles, had invited him in to 'inspect her facilities', as she had put it. He had assured the bemused Murdoch that he would find everthing to his satisfaction, neat, clean and readily available, including the use of her telephone in the front parlour – on the strict understanding that she would not be called upon to foot the bills, and would be paid adequately for the accommodation provided.

'Tell me, Mr Murdoch,' she enquired archly as he headed for the front door, 'are ye a married man?'

'Aye, that I am,' he affirmed stoutly, 'wi' two bairns an' a third on the way. Now, good day tae ye, Mistress Cameron, for the time being, looking forward tae seeing ye later.'

Returning to the car, 'We're in, sir,' he announced triumphantly, 'at a house called

"Cove View" owned by a Mrs Cameron. It's a tad overfurnished, but cosy.' He went on to explain that the front parlour was available to them, plus bed and breakfast and an evening meal. So to all intents and purposes they would appear to be a couple of end of season visitors in need of a seaside holiday. 'We could pretend to be related, sir, if that would help,' Murdoch added, feeling guilty. 'I could call you uncle; say you'd been ill and needed me to keep an eye on you.'

'Keep an eye on me? Why, for God's sake?' Moncrieff demanded in amazement. 'What's the matter with you, Murdoch? You did tell this Mrs Cameron we'd require separate rooms, I hope?'

'Well no, I didn't. The fact is, sir, she's a bit flirtatious: wanted to know if I was married. I said yes, married with two kids and a third on the way.'

'And you figure that with you spoken for, she might have a go at me, is that it?' Moncrieff burst out laughing. 'Wait 'til my wife hears about this. She'll be chuffed to bits when I tell her I'm being pursued by another woman. What's she like, by the way?'

'Seventy, at a rough guess, as thin as a rail with pince-nez specs, buck teeth and a bun.'

'Hmm,' Moncrieff chuckled deeply, 'it sounds promising. Just my cup of tea. Wonder how she'll react when I tell her you're not even engaged, much less married, just playing the field, on the look out for a nice little widow with a home of her own and a canny wee nest-egg tucked away in the Post Office Savings Bank.'

'You wouldn't, sir, would you?' Murdoch asked nervously.

'As if. Now stop playing the fool and start acting like a policeman. Time's getting on and we have more to worry about than a seventy-year-old nymphomaniac with buck teeth and a bun. We have a serious job of work to do, and the sooner we get started, the better. Understood?'

'Yes sir. Sorry sir.'

'Huh, uncle indeed,' Moncrieff commented scathingly as Murdoch nosed the bonnet of the car down a steep incline leading to Cove View Cottage.

'Look, Bill darling,' Gerry said, 'I've got to go out. Find a chemist's, I'm running out of painkillers and other things besides.'

'But what if you're not allowed to leave?' Bill argued, dreading the thought of her walking alone in the rain, with no clear idea of where she was going. 'And what if you can't find a chemist's? Please, darling, don't do this. Stay here where you'll be safe and dry, where I can keep an eye on you.'

'No Bill, I'm sorry but my mind's made up, and if there's a policeman on duty I'll ask him the way. Think about it, darling, there must be shops, a village of some kind close at hand. Even Glencochlin must need shaving cream, razor blades and toothpaste once in a while. Besides which, your socks and shirts and my undergarments need washing, so does my hair, and the soap's almost run out. So stop fretting, lie back and rest that foot of yours, and I'll be back before you know it.'

Oh God, he thought, when she had kissed him goodbye, curse this bloody foot of his. Curse this blasted castle, the continually overcast skies and the steadily pouring rain, the sheer boredom of having nothing to do. Nothing to look forward to except stodgy, unimaginative food served in a stone cold dining room in the company of boring strangers and an outwardly charming, bizarre looking host who, quite frankly, put the fear of God into him.

There was no policeman on duty. Rain was still coming down quite heavily, but Gerry was well wrapped up, wearing slacks, stout walking shoes, and with the hood of her anorak covering her hair.

Crossing the forecourt, she set off down a steep road which, she reckoned, must lead to the shore where she would hopefully find a fishing village with a few shops to supply the needs of a local community wanting fresh bread, eggs, bacon, meat or other essentials.

Walking briskly, she passed the turning Bill had taken on the day of their arrival at Glencochlin Castle and plodded on determinedly downhill until she came to a red-brick chapel, with worn steps, on the right hand side of the road. Next to it stood a slate roofed dwelling with the name 'Wesley House' above the front door.

Gerry felt like singing. Soon, taking a bend in the road, she saw, to her relief, a cluster of cottages grouped about a grey stone harbour with fishing vessels anchored alongside the quay. There were groups of gossiping women wearing headshawls and men busy about their boats; seagulls clamouring noisily for fish-guts thrown overboard into the rain-lanced sea.

Aware that she was being watched, a stranger in their midst, feeling like the proverbial 'sore thumb' and not wanting to appear stand-offish, she enquired pleasantly, 'Excuse me, but are there shops hereabouts?'

'Aye, across yonder,' came the grudging response from a stony faced woman. 'Ye canna verra weel miss 'em, not if ye've got eyes in yer head.'

Gerry's wicked sense of humour came uppermost. 'Ah weel,' she said wistfully, 'ma sight's not what it was afore the removal of ma cataracts. Like peeling the skin off a coupla grapes, it were. Verra, *verra* painful!'

Smiling bravely, she added, 'Ah prefair not tae use ma telescope if I can help it. but they've promised me binoculars, if ma condition worsens.'

So saying, she headed across the road to the shops – a small parade comprising a mini-market, a chemist's and a butcher's – her arms held out stiffly before her, thinking gleefully, serve her damn well right, the patronizing old biddy.

Entering the chemist's shop, she purchased a bottle of liniment, a packet of sleeping pills, a box of Anadin, shampoo and a roll of crepe bandage, plus a couple of tablets of soap, razor blades and a tube of shaving cream. In the mini-market, she bought washing powder, candles and matches, four bananas and a packet of gingernuts.

So far so good, Gerry thought, now for the tricky part of the venture. First she must strap her carrier bags about her to leave her hands and arms free when it came to rounding the base of the promontory on which Glencochlin Castle was perched. Bill would have a fit if he knew what she was up to but she simply wanted to sneak up on the castle, so to speak, to find out if the castle and the boathouse were conjoined. If so, chances were that access to the turret room would be possible by way of steps and passageways leading up to it. When all was said and done, she couldn't very well march up to the turret room by the usual means, knock on the door and ask the countess if she was OK, *could* she?

Her intrepid, fictitious heroine Virginia Vale might well have done so, but Gerry wasn't intrepid, and she was certainly not Virginia Vale – as lithe as a mountain lion, as slim as a wand, as resourceful as a monkey. Furthermore, Virginia would not have made such a pig's ear of strapping carrier bags about her waist by means of her trouser belt – or rather Bill's trouser belt which she had surreptitiously removed from his grey flannel slacks earlier on that morning.

Looking like a Michelin Tyre Man when the bags were in place, Gerry descended a flight of steps leading to the rocks beneath Glencochlin Castle where she stood still for a while surveying the hazardous route ahead of her: moss covered rocks with bubbling pools of seawater between. She doubted her ability to retain her balance once she had embarked on her perilous journey to the cove beneath the castle; that curved, rock littered crescent of sand on which Penny Douglas had been so brutally murdered. Of this, Gerry was quite certain. Now it seemed equally certain that the life of another human being also stood in jeopardy if she failed in her mission to rescue the countess: remembering the poor woman's plea, 'Please, help me before it is too late.'

Drawing in a deep breath, plucking up every ounce of her courage, concentrating deeply on the task in hand, Gerry picked her way, step by step, inch by inch, towards Glencochlin Cove. Slipping and sliding; her heart pounding with rain and perspiration streaming down her face, the carrier bags slapping against her thighs, she felt rather like a child in a paddling pool, wearing water wings.

Grimly determined, Gerry continued on towards her destination, stopping now and then to lean her aching back against the wall of the promontory towering above her. Pausing to wipe her glasses and to scrape the soles of her shoes free of algae, she thought of Bill, and how pleased he would be on her safe return, based on the supposition that she would arrive back at Glencochlin Castle still alive and kicking.

Realizing that the tide was now on the turn, and the rocks beneath her feet would soon be swallowed up if she didn't get a move on, making one last desperate bid for safety, she suddenly, blessedly, felt sand beneath her shoes, and knew that her mission had, miraculously, been accomplished. Or had it?

On the far side of the beach, a scene of activity was taking place near the boathouse. Keeping well hidden, Gerry saw that the doors of the boathouse were being dragged open by the manservant Harker and a much younger man; stockily built, with a mane of dark hair, and wearing oil-skins and sea-boots. The tide was coming in fast, swallowing up the sand, increasing the odds against her safe return to the castle via the cliff path to the forecourt. She could scarcely bypass Harker and his henchman, hefting her shopping bags, with a foolish smile on her face and a cheery 'good day' greeting.

Weighing up the pros and cons in her mind, Gerry considered she could always ditch her shopping, stash it away behind a boulder, sally forth from her hiding place and pretend she'd been for a leisurely stroll along the sand. What? And waste those gingernuts and bananas? No way. She was simply curious to find out what was happening near the boathouse.

Thankfully, she hadn't long to wait. Harker and the man she labelled the Troll, having opened the doors, went into the boathouse – to do what? she wondered. The answer was now obvious. The boat was being launched. Glencochlin was at the wheel. As the vessel slipped into view, Gerry smothered a cry of anguish. The Troll was in the stern: beside him huddled a grey-haired woman, the collar of her fur coat framing her face. The countess, Gerry thought bleakly. But where were they taking her? And *why?*

Harker, she reckoned, must have gone

back to the castle via the internal passageways leading from the boathouse. No prizes
for guessing that the countess had been
brought down to the boathouse by the same
route, more than likely drugged to prevent
her from struggling and calling out for help.
Seldom had Gerry felt as useless as she did
now, having failed to help the countess as
she had intended. Too late now.

Emerging from her hiding place, glancing
out to sea, she saw the motor launch as a
mere speck on the horizon, heading, presumably, to some much larger vessel lying at
anchor beyond the three-mile exclusion
zone, awaiting the arrival of the motor
launch, no doubt, and the helpless woman in
charge of her captors, Glencochlin and the
Troll. Why, Gerry hadn't the faintest idea,
she could only surmise that the countess's
future looked grim, if, indeed, she had a
future.

When the coast was clear, unhitching her
shopping bags, Gerry hurried along the
beach to begin the steep ascent to the castle
forecourt. Looking and feeling like the
'Wreck of the Hesperus', having reached her
destination, she entered the castle and stumbled upstairs to discover Bill standing at the
door of their room, a worried frown creasing
his forehead, demanding to know where she
had been.

'Shopping, I took a bit of a short cut, that's

all. Here, have a banana,' Gerry said ingenuously, gasping for breath and dumping her carrier bags on the carpet. 'I'm sorry, Bill. I didn't mean to be facetious. Please, sit down, there are things I need to tell you. I should have told you sooner, but I didn't want to worry you when you were in so much pain with your poorly ankle, an' all, so I kept it to myself—'

'Kept *what* to yourself?' Bill asked, perching on the edge of his bed. 'Come on, Gerry, spill the beans. I guessed there was summat up, but I'm not a mind reader. In any case, I've been in a stupor most of the time from those "painkilling tablets" you've been feeding me. Sleeping pills, more likely. I'm right, aren't I?'

'Well it said on the packet, "These tablets may cause drowsiness", which they did, and I figured that, asleep, you'd forget about the pain in your foot. Now, do you want an argument or to hear about the countess?'

'The *countess*? Who the hell is she, for Pete's sake?' Bill's frown deepened.

'Glencochlin's "auntie",' Gerry explained impatiently, 'who I chanced upon in the boathouse, when I stumbled in backwards, if you recall?'

Bill, who hadn't a clue what she was on about, said levelly, 'Look. Gerry love, calm down and begin at the beginning. Forget you're a bestselling crime novelist, pretend you're in the witness box at the Old Bailey and take it from there. OK?'

'Yes, Bill. Sorry. Well, here goes.' Perching next to him, she began.

Listening intently, Bill pieced together the whole dramatic story, groaning slightly when Gerry embarked on the tale of her perilous journey round the rocks of the Glencochlin peninsula with her carrier bags of groceries strapped to her waist, thinking how easily she might have been swept away by the incoming tide. Yet maintaining his silence until she had finished speaking when, gathering her into his arms, he said huskily, 'Thank God you're still alive and kicking. When I think how close I came to losing you.'

'Oh, never mind about me. What about the countess? What about the ghastly goings on here in Glencochlin Castle?' Gerry reminded him. 'If what I suspect about a drug smuggling racket is true, the sooner we decide what to do about it, the better.'

'Such as what, for instance?' Bill responded patiently. 'Gerry, my love, you know as well as I do, perhaps even better, that the police need facts, not guesswork. Tell them what you suspect by all means. DCI Moncrieff struck me as being a reasonable, approachable human being, but even his hands would be tied without facts to go on.'

Gerry knew Bill was right, and said so. Getting up, she went to the bathroom to make herself presentable before lunch, wondering how long this house party nightmare was destined to last. What would happen if she and Bill packed their belongings and headed back to London? She would have to do the driving, of course, but they could take their time, stopping as and when they felt like it: knowing, as the thought occurred, that to leave here now would be impossible. How could she go without knowing what had become of the countess, why Sam MacNally had been murdered and how Penny Douglas had met her death? Without telling DCI Moncrieff of her brief encounter with a woman who had begged her for help – before it was too late?

Gerry knew she could not. Up to her neck in the sinister goings on at Glencochlin Castle, come hell or high water, she must see this thing through to the bitter end. But where, oh where, were DCI Moncrieff and his sidekick DS Murdoch? Had they simply disappeared into the wild blue yonder, when she so desperately needed to talk to them again?

Eight

Now what was Gerry up to? Bill wondered. Apart from sitting cross-legged on her bed, eyes closed, a scowl of concentration on her face, and muttering what sounded like an incantation.

'Sorry, darling,' she sighed when Bill enquired, opening her eyes, 'I'm doing a spot of thinking.'

'About – *what*?' he enquired anxiously. One never quite knew for certain, so far as she was concerned, exactly what was going on in that astute mind of hers.

'About servants,' she enlightened him, 'or rather the lack of them. Who, for instance, sweeps the dust under the carpets? Who makes the beds? Lights the drawing room fire, helps with the washing up? Apart from Harker, the "Wardress" and the "Troll", I haven't, so far, clapped eyes on anyone else even remotely resembling a servant. As for the "Troll", how does he fit into the picture?'

Warming to her theme, she continued, 'Another thing that bothers me, that turret room. As sure as eggs is eggs, there's a secret passage leading from it to the boathouse. I'm not being fanciful, Bill. How else could the countess have appeared in that boathouse, her clothing as dry as a bone, the first time I saw her? It was pouring down with rain at the time. Had she been outdoors, that fur coat of hers would have been wet, not dry.' I'm right, Bill, aren't I? No-one can walk in the rain without getting wet, can they?'

'Not without an umbrella. Not always with one either, if it happens to be my golf umbrella with you under it.' Bill spoke lightly to divert Gerry's mind from the turret room and the possibility of there being a secret passage, dreading the thought of her attempting to find out if such a passage existed. He said despairingly, 'Please, Gerry, promise me you'll steer well clear of that room. Why poke and pry into matters that don't concern us?'

Abandoning her buddha-like position with some difficulty, wishing she had not assumed it in the first place and massaging her knees as she got up to cross over to Bill's bed, she said, 'You don't get it, do you? It's my belief that, had we stayed in that turret room, *I* might well have disappeared without trace. I'm deadly serious, Bill! Don't ask me why, but we were invited here for a specific purpose – to get rid of me.'

Bill looked stunned. Deeply shocked, he said, 'Gerry darling, you *must* be mistaken.

111

Why *you*, of all people? Dammit, you – we – had never clapped eyes on Glencochlin until that day we saw him on the quayside.'

'I know, Bill. As I said before, I haven't the faintest idea. All I know is the look of hatred I saw on his face when he handed me a glass of gin and tonic when we joined this ghastly house party of his. My blood ran cold, I can tell you.' She shuddered slightly at the recollection. 'That was why I begged you not to confront him over the turret room stairs. I knew, even then, that Glencochlin was dangerous. It all began with the murder of Sam MacNally. I'm certain Glencochlin believes that Sam knew his life was in danger and why; that the poor old man divulged the name of the person he was afraid of – I also believe that the laird, realizing I had over-heard his conversation with the countess, wanted rid of us and as quietly as possible. You see, Bill, I think that Glencochlin is a cold-blooded murderer. My belief is he killed Sam MacNally and Penny Douglas. Well, that's it in a nutshell!'

If only he hadn't crocked his ankle, Bill thought, blaming himself, not Gerry, for their present dilemma, the extent of which he had not fully realized until now. He said hoarsely, 'Look, darling, we *must* get away from here. No excuses necessary, we'll just get into the car – and go. As simple as that. If the police come after us, so much the

112

better. We'd be a damn sight safer in custody than we are here. Frankly, I'd welcome being locked up, behind bars, rather than remain in this bloody awful – fortress – a moment longer than necessary.' He shuddered, 'Talk about the Bastille!'

Gerry said fearfully, 'But Glencochlin and the Troll, not the police, would come after us. Trust me, Bill, I *know*. We'd probably end up dead in the wreckage of the car, the way Sam MacNally ended up dead in his land-rover. No evidence of foul play, of course, not murder as such, just an unfortunate accident, with the car wrapped round a tree and a couple of dead bodies in the front seats. We'd best stay put for the time being and pray that DCI Moncrieff will turn up again soon.'

Bill groaned. 'With our luck it will probably be Sergeant Kirk.' But he was wrong.

As Kirk left his office late that night, he glanced over his shoulder, turned up his coat collar against the wind and rain, and thought he'd be glad of a warm fire, a bite to eat and a wee dram before bedtime. He had stopped walking suddenly to peer into the darkness, almost certain he'd heard footsteps behind him; stealthy footsteps. 'Who's there?' he'd called out. Then, 'Oh, it's you.' The last words he ever spoke. Momentarily, shockingly, he'd been aware of a raised arm, the swift descent of an iron bar before death claimed him, when his lifeless body had sprawled forward, streaming blood and brain matter from the heavy blow to his cranium, which his police cap had done nothing to deflect.

Indeed, so violent had been the attack that Constable Mitchell, who had discovered the body in the early hours of next morning, had thrown up when he saw that Kirk's cap had been driven into his skull by the severity of the blow, and appeared to be glued to his scalp by the congealed blood issuing from the wound.

Pale and shaken, Mitchell had stumbled into the office to contact DCI Moncrieff, whose phone number had been scrawled, by Kirk, the day before when the DCI had rung him about the newly established incident room at Cove View Cottage. Later, when Moncrieff and Murdoch had arrived at the scene of Kirk's murder, Mitchell had been taken to hospital, suffering from shock.

'A nasty business, this,' Moncrieff said distastefully, awaiting the arrival of a SOC team from a police station based in Harris, which Moncrieff had contacted earlier to request help in his present dilemma relating to the brutal murder of a fellow officer, lately in charge of the Stornoway Constabulary.

'You mean Sergeant Kirk?'

'Yes, sir.'

'And you are—?'

114

'Detective Chief Inspector Moncrieff of Divisional Headquarters, Glasgow, here to investigate the murder of one Samuel Mac-Nally, the probable murder of a Mrs Penny Douglas, and what I can only describe as sinister goings on at a certain Glencochlin Castle, if you've ever heard of it?'

'Heard of it? My dear fellow, who hasn't? So Glencochlin's back in residence, is he? Well, take my advice, Moncrieff, tread warily. Glencochlin's a slippery customer and no mistake; as cunning as a fox and as clever as a monkey, always one step ahead of the law. That's all I'm prepared to say for the time being, except I pray to heaven that the law will catch up with him as quickly as possible.'

When the SOC team had finished their work, taking photographs and measurements, and cordoning off the alleyway in which the murder had occurred, the chief in charge of the Scene of Crime Squad told Moncrieff, 'No sign of the murder weapon, sir, and no relevant fingerprints neither. It's my guess that the murderer took the murder weapon with him after the fatal blow had been struck: a crowbar, the MO reckons. Well, sir, since there's nothing more to be done here, with your permission I'd like to head back to Tarbert, leaving two of my team here to stand watch, to man the office and so

115

forth. They'll need somewhere to stay. Can that be arranged? Constable MacKenzie has volunteered for the night watch, Constable Mackie will relieve him first thing tomorrow morning, if that is in order, sir?'

'Yes indeed, Sergeant, and thank you. There's a small hotel not a stone's throw from here. I'll have a word with the landlady, make sure your men are well taken care of; see if I can rustle up pyjamas, razors and so on. Detective Sergeant Murdoch and I have established an incident room in the vicinity. You'd best make a note of the phone number.'

'I have it here, sir,' Sergeant Lansdale said briskly, 'and you'll find my incident report on the office desk.' Saluting smartly, he and the rest of his team headed towards the police vehicles parked in the town square, pushing their way through a silent crowd of onlookers gathered there to witness events stemming from the tragic death of Sergeant Kirk, a well known figure in their midst: not well liked, but feared.

Following their departure, Moncrieff had a word with the two constables left on duty, after which he walked to the hotel to arrange overnight accommodation for them, possibly two nights, explaining the nature of their requirements. 'Och, nae need tae worry,' the landlady assured him, 'I've menfolk of ma own, plenty o' clean pyjamas an' spare razors. They'll be just fine here.'

Walking back the way he had come, he paused to tell the two constables the name of the hotel. Meanwhile Murdoch emerged from Kirk's office to impart the news that Constable Mitchell would be back on duty the next day; having been given the all clear by the doctor who had treated him for shock – suffered on his discovery of Kirk's body.

Moncrieff nodded in satisfaction at Mitchell's recovery. On their way to Cove View, he reminded Murdoch that they would need to question Kirk's sidekick about events prior to the sergeant's murder. Meanwhile he had begun enquiring into the backgrounds of Glencochlin's houseparty guests, his servants, and the man himself, information which would be relayed to him by telephone from Glasgow – a lengthy procedure but the best he could hope for without access to his own computer.

A verbal tussle had ensued with Mrs Cameron when Moncrieff had requested the removal of surplus ornaments from the incident room. 'This is ma hame, ye ken,' she said stiffly, 'I see nae airthly reason why I should remove ma bits an' pieces at your say so.'

'For safe keeping, ma'am,' Moncrieff said urbanely, 'in case of accidents. Young Murdoch takes up a lot of space, as you've probably noticed, with a habit of waving his arms about and blundering into the furniture in moments of excitement or stress.'

'Weel, yes, now ye come tae mention it, he is a verra weel built young man,' the landlady concurred with an admiring glance in Murdoch's direction. 'Hot blooded, I daresay, when the mood tekks him.' Sighing deeply, she added, 'As the saying gaes, youth must hev its fling.' Secretly wishing that Murdoch would fling himself in her direction in moments of excitement or stress. As to his habit of blundering into furniture, he'd be more than welcome to blunder into her bedside table any time he felt like it...

And so the matter of the extraneous ornaments had been resolved to Moncrieff's satisfaction when they, and Mrs Cameron's china cabinet had been removed from the incident room to her back parlour by the long suffering Murdoch, upon whose return Moncrieff said expansively, 'Ah, that's better. Now, let's get down to business, shall we? Catch ourselves a killer or two, possibly even three, if my thinking is correct.'

'You mean you know who murdered Sam MacNally, Mrs Douglas and Sergeant Kirk?' Murdoch asked respectfully.

'Put it this way, laddie,' Moncrieff replied, smiling grimly, 'I have my suspicions. No proof, as yet, but I shall have, given the time, patience and the information I need to bring this case to a barn-storming conclusion.'

'Won't you at least give me a hint, sir?' Murdoch frowned.

'No, laddie, that I shall not. You are the Sherlock Holmes buff. Work it out for yourself. Now we'd best be on our way to Glencochlin Castle to conduct further enquiries concerning one person in particular.'

'You mean Glencochlin?'

'No, son. Not Glencochlin. The person I have in mind is Mrs Geraldine Bentine. According to the Glasgow computer, a woman of some standing with our Scotland Yard colleagues as an undercover agent, instrumental in solving at least two headline murder cases, at considerable risk to her own life and limb. A bestselling crime novelist to boot. A woman of integrity, vouchsafed by no less a personage than DCI Brambell of the Yard, himself the acme of decency and honour. He is a force to be reckoned within the annals of crime solution; recipient of an OBE and, the highest honour of all, a George Cross for bravery in the line of duty in his younger days.'

Later, Murdoch repressed a shudder at the sight of Glencochlin Castle looming through the mist as he bowled the car into the forecourt, dreading a further encounter with bizarre Laird of Glencochlin who, quite frankly, gave him the creeps.

'Bear up, laddie,' Moncrieff advised him, getting out of the car to ring the doorbell, 'keep your eyes open and your mouth shut: your notebook and biro at the ready.'

Harker greeted them impassively and ushered them into the drawing room to await the arrival of the laird who, he explained, was in his private quarters at the moment. 'I'll tell him you're here, sir,' he said. 'Is he expecting you?'

'No. This is a passing visit. We shan't stay long. A word or two will suffice for the time being,' Moncrieff said briefly. Holding his hands towards the fire when the man had departed, 'I wouldn't mind a look see at the laird's private quarters,' he told Murdoch, glancing up at the mounted stag's head over the mantelpiece with distaste at its moth-eaten appearance.

'We could apply for a search warrant,' Murdoch suggested eagerly, glancing over his shoulder to make certain the laird hadn't materialized like the demon king in a pantomime.

'All in good time, laddie. All in good time,' Moncrieff replied grimly, 'when we are sure of our ground. Wisht now: I think he's coming.'

Glencochlin entered the room with a flourish, a formidable figure in his usual black get-up. 'Ah, gentlemen,' he said expansively, 'an unexpected pleasure. How may I help you?'

'That depends, Laird,' Moncrieff replied levelly, 'on your co-operation in matters pertaining to our enquiries into the deaths of Sam MacNally, Mrs Penny Douglas and now the murder of Sergeant Hamish Kirk, a man you knew well, I believe?'

Glencochlin appeared stunned momentarily. 'Kirk?' he uttered hoarsely. 'You mean to tell me that he's dead? But when did it happen? This is appalling news. Of course I knew the man, not well as you suggest, but in his official capacity as a law enforcement officer. As you know, he was here recently in connection with the Penny Douglas affair, and he was, to the best of my knowledge and belief, also involved in enquiries into the unfortunate death of Samuel MacNally.'

'Ah yes, MacNally,' Moncrieff nodded. 'An employee of yours, I understand? I am right in thinking that you are the owner of an estate agency, am I not?'

Glencochlin smiled indulgently, 'Nothing of the sort, Inspector. I merely dabble in making available my own properties to visitors during the summer months. Let me explain. Apart from the castle, from which I absent myself from February until October to pursue my main business interests in Queensland, Australia, my estate includes several houses and cottages, both ancient and modern, which benefit greatly from occupancy by tourists to the island when I am far away from home.

'I employed Sam MacNally, on a part-time basis, to deal with incoming requests for accommodation, to meet visitors on their arrival and hand them the keys. His duties included making certain that all was in apple-pie order beforehand. It beggars belief that he was murdered. *Why?* He was such an inoffensive old man. Why on earth should anyone have wanted him dead?'

'His murderer presumably did,' Moncrieff commented drily. 'The reason why we're here, to discover the identity of that murderer!'

'Of course, Inspector. And you can count on my full cooperation and support,' Glencochlin promised smoothly.

'Good. In which case I should like a word with one of your house guests, Mrs Geraldine Bentine, now if at all possible.'

'I think that can be arranged. My man will ask her to come down. By the way, this house party's going a bit stale. My guests are showing signs of irritation at being incarcerated, as it were, waiting for – what exactly?'

'The inquest on Mrs Douglas,' Moncrieff explained, 'when the coroner will examine the evidence pertaining to her death and make clear his views on whether she drowned accidentally or if she was murdered.'

'*Murdered?* But that's ridiculous.' Glencochlin's eyes narrowed. 'Good grief, man, the woman was lying with her face in a pool of water. The inference was clear. She must have stumbled and fallen accidentally. Your murder theory is nothing short of ludicrous. Mrs Douglas was an extremely popular, attractive young woman with everything to live for. Who, in their right senses, would have wanted to kill her?'

Turning abruptly, he tugged at a bell-pull near the fireplace to summon his man-servant. When the man appeared on the threshold, 'Ask Mrs Bentine to come down to the drawing room at once,' he ordered. 'Tell her, with my compliments, that Inspector Moncrieff wishes to speak to her.'

When Harker had gone to do his master's bidding, Glencochlin said coldly, 'Now, Inspector, if you'll excuse me, I have work to do.' So saying, he strode out of the room without a backward glance in Moncrieff's and Murdoch's direction.

Minutes later, Gerry came in. Her opening words were, 'Oh, thank God you are here.' Her relief was obvious. 'I have something very important to tell you. It's the countess, you see? She's gone missing.'

Nine

'*The countess?*' Moncrieff looked mystified, as well he might. This case was assuming nightmare proportions. 'Sit down, Mrs Bentine,' he advised her. 'Take your time. Now, tell me, who is the countess, and what leads you to believe she's – gone missing?'

'Because the last I saw of her, she was in Glencochlin's motor launch, heading for the open sea, in charge of the "Troll". It's my belief she'd been drugged, bundled down from the turret room under sedation, dumped in the stern like a sack of potatoes, and where she is now I shudder to think, the poor woman.'

'*The "Troll"?*' Moncrieff's frown deepened. 'Are you by any chance referring to the Harkers' grandson, Ian?'

'I don't know! I'd never clapped eyes on him before. I didn't know that Harker had a grandson, or a wife, come to that.' Gerry paused momentarily to weigh up the pros and cons, then, 'Oh, God,' she uttered fearfully. 'You mean the "Wardress".' Light had dawned suddenly upon her hitherto mud-

124

dled thought processes. 'Of course! Why didn't I think of it before? The "Wardress" must have been none other than Mrs Harker. Sorry, Inspector, if you'll bear with me, I'll begin at the beginning and go on from there.'

Moncrieff and Murdoch listened intently as Gerry, now fully in control of her mental faculties, regaled them with the tale of the countess from beginning to end, including the row she had overheard in the turret room between her and Glencochlin. She strongly believed that the countess, having become a thorn in the laird's flesh, had been held prisoner in the turret room before more permanent arrangements were made for her, on her removal from Glencochlin Castle.

When Gerry had concluded her story, uncertain whether or not to believe it, it sounded so bizarre, and taking into account that she was, by profession, a crime novelist with a lively imagination, Moncrieff tried a fresh approach from a different angle. 'Tell me, Mrs Bentine,' he said quietly, 'have you formed a theory of what exactly is going on here?'

'Well, yes, a racket of some kind. Drug smuggling more than likely, in which Glencochlin's house guests are all somehow involved. Why else would they have come here from as far afield as Italy, Germany, and New York, if not to – talk turkey? That's fairly

125

obvious, isn't it? Hardly likely they'd have foregathered in this God-forsaken spot to enjoy the laird's notion of hospitality, to eat indifferent grub and half freeze to death in stone cold bedrooms, with no servants to wait on them hand and foot?' She continued, speaking levelly yet forcefully, 'Think about it, Inspector! Had it not been for the murder of Penny Douglas, the house party would have been a one night stand, not the long drawn out endurance test it has become, with the guests at daggers drawn, and I should know. I'm one of them, for Pete's sake. Well, almost. Not quite.' She smiled, 'Call me Gerry, by the way. Mrs Bentine sounds so formal, and I'm not used to it yet.'

'Why did you come here – Gerry?' Moncrieff asked her.

'I, that is we, Bill and I, were invited. We were in a Glencochlin-owned bungalow at the time, when the man himself appeared with an offer we could scarcely refuse.'

'What kind of offer?' Moncrieff spoke sympathetically.

'The offer of a stone built cottage in exchange for a modern bungalow with a slate roof and a dodgy hot-water supply. He apologized that the agent, Sam MacNally, had handed us the wrong keys apparently.'

'Sam MacNally?' Moncrieff's interest quickened. 'Tell me about him.'

'There isn't much to tell,' Gerry replied.

'He simply gave us the keys, said there was a storm brewing, got into his landrover and set off back to Stornoway. In any case, it's all in the statements Bill and I gave to Sergeant Kirk after his visit to the bungalow, next day. He's certain to have kept copies, being the conscientious type. Why not ask him for a look?'

Moncrieff said quietly, 'Unfortunately, Sergeant Kirk is no longer with us. He's been murdered.'

'*Murdered?* Ye gods! But *why*? By whom?' Gerry looked stricken. 'First Sam MacNally, then Penny Douglas, now Sergeant Kirk! What's going on here? It doesn't make sense! Have you no clues, Inspector? Nothing to go on? And what about the countess? What if she also has been murdered? What, if anything, are you going to do about it?'

Moncrieff said patiently, 'So far as the countess is concerned, there is nothing we *can* do for the time being. Think about it, Gerry, we have no proof whatever that the woman was kept here, under duress, much less that she was abducted, against her will, just as we have no positive proof that Penny Douglas's death was deliberate, not accidental. Not, at least, until tomorrow, at the coroner's inquest into her demise.' He added briefly, 'I take it you'll be there, at twelve o'clock precisely, in the Methodist Church Hall?'

'Wild horses couldn't keep me away,' Gerry assured him grimly.

The church hall was packed to capacity. A tin-roofed building, it stood in a field opposite the church itself, and the manse Gerry had passed that day she had embarked on her hazardous journey round the Glencochlin peninsula, lumbered with her shopping bags.

The coroner, a thin, elderly man, was seated at a trestle table at the far end of the room, apparently absorbed in perusing the contents of a manila folder in front of him. A good sign, Gerry thought, at least he was doing his homework, taking no notice of the occupants of the rows of chairs ranged up in this makeshift courtroom, or those seated to right and left of him, on whom he would call, in due course, to give evidence relevant to the death of Penny Douglas. Glencochlin, Penny's husband, Brian, Gloria and Arnold Crowther, Tony Cannelli, Constable Mitchell, the police medical officer – herself and Bill were all seated at the long wooden table.

Wondering if she should apologize for their last minute arrival, Gerry decided to remain silent, thinking it best not to mention the struggle she'd had to stuff Bill's right foot into its sock and to lace up his shoe once the sock was in place. No way, he'd protested vehemently, was he prepared to attend an official inquiry wearing his slippers. No lame excuses for him.

They had just sat down when a clock somewhere struck twelve, and the proceedings began. When the tinny notes had died away, the coroner looked up from his homework, cleared his throat, adjusted his silver-framed spectacles, and reminded his audience of the solemnity of the occasion, and the responsibility resting on his shoulders to determine the cause of death of a Mrs Penelope Douglas – a member of a house party at Glencochlin Castle, whose body had been discovered, face down in a pool of seawater, to which end it was his duty to question witnesses, here present, to arrive at the truth of the matter. Whereupon, instructing his clerk of court to summon the first witness, Brian Douglas rose unsteadily to his feet to take his place in the witness box – a podium on which stood a kind of lectern embellished with a bible.

Gerry's heart sank. The poor young man looked so lonely, so bereft, standing there to give evidence leading to the discovery of his wife's body lying face down in that pool of water.

Had Mrs Douglas given any reason why she wished to go out alone on the afternoon of her death? the coroner asked intently.

'She said she fancied a breath of fresh air,' Brian answered in a low voice.

'Didn't it strike you as odd that she didn't ask you to go with her?'

'No, not really. Penny was an independent person, and I was in bed at the time. A bit under the weather, to be honest, having drunk more than was good for me, I guess.' He buried his face in his hands, his shoulders heaved with unsuppressed emotion. 'When I woke up and realized how long she'd been gone, I hurried down to the drawing room to alert the other guests.

'Immediately, our host, Laird Glencochlin, organized a search party to look for her. Oh, God! Need I go on? There she was, my darling girl, beyond human aid. The sea was coming in, rain was falling, daylight fading fast. I lifted her up in my arms and carried her to a boathouse further along the beach, and stayed with her all night long, just praying for a miracle to happen, that I'd wake up to find it had all been a bad dream. That Penny would wake up too, saying she was hungry and we'd be late for dinner if we didn't hurry. You see, I couldn't bring myself to believe that she was really dead, and I still can't, God help me! I still can't believe that I'll never talk with her, laugh with her, ever again. We were so happy together and I loved her so much. So very much.'

Following a brief consultation with his clerk, the coroner ordered the removal of Brian Douglas from the courtroom to spare the witness further distress or embarrassment, to Gerry's infinite relief. Watching the stripping bare of a fellow human's emotions had been a nerve-wracking experience, giving rise to the fear that young Brian Douglas might never recover from the loss of his wife.

Next to be called to the witness stand was Glencochlin, a towering, bizarre figure in his all-black clothing, who calmly testified that he had, indeed, organized the search party which had led to the discovery of Mrs Douglas's body lying face down in a pool of water, her neck tethered to an outcrop of rock by a heavy gold chain she happened to be wearing at the time of her death.

'Tell me, Laird,' the coroner queried, 'what significance did you attach to that particular item of jewellery?'

'Why, simply that the poor lady might well have survived had she not had the misfortune to become entangled with that jutting spur of rock. Obviously, she had struggled to free herself and, when she could not, she simply drowned.' Glencochlin shuddered slightly. 'A horrible, accidental death which no-one could possibly have foreseen – or prevented, in my view – since she was out walking alone at the time.'

'Thank you, Laird. You may step down now,' the coroner acceded, well aware of Glencochlin's standing in the community, yet in no way impressed by his outré appearance or his ill concealed arrogance in the witness box when expressing his own view that the death of Mrs Douglas had been purely accidental.

Gerry's blood almost froze in her veins when the clerk of court intoned impassively, 'Will Mrs Geraldine Bentine now please take the stand.'

Leeching on to Bill's sleeve, 'I'm scared of messing this up,' she hissed. 'What on earth shall I say?'

'You'll think of something. Go on, sock it to 'em about why you think Penny's death was no accident.'

Knees knocking, Gerry mounted the podium to face her ordeal.

Asked if she had been a member of Glencochlin's search party, present at the discovery of Mrs Douglas's body on the afternoon of her death. Gerry replied in the affirmative. 'Yes, I was present on that occasion.'

'Can you describe the scene for us?' The coroner's glance was direct yet sympathetic. 'Take your time, Mrs Bentine.'

'Well, we were all deeply shocked. Mrs Douglas was lying, face down, in a rock pool. She was obviously dead.'

'Quite so. And did you notice anything – untoward – which led you to believe that Mrs Douglas had died other than accidentally?'

Drawing in a deep breath, 'Yes, sir, I did,' Gerry responded quietly. 'I noticed that the heavy gold chain and cross she'd been wearing at lunchtime, had become attached to a spur of rock much higher than the victim's head, suggestive of the fact that it had been placed there by someone else, inflicting dreadful injuries to her throat and neck area, in a vain attempt to free herself from the throttling restraints of her jewellery. In a state of exhaustion, the poor woman had finally fallen forward to drown in less than six inches of water.'

'Leading to what conclusion on your part?' the coroner asked intently.

'That Mrs Douglas was not alone on the beach at the time of her death,' Gerry said doggedly. 'It's my belief that she went out, that afternoon, to meet someone who wanted her dead.'

'I see. Thank you, Mrs Bentine, you may step down now,' the coroner said levelly, turning to his clerk of court to summon the next witness. The medical officer, who had performed the autopsy on Penny Douglas, moved towards the podium. Having first supplied details of his qualifications as a long standing member of the medical profession, he went on to state, categorically, that in his opinion, Mrs Douglas *had* met her death by drowning, a fact consistent with the amount of seawater found in the victim's lungs – proving beyond a shadow of doubt that she had been alive and breathing prior to her inhalation of the seawater in the rock pool.

'I see, Doctor Marriot,' the coroner commented impassively, duty bound, by law, to accept the findings of an expert witness into the manner of death of the deceased, yet free to make up his own mind regarding the verdict.

With this thought in mind, 'Tell me, Doctor,' he persisted, 'what conclusions did you draw from the injuries to the throat and neck of Mrs Douglas?'

'Why, simply that she had struggled desperately to free herself from the heavy gold chain and cross she was wearing at the time of her death, which had somehow become attached to a spur of rock adjacent to the rock pool,' Marriot replied edgily, obviously rattled by the coroner's cross-questioning when he had already stated the cause of death.

'In your opinion, Doctor Marriot,' the coroner pursued relentlessly, 'could Mrs Douglas's injuries have been caused by someone? Could the injuries have been suffered in a desperate struggle for life, and could these injuries have weakened her to the extent of her falling, face down, into that rock pool?'

'It might well have done so,' Marriot conceded ungraciously. 'But I deal with facts, not supposition. I, sir, am a doctor, not a clairvoyant!'

Seemingly satisfied, the coroner, Charles Maxwell, dismissed Marriot from the witness stand and began his interrogation of first, Tony Cannelli, then the Crowthers, Arnold and Gloria, and finally Bill, all of whom had been present, as members of Glencochlin's search party, at the discovery of Penny Douglas's dead body on the beach below Glencochlin Castle. None of whom, apart from Bill, was prepared to shed a glimmer of light on the happenings on that fateful afternoon in which they had all been involved to some extent. Not one of them had ever met or talked to Penny Douglas, or her husband, prior to their arrival at Glencochlin Castle as fellow guests at the laird's house party.

Called to the witness stand, Bill said clearly, 'Mrs Douglas and I were next to each other at luncheon. She talked, I listened.'

'What was the gist of the conversation?'

'Mainly money: possessions, her love of shopping, a new apartment overlooking Central Park. She mentioned that she had recently purchased the heavy gold chain and cross she was wearing, from Tiffany, for a mere twenty thousand dollars.'

'The item of jewellery she was wearing at the time of her death?' Maxwell pursued intently.

'Yes,' Bill replied quietly.

'And what conclusions did you draw from the appearance of that item of jewellery's attachment to a spur of rock adjacent to the pool of water in which the deceased had so sadly met her end?'

'Why, simply that, considering the sheer weight of it, it struck me as odd that it had become entangled, accidentally, with that spur of rock. If Mrs Douglas had tripped and fallen into that rockpool by accident, the cross and chain would have been trapped beneath her body, not floating free – like a feather in the breeze – to attach itself to a conveniently situated splinter of rock.'

'In other words, Mr Bentine, are you suggesting that the death of Mrs Douglas was not accidental, but deliberate?'

Drawing in a deep breath, meeting Gerry's eyes across the table, trusting implicitly in her hunch that the death of Penny Douglas had not been accidental, but a case of cold-blooded murder, he answered succinctly, 'Yes, sir, that is precisely what I'm suggesting.'

'Thank you, Mr Bentine. You may step down now.'

Bill did so cautiously, deeply aware of the pain in his right ankle, as he hobbled back to his wife, who murmured ecstatically, as he slumped down beside her, 'Oh, well done, darling. You were nothing short of magnificent.'

The testimony of Bill and Gerry Bentine had caused quite a stir in the courtroom. The inquest alone had injected an aura of excitement into the mundane lives of the fisherfolk eking a precarious livelihood in the shadow of Glencochlin Castle, known locally as 'the 'Big Hoose', from which news of a drowning accident had filtered down to them via the 'Postie', who delivered their letters and liked nothing better than to engage in a bit of gossip. 'Ah, sich goin's on as ye wudna believe,' he would tell his listeners, leaning against his bicycle and rolling his eyes heavenward. On the day following the drowning, 'Perlice cars in the forecourt, no less. Tek ma wurrd for it, there's trubble brewin' for 'is lairdship.'

Now, it would appear, Postie's dire predictions concerning Glencochlin's troubles were entirely correct. The frozen expression on the man's face as the coroner announced his findings, scarcely succeeded in disguising the laird's innate fury and frustration that the 'open verdict' had failed utterly to end speculation over the death of Penny Douglas, giving rise to further police enquiries into her demise, doubts promulgated in the coroner's mind by the evidence given by Gerry and Bill Bentine.

Rising to his feet at the conclusion of the

inquiry, Glencochlin pondered grimly that the time had come to put paid to the Bentines once and for all.

Ten

Members of the house party made their way back to the castle, after the inquest, to partake of a far from heart-warming luncheon of cold meat, salad and ice cream, served in the ice cube atmosphere of the dining room.

Acting as a kind of spokesperson for her fellow guests, Gloria Crowther enquired charmingly of Glencochlin, 'Are we free to leave now? Not that we are in any way demeaning your hospitality, but we do have urgent business matters to attend to, travel arrangements to make, belongings to pack. You do understand, don't you?'

'Most certainly,' he responded graciously. 'However, since today is well advanced, I suggest that you postpone your leave taking until tomorrow. Join me, this evening, in a farewell drinks party, preceding a celebratory dinner.'

'Yes, of course,' Gloria enthused. 'What a brilliant idea. Everyone in agreement?'

All eyes, except Gerry's, were on Gloria. It

was then she noticed something decidedly odd.

Later, attending to Bill's foot, 'How old is Gloria Crowther, do you imagine? Go on, hazard a guess,' Gerry said.

Mystified, 'I haven't a clue,' he admitted. 'Difficult to tell under all that makeup she wears. Oh very well then, middle to late fifties at a rough guess. Why do you ask?'

'And how about Professor Telemann?' Gerry persisted.

'*Telemann?*' Bill frowned. 'Look, love, what's this all about?'

'I'll tell you later. Just bear with me and answer the question.'

'Oh lord, late seventies to early eighties by the look of him; bent double with arthritis, as deaf as a post and as blind as a bat, I shouldn't wonder, hence those pebble-lens glasses of his. How he made it here without a minder and a wheelchair in tow, beats me.'

'It's my belief that he has no need of either,' Gerry said levelly, 'that he hasn't an arthritic bone in his body. I'd also bet my bottom dollar that he's no more than forty.'

Bill snorted. 'You're kidding. Are you saying that Telemann's an imposter? What on earth put that idea into your head?'

'His hands! At luncheon, when Gloria was holding centre stage, and when he thought no-one was looking his way, he uncurled the fingers of his right hand to crumble a bread

139

roll. Believe me, Bill, it was the hand of a young man, not that of a gnarled and knotted octogenarian.'

'But surely, what I mean is, if the professor *is* here under false pretences, presumably in heavy disguise, how has he managed to get away with it? He's either a consummate actor or a darned fool with a death wish.' Unwilling to pursue the topic, tentatively, Bill wiggled his toes.

Replacing Bill's sock and shoe, 'Try standing up,' Gerry suggested, 'walking, not limping. Go on, you can do it! Your toes are back to normal now. Well, tell me, how does it feel?' No use flogging a dead horse, she thought ruefully.

'Fine! Much better. Thanks, love,' Bill acknowledged, crossing the room to the window and looking out at the forecourt, not daring to limp.

'Know what, Bill?' Gerry said wistfully, getting up, overwhelmed by a sudden longing to go home, back to her Hampstead eyrie, her workroom, her typewriter, her little red Mini, 'I'd rather give the drinks party and the celebration dinner a miss, if you don't mind. Let's just bung our belongings in the car and catch the early morning ferry to the mainland. Frankly, I can't wait to see the back of this benighted castle and its inmates. So let's get going, the sooner the better, shall we?'

Turning away from the window, Bill said bleakly, 'Come here, darling. Take a look. Forget about the car. It's *gone!*'

The drinks session was in progress when Gerry and Bill went down to join the party. What other option had they but to find out what had happened to the hatchback? 'That man can't keep us here against our will,' Bill railed angrily, following the initial shock of losing his car, 'and I'll tell him so in no uncertain terms. He had no right to move my property without my knowledge or permission.'

Gerry agreed wholeheartedly, but her concerns lay deeper than the confiscation of their transport. Above all, why were they being kept against their will? What had Glencochlin in store for them? A quick trip to the open sea in a motor launch? Yet another drowning 'accident'?

She whispered, as they entered the drawing room, 'Play it cool, darling. No use making a crisis out of a disaster.'

'Ah, here you are at last.' Glencochlin stepped forward to greet them, smiling affably. 'By the way, before you "name your poison" so to speak, I owe you an apology. Your car was leaking oil rather badly, so I took the liberty of removing it to my garage for a check-up. I realize, of course, that I should have asked your permission to do so. But well,' with a dismissive shrug of his shoulders, 'I have been somewhat preoccupied of late, what with one thing and another: the inquest above all, and preparations for this evening's farewell festivities, for which I beg your indulgence. Now, what'll it be? Whisky for you, Bill? Gin and tonic for you, Gerry?'

So what exactly was he up to? Gerry wondered, accepting her gin and tonic. Why the affability, the bonhomie? He must have something, apart from his arm, up his sleeve, she reckoned, sniffing her drink suspiciously before venturing to taste it, and glancing about the room at her fellow guests; the Crowthers, Cannelli, Brian Douglas and, seated in a high backed chair, well away from the fire, Max Telemann – or his lookalike, she surmised.

He alone was seated, the rest were standing, nursing drinks, engaging in reasonably animated conversation for a change, obviously relieved by the thought of freedom ahead of them, come tomorrow, of shaking the dust of Glencochlin Castle from their feet and returning to whichever spot on the map they called home. Home, Gerry thought longingly. She said coolly to Glencochlin, 'Strange about that oil leak. The car was given a full service at our local garage a short time ago, and there was nothing wrong with it. So how long will it take to fix? You see, Laird, Bill and I plan to leave here the first thing tomorrow morning, along with the rest of your house party guests.'

Glencochlin said urbanely, 'That would seem a pity, considering the surprise I have in store for you. That honeymoon cottage you had your heart set on, remember?' He smiled grimly, 'I venture to say you'll adore its splendid isolation amid acres of moorland, where you and Bill will be well and truly alone at last. A dream come true, wouldn't you say?'

Sensing danger, a hidden menace in the laird's demeanour, 'Well no,' Gerry replied tautly. 'Thanks, but no thanks. We'd much prefer to go home, back to London, to get on with our lives, if you don't mind.'

'Ah, but I shall mind, a great deal, if you choose not to accept my offer of a fitting conclusion to your honeymoon. Need I say more? Indeed, I've been to great lengths to ensure the success of your stay at Brook Cottage, and I refuse to take no for an answer. I shall drive you there myself tomorrow, after breakfast, is that clearly understood?'

Gerry remained silent, realizing the full implications of the man's words, with the dawning awareness that she and Bill were virtually prisoners of Glencochlin. Obviously, she thought he regarded them as a threat to his security, a threat to the masterminding of whatever diabolical racket he was engaged in. Almost certainly drug smuggling, with sidelines of abduction and cold blooded murder.

At that moment, Harker entered the room to announce that dinner was served.

Seated next to Telemann, taking a calculated risk, Gerry whispered urgently, 'Please, if you can hear me, give me a sign. Knock over your wine glass. *Anything!*' She daren't say more for fear of being overheard, but she had chosen her time precisely to coincide with the moment Glencochlin rose to his feet to carve the leg of roast lamb that Harker had brought to the dining table before returning to the kitchen to bring in the tureens of vegetables.

But what if she'd been wrong in her assessment of Telemann as an imposter? Gerry thought bleakly. What if he really was a long in the tooth octogenarian, as deaf as a post and as blind as a bat? Not a potential ally but a deadly enemy? Then, if so, what of it? she thought fatalistically, she would have to rely on herself to rid Glencochlin of his notion that he could put paid to her and Bill by the simple expedient of robbing them of their car and driving them to an isolated, so called honeymoon cottage, in which he fully intended to rob them of their lives. Huh. Over my dead body, she decided grimly. If Glencochlin imagined that he could get rid of her and Bill so easily, he had another think coming. She'd outsmart the bastard some-how. Just how, at the moment, she hadn't the faintest idea.

And then the miracle happened. Suddenly, dramatically, reaching out for the gravy boat, Telemann knocked over his wine glass, muttering darkly to himself as he did so, berating himself for his clumsiness as he mopped up the spillage with his table nap-kin. Not that anyone else noticed, not with Gloria Crowther holding centre stage, as usual, praising to the skies the tenderness of the roast lamb, and saying, in her loud, grating voice, how much she and her husband had enjoyed their extended visit to Glencochlin Castle: how sorry they would be to leave.

Bill was aware of something going on, a kind of undercurrent of hostility between Gerry and the laird, and was harbouring the familiar feeling of being kept in the dark. 'Look, Gerry love,' he demanded edgily upstairs in their room after dinner, 'if there's something you're not telling me, for Pete's sake spit it out!'

'All right, Bill. But you're not going to like it—'

She was right. He didn't, not one little bit.

When Gerry had finished speaking, 'You honestly expect me to believe that Glencochlin means to kill us? But that's ludicrous. Why, for God's sake, unless the man is completely mad.'

'He *is* mad,' Gerry assured him. 'Completely bonkers and dangerous. I told you some time ago, if you remember, that it was me he was after. You didn't appear to be taking it in, as I recall.'

'Huh! I'm not surprised, with all those tablets you kept on slipping me. Talk about the Sleeping Beauty.'

Gerry chuckled, 'Well, sleeping, anyway.'

'This is no laughing matter, young lady,' Bill reminded her, trying hard to keep a straight face and failing to do so in view of his wife's optimism; her bubbling sense of humour, never far from the surface even in the direst of circumstances. The reasons why he loved her so much, his brave, amazing Gerry Bentine – née Mudd – who had imparted a kind of glow to his life from the moment they'd met in that Greek restaurant. When, in her naivity, following his suggestion of ordering a dish wrapped in vine leaves, she'd later confessed to a preference for steak pie and chips, not knowing what to do with the vine leaves, whether to eat them, leave them on her plate, or to drape them round her lugholes, like earrings.

He hadn't been in love with her then – a fat, plain little lass with a Cockney accent. Aware of her, yes, of her potential as a bestselling author, most certainly. In a sense, Gerry had simply 'grown on him' until he had known, beyond a shadow of doubt, that his life would seem pointless and empty without her. He knew he was, as sure as Christmas Day falling on the 25th of December, passionately in love with her. And if that bastard, Glencochlin, imagined for one moment that he could get away with two more murders to add to his repertoire of crimes so far, he had another think coming.

How exactly he would thwart the man, Bill hadn't the faintest idea. Not a violent person by nature, he couldn't quite picture a punch up with Fergus and his henchman Harker in some crackpot cottage in the middle of nowhere. Why the cottage? he wondered, putting the question to his better half whose power of imagination far outstripped his own and which, indeed, ran away with her, at times; that notion of Telemann being an imposter, for instance, which seemed highly unlikely to Bill's way of thinking.

'Ah, the cottage? I've been trying to figure the answer to that myself,' Gerry admitted.

'And what, if anything, have you come up with?'

'Hmmm. First and foremost, if we're destined for the chop, sure as hell old Glencochlin won't want our bodies found here. I'm pretty damn certain we are to be put to sleep painlessly, he wants our bodies found far away from Glencochlin Castle. And he'll try to make it look like natural causes – no bullet holes, no blood-letting.'

'Thank God for that,' Bill said fervently. 'I never could stand the sight of blood, especially my own. Ask ma, if you don't believe me. I'd blubber like a baby if I nicked my chin, shaving, and I was seventeen years old at the time.'

'Know what?' Gerry chuckled admiringly. 'If we come out of this mess alive, you could earn a living as a gag-writer for Ken Dodd.'

'Whaddayou mean by *if* we come out of this mess alive?' Bill said determinedly, 'No way am I prepared to set foot in that bloody holiday cottage, to die of starvation, or whatever. So let's get the hell out of here right now, shall we? After all, what's to prevent us finding our car, under cover of darkness, to catch the early morning ferry to the mainland?'

'I can think of several reasons why not,' Gerry said bleakly, sitting beside him on his bed in the shadowy room lit only by the pool of light cast from a meagre 40-watt bulb in the parchment shaded table lamp on the bedside cabinet. 'Unless I'm much mistaken, I daresay the hatchback has already been demobilized by Harker or his grandson, Ian. And I bet one or the other of them is standing guard on the landing outside our room to ensure that we stay put until morning. In which case, we'd best get a bit of shut eye.'

Switching off the bedside lamp, and snuggling up to Bill, dog tired yet unable to sleep, Gerry thought that whatever tomorrow might bring she had, at least, a wealth of happy memories to sustain her, a love affair to remember.

Bill's arms about her her head cradled against his shoulder, she relived their wedding day, recalling every detail of the happiest day of her life; the scent of roses and carnations, the swish of her wedding dress about her ankles as she had walked down the aisle towards him, the light of love in his eyes when he had placed the wedding ring on her finger. Remembering that heart-stopping moment of bliss when the parson had solemnly pronounced them husband and wife: ending the service with the age old words: 'Whom God hath joined, let no man put asunder.'

With those words uppermost in her mind, aware of the steady rhythm of Bill's heartbeat so close to hers, Gerry determined to fight Glencochlin tooth and claw rather than succumb to his threats of extinction. She'd been in life-threatening situations before today – had been shot at, imprisoned, abducted, damn near smothered to death – but she was still here, alive and kicking, and she intended to remain so. Life was sweet, and she didn't fancy herself and Bill ending up as rag-draped skeletons, six months hence, when, presumably, Glencochlin would be back in Aussieland, living the life of Riley. Well, not if she could help it.

She was trying to figure out how the laird planned to do away with them when, around two a.m., she heard a muffled sound in the darkness. Immediately alert, and sitting bolt upright in bed she hissed, 'Who's there?' fearing the worst.

'Hush,' came a voice from the far side of the room, 'do exactly as I tell you. Get up, put on your oldest clothes. Don't switch on the light, I have a torch. And please hurry. Time is of the essence.'

Bill stirred and opened his eyes. 'What's happening?' he asked drowsily.

'Another miracle,' Gerry breathed ecstatically.

Finding and donning their oldest clothes presented few, if any problems, since their evening finery had been hung in the wardrobe, and their thick-knit sweaters, woollen socks, scarves and anoraks had been placed, conveniently, on the various chairs scattered about the room. Their boots, Gerry's caked in mud, were lying near the bedroom door, next to Bill's – so far unworn.

Bewildered, Bill, still half asleep, managed to manoeuvre himself into his clothes, aided

150

by a pencil beam of a torch held by the unseen presence in the room. No one spoke, apart from Bill who muttered 'Ouch' when he thrust his foot into his right hand Wellington boot, and 'Blast' when his anorak zipper stuck halfway. It all felt so unreal he wondered if he was still asleep and dreaming, until a sharp pinch from Gerry, on his backside, accompanied by her hissed exhortation to stop farting about and get a move on, convinced him otherwise. Get a move on? But where to? Well, he thought pessimistically, he was bound to find out sooner or later...

Eleven

At Maggie and Barney Bowler's Hamburger Joint in London's Old Kent Road, having hung the Closed sign on the cafe door, Barney said anxiously, 'Look, Maggie love, I wish you'd tell me what's bugging you. You've been like a cat on hot bricks these past few days an' nights tossin' an' turnin' in bed: gettin' up at the crack o' dawn to collar the postman. Mekkin' yerself porely fer no good reason, if you arsks me. What I mean to say is, stands to reason, don't it, that a bride on her 'oneymoon wuddn't be bothered to send picture postcards to all an' sundry?'

'That's just it. That's what's bugging me,' Maggie replied emotionally, tired out from all her sleepless nights and her early morning excursions to await the arrival of the post-man bearing a message of some kind from the girl she regarded as dearly as her own flesh and blood: the daughter she'd always longed for, and never had. 'Gerry would've moved heaven an' earth to send us a postcard, an' you know that as well as I do, Barney Bowler, so don't pretend you don't.'

She added fearfully, 'I can't help thinkin' she's in trouble of some kind. In need of help. I just wish I knew what to do about it, that's all!'

'Then why not have a word with that nice Scotland Yard bloke we met at her wedding?' Barney suggested eagerly. 'Detective Chief Inspector Brambell, as I recall. Now, come to bed an' stop worrying. We have another long hard day ahead of us termorrer, think on, an' the way you are now, you're about as much use as – a chocolate teapot!'

'Eh, I can't go bothering Scotland Yard,' Maggie demurred. 'What the heck would I say?'

'You could ask him for his wife's favourite chutney recipe, I suppose,' Barney said drily, 'or you could just arsk 'im, point blank, if 'e's 'eard from Bill an' Gerry. If 'e says yes, then no need to worry. If 'e says no, then tell 'im what you told me, that you think they're in trouble of some kind: in need of 'elp, an' let *'im* do the worryin'.'

First thing the following day Maggie entered the portals of New Scotland Yard and asked for a word with Detective Chief Inspector Brambell: feeling as nervous as a kitten as she did so, wishing she'd rung up before-hand to book an appointment, same as she did at the hairdresser's when her roots need-ed retouching. An' what if the Inspector didn't remember her? After all, he was a very busy man with a lot on his mind.

But Detective Chief Inspector Brambell was not the kind of man to forget a name or a face, she discovered when, ten minutes later, he emerged from his office, a hand extended in greeting, and with a warmly uttered, 'Mrs Bowler. How nice to see you again. Please, do come in, sit down, and tell me what I can do to help you; assuming, of course, that you are in need of help?'

'Well yes. That is, I'm not quite sure,' Maggie confessed as Brambell led her into his office and she sank down in a chair opposite his own swivel chair, behind a vast mahogany desk littered with folders, tele-phones, and, glory be, a tray containing a cafetière of coffee, two cups and a plate of chocolate biscuits.

Brambell said, with a twinkle, 'Shall I be Mother?' Maggie could have wept with the relief of knowing that she had come to the right place, to the right person, at the right time, as she unburdened her fears for Gerry and Bill's safety to the Chief Inspector. He listened intently as she voiced her gut feeling that the pair of them were in some kind of danger – in dire need of help.

'Do you think I'm just a barmy old woman letting my imagination run away with me?' she asked tearfully, at the conclusion of her outpourings.

Brambell said decisively, 'No, not at all, Mrs Bowler. Now, take my advice, go home, get on with your life, try to stop worrying, and leave the rest to me. You have my word that I shall move heaven and earth to discover the present whereabouts of Gerry and Bill. Need I say more?'

Brambell meant what he said. After Maggie had gone, via a police car driven by a smart young constable who had treated her like royalty en-route to the hamburger joint, he rang the switchboard and asked to be connected to Glasgow Headquarters, wanting a word with an old friend and colleague of his, Detective Inspector Bruce Moncrieff.

When the connection with Glasgow had been made, an apologetic voice came on the line. 'Sorry, sir, but DCI Moncrieff's no here at the moment,' the voice explained. 'He and DS Murdoch are investigating a series of murders in the Outer Hebrides, either Lewis or Harris, though I cudna say for certain which one, the pair of them being conjoined, so to speak.'

Brambell's pulse quickened. The Outer Hebrides? Bill and Gerry's honeymoon destination. He said abruptly, 'Then I suggest you find out which one as quickly as possible. We are not into guessing games here at Scotland Yard. We deal in facts, not fantasy. As a matter of urgency, I need to know the exact whereabouts of DCI Moncrieff and DS Murdoch, is that perfectly clear?'

'Sir.'

Hanging up the receiver, Brambell experienced an uprush of trepidation, a sinking feeling engendered by the revelation that a series of murders had taken place in a remote spot on the map, in which Bill and Gerry might somehow have become involved. Almost certainly so, knowing Gerry. The girl had a nose for trouble – murder in particular.

The call Brambell was expecting, came ten minutes later from a desk sergeant, who told him that DCI Moncrieff and DS Murdoch had established an incident room in a cottage near Stornoway, and gave him their telephone number. Brambell thanked him, hung up the phone, and sat back in his swivel chair to consider his next move. Obviously a phone call to Moncrieff's incident room to find out what was going on up yonder in Bonnie Scotland, and then what? Only time would tell.

When Moncrieff picked up the receiver, the friends exchanged greetings as they had done, often, in the past, albeit long distance this time. When news of family and friends had been dealt with satisfactorily, 'Now, tell me what you and Murdoch are doing in the Outer Hebrides,' Brambell asked.

'Besides freezing to death, you mean?' Moncrieff responded gloomily. 'Getting nowhere fast, in my opinion. Have you ever tried catching an eel with your bare hands?' He sighed deeply. 'The man I'm after is a big fish and as slippery as an eel. Perhaps you've heard of him? Fergus Glencochlin?'

Brambell whistled softly between his teeth. 'Glencochlin, eh? I'll say I have. We have a dossier on him here at the Yard. The owner of a broken down castle, a Bugatti motor car, a second home in Australia, a dabbler in the occult, a drug runner, I shouldn't wonder, or something even more diabolical to my way of thinking. Not that anything has been proved against him, worse luck. Perhaps he's in league with the devil. But go on, old chap, what's he been up to this time?'

'How long have you got?' Moncrieff

enquired, sounding more cheerful.

'As long as it takes,' Brambell assured him.

Leaning forward in his chair, Brambell listened intently to Moncrieff's saga of events, gaining an overall impression of what his colleague was up against. In Brambell's opinion two murders, one suspicious death and a possible abduction seemed more than a fair workload for one senior officer and a detective sergeant to shoulder, without recourse to computers and a solid back-up team for the leg work.

So far, Moncrieff continued, there had been no breakthrough in the murder of one Samuel MacNally whose body had been discovered on the back seat of his landrover, nor in the murder of Police Sergeant Kirk of the local constabulary, whose body had been found in an alleyway near his headquarters. He then described, in detail, the death of a Mrs Penny Douglas, by drowning, an accidental death at face value, but not according to a young couple, house guests of Glencochlin and members of the search party who had discovered the body lying face down in a rockpool. They had stated categorically that the victim could not have died accidentally, that she'd been murdered, and had, moreover, come up with good and sufficient reasons in support of that theory.

Brambell's heart skipped a beat. 'A young couple, you say? Not a honeymoon couple by any chance?'

'Yes, as a matter of fact. But how the hell did you guess?' Moncrieff knew that Brambell was an astute old devil. But a clairvoyant? No way. He added, 'Come on, Foxy. Spill the beans. Is there something you're not telling me?'

'No. You have my word. I'm just curious to know how they became involved with Glencochlin: what they are doing in that crumbling, so called castle of his, when they should be doing what honeymoon couples usually aim for – that is to say, being alone together, not getting mixed up in house parties and murder.'

Seriously worried, Brambell wondered if Maggie Bowler could have been right in thinking that Bill and Gerry were in danger. Only one way to find out.

He said brusquely, 'Look Bruce, find me a billet of some kind, would you? Bed and breakfast will do. Any old hole or corner as long as it's reasonably clean and comfortable. With a modicum of luck, I should be with you tomorrow. Not to worry, I shan't interfere in your enquiries. It's just that I need to find out about Gerry and Bill Bentine, who may well be in trouble; danger of some kind. You understand?'

'Not entirely,' Moncrieff confessed bemusedly, 'but you can rely on me. Bed and breakfast, and an evening meal? I know just the place. Shall I meet you at the ferry landing?'

'No need,' Brambell assured him. 'This time I'm pulling out all the stops. Commandeering a helicopter, no less.' He added, with a chuckle, 'Don't ring us, we'll ring you.'

Overcoming her fear of confined spaces would take some doing, Gerry realized as the door of the secret passage swung shut behind her. The beam of a more powerful torch revealed the dank stone walls of a narrow tunnel cut deep into the heart of Glencochlin Castle, with slippery, roughly hewn steps leading down to a pit of blackness beyond the circle of torchlight. The torchbearer, a mere presence wearing dark clothing, said quietly, 'Tread warily, my friends. We have a long haul ahead of us, with no guarantee of success if we fail to get out of this hell hole before daybreak.'

Suppressing a shudder, Gerry uttered hoarsely, 'And if we don't, then what, Professor? You *are* Professor Telemann, aren't you?'

'Let's not dwell on that. My name is Frank Dawson, by the way. I'm an officer with Interpol. A spent force now Glencochlin's on to me. It was bound to happen. The deception went on too long.'

'You mean the house party went on too long?' Gerry said astutely.

'Precisely.' Dawson replied. 'As the saying goes, you can fool some of the people some of the time, not all the people all of the time. The murder of Penny Douglas complicated matters.'

'Then it *was* murder?' Gerry asked.

'Oh yes, as you were quick to spot, Mrs Bentine. Police involvement was the last thing I needed at that point however,' Dawson continued, 'Impersonating an old man was a risky business from the start. I knew that. The thick lensed glasses helped, so did the dentures and the cheek pouches. I relied heavily on a speedy departure once I'd gleaned the information I wanted.'

They were in single file, Gerry sandwiched between Dawson and Bill, speaking spasmodically, Gerry wishing to heaven she had never dreamed up this Highland honeymoon in the first place, otherwise she and Bill might have been in a gondola, right now, hearing the strains of 'Just One Cornetto' belted out by a gondolier bearing a striking resemblance to Luciano Pavarotti. If only...

She said apologetically, 'Sorry I landed you in it, Mr Dawson...'

'Not to worry, Gerry. And you can forget the Mister. Call me Dawson. OK?' A pause, then, 'How's your foot, Bill?'

'Dunno. I'll ask it when it wakes up,' came Bill's reply. 'Where are we heading, by the way?'

'For the boathouse. Quiet now, we're almost there. Just keep your fingers crossed that Harker isn't on duty – armed with a shotgun.'

Oh gawd, Gerry thought, that's all they needed, a cadaver wielding a lethal weapon. Despite the dank, chilly atmosphere of the tunnel with its slippery steps, moss embellished walls and cobwebby arches, she felt a tide of warm, sticky perspiration trapped under her corselette, the way she had done during the Antiques Murders, the day she'd visited the arty farty galleries of the serial killer, Christian Sommer.

Now, clinging tightly to Bill's hand in this present, nerve wracking dilemma, what she most deeply regretted was not having brought with her a spray can of deodorant. At least Bill was with her this time. She'd been alone that day at Christian Sommer's galleries, he'd been in Wiltshire on that occasion: in Stuttgart when she'd been abducted during in what the press had been pleased to call 'The Matinee Idol Murders', in view of the theatrical background of the serial killer, Aubrey Sandys. What the press would dub the murders of herself and Bill if they failed to emerge from this present dilemma she could only surmise. 'The Honeymoon Murders' most likely. Now for the boathouse...

From the passenger seat of the police

helicopter, Brambell gazed down at the counties of England spinning away beneath him, marvelling at the speed of flight, feeling like Gulliver seeing everything in miniature: towns, cities, rivers and motorways, the patchwork of fields in open country, the craggy hills and shining lakes of the Lake District. Finally he saw the waters of the Little Minch which separated the mainland of Scotland from the Outer Hebrides, where, on a deserted stretch of moorland within striking distance of Stornoway, the helicopter pilot landed his craft as sweetly and gracefully as a bluebottle landing on a dung heap. And there, Brambell discerned delightedly, was a police car awaiting his arrival, the driver of which had been detailed to convey a senior Scotland Yard official to his Cove View destination. DCI Brambell was wearing a shabby raincoat and a battered brown trilby hat more in keeping with a country doctor than a mastermind detective, to the driver's way of thinking.

Moncrieff had been alerted to Brambell's arrival. Indeed he had heard the unmistakable sound of the chopper's approach and witnessed its descent with a sweet feeling of relief at the prospect of a good heart to heart talk with his old friend and colleague.

Agog with excitement and self importance, Mrs Grace Cameron had insisted on providing accommodation for so important a personage as a Scotland Yard Inspector. 'Och, it's nae bother,' she'd assured Moncrieff gaily, when he'd expressed his concern that she might overtax herself in taking in another lodger in so limited a space, 'I've a nice wee spare room along the landing, an' I can easily slip anither egg an' a coupla rashers in't skillet, come brekfust.'

'Well, if you're quite sure,' Moncrieff demurred, to no avail in face of Mistress Cameron's determination to fit a quart into a pint pot.

Now, as Brambell's car nosed down the lane and Moncrieff hurried forward to greet him and to lead him into the incident room, Grace appeared on the threshold carrying a tray of coffee and freshly baked oatmeal biscuits, ogling Brambell as she set down the tray on a sidetable, to Moncrieff's embarrassment. Not that Brambell appeared to notice the widow's come hither glances as he acknowledged the introduction and complimented her on her cooking.

When she had drifted away on a cloud of euphoria, Moncrieff said fondly, 'I'd like you to meet my sidekick, Ted Murdoch, a Sherlock Holmes buff, still a bit wet behind the ears, but a quick learner and a great legman.'

'A pleasure to meet you, sir,' Murdoch said boyishly, flushing slightly as he shook hands with Brambell, a present day hero of his.

163

'You too, son,' Brambell said easily, liking the young man's quiet demeanour and his air of dependability. 'Well, let's have our coffee and biscuits, shall we? Then we'll get down to business.'

Nearing the boathouse, switching off his more powerful torch in favour of the pencil-beam, Dawson said quietly, 'You wait here, I'll take a look. If the coast's clear, we'll cut through to the cove and make for the headland. The tide's on the ebb so we should be able to negotiate the base when it's light enough to see our way. It'll be tricky, not to say dangerous, but our only hope lies in reaching civilization, of hiring a vehicle of some kind, a car or a coble.' He paused, then, 'Not to worry, Gerry, Bill and I will help you.'

'Oh, that's all right,' she said matter of factly. 'It's not too dangerous. I came that way from the village a few days ago. The tide was coming in at the time, and I was a bit hampered by my shopping bags. It should be a doddle with the tide going out.'

Twelve

Murdoch listened enthralled as Brambell and Moncrieff got down to business: responding intelligently when asked for his opinion. Having typed the case-notes on the Stornoway office computer – taking care to get things in chronological order, and adding his own deciphered shorthand notes to the dossier – he felt qualified to offer his opinions when invited to do so.

Heeding Moncrieff's advice, on his arrival at Glencochlin Castle, Murdoch had kept his eyes open, his mouth shut, and his notebook and pen at the ready. He had scrupulously recorded verbatim accounts of the testimony given by the servants and the house party guests concerning the death of Penelope Douglas – leaving nothing to chance in the event of their statements providing conflicting evidence of their whereabouts on that occasion.

None had done so, and the consensus had been that the woman had died accidentally. At least until Mrs Geraldine Bentine had come up with a plausible theory to suggest otherwise, supported and endorsed by her husband Bill.

Trust Gerry, Brambell thought resignedly, perusing the dossier, to wade in at the deep end, all flags flying. But how had she and Bill become involved with Glencochlin in the first place, and where the hell were they right now? Well, that was why he had come here, to find out, hence his preoccupation with the names of the laird's houseguests, their occupations and countries of origin; Italy, Germany, South Africa, America. According to the dossier, the Crowthers were of South African extraction, born in Johannesburg, emigrants to Britain in the 1980s, presently residing in Yorkshire, their wealth deriving from the manufacture of textiles.

The Italian, Tony Cannelli, born in Milan, had described himself as an entrepreneur of independent means, a dabbler in works of art, antiquities, rare books and manuscripts; an inveterate traveller and a connoisseur of fine wines; owner of a town house in Milan, an apartment in Paris, and a pied-à-terre on the shores of Lake Como.

Brian Douglas, husband of the deceased woman, a Mancunian by birth, a clever lad by all accounts, had won a scholarship to Queen's College, Oxford, where he'd been awarded First Class degrees in Electronics, English Literature and Modern Languages and had, subsequently, decided to accept the offer of a job as an electronics engineer in

New York, where he had met, and ultimately married, his wife Penny.

Brambell's interest in the dossier had quickened when he came to the name – Max Telemann. To the best of his knowledge and belief, a man in his late seventies or early eighties, presently under surveillance by Interpol on suspicion of procuring young women as prostitutes in far flung corners of the globe, mainly Thailand where rich business tycoons had a fondness for European girls. Nubile blondes in particular, the DCI thought disgustedly, pondering Telemann's involvement with Glencochlin. What was the reason behind the laird's bizarre house party, his even more bizarre assembly of guests, bearing the hallmarks of a summit meeting of partners in crime.

And yes, by George, that was *it*, he realized triumphantly. And had it not been for the death of Penny Douglas, Gerry and Bill's refusal to accept the accidental drowning theory, there would have been a complete cover up of that meeting of criminals. Glencochlin's cohorts would have melted away like mist on a May morning, with none the wiser – except Bill and Gerry, Harker and his grandson Ian and Mrs Harker. Especially after Sergeant Kirk's murder which had really put the cat among the pigeons.

'Did you gain the impression that Kirk and Glencochlin were in cahoots?' Brambell asked. 'What I'm getting at is if Kirk hadn't "copped" it, so to speak, do you think your enquiries into Sam MacNally's murder would have extended to the castle? And if they had not done so, if Gerry had not raised doubts about the so called accidental death of Penny Douglas, would you have pursued the matter further?'

'Probably not,' Moncrieff admitted ruefully, 'but the fact remains that Kirk *was* murdered and as he had recently led the local inquiry into the death of Mrs Douglas at Glencochlin Castle, we enquired into his known movements prior to his demise. It was simply a matter of routine. Besides which, we had another murder to investigate, we knew old Samuel MacNally was well known locally, almost certainly to Sergeant Kirk, and it had occurred to me that the two murders might be linked in some way.'

'Rightly so.' Brambell nodded his approval. 'I've a hunch that whoever killed MacNally and Sergeant Kirk was one and the same person, not necessarily the same person who killed Mrs Douglas. The murders of MacNally and Kirk suggest a strong man, of limited intellect. The murder of Mrs Douglas was far more subtle. Agreed?'

Murdoch cleared his throat and flushed slightly before speaking. He said, 'With respect, sir, I forgot to mention it before but Constable Mitchell said when he came back on duty after his spell in hospital, "The Laird will be lost without him" meaning Sergeant Kirk. Kirk was, perhaps, receiving "back handers" from Glencochlin to do as he was told.' He added, apologetically, 'Sorry, sir, but I thought you ought to know.'

'Thanks, Murdoch. Every scrap of information is vital,' said Brambell getting up. 'Now I'd best be making my way to my billet.'

'You're staying here, if that's all right,' Moncrieff said. 'Mrs Cameron wouldn't take no for an answer. You're in the spare room, so lord only knows what you'll be up against – the walls most like.' He sighed deeply, 'I didn't even know she had a spare room.'

'I've had a look,' Murdoch said eagerly, 'and it's nae so bad. A bit on the snug side, but there's a bedside lamp and a bitty chest of drawers, an' a plastic bag behind the door to hang up your suit.'

Brambell said drily, vastly amused by the thought of the plastic bag, 'Just as well I didn't bring my evening dress suit then, isn't it? Otherwise I'd have needed a spare hanger.'

'Oh damn and blast!' Dawson muttered savagely. 'Someone's there. Harker, I suspect. A change of plan. We'll have to try the

169

kitchen exit. He's bound to be armed and the last thing we need is a confrontation with a trigger happy henchman of Glencochlin.'

'Don't get much kip, do they?' Gerry observed mildly. 'What I mean is, being on duty twenty-four hours a day must take it out of them one way or another.'

'If you're thinking what I think you're thinking,' Bill groaned, 'forget it!'

'But there's three of us, only one of him, and I really don't fancy another tunnel. My claustrophobia's getting the upper hand.'

'But he's armed, we're not.'

'Is he sitting or standing?'

'Sitting,' Dawson hissed, 'as far as I can make out.'

'Oh good. He won't feel a thing.'

'I'm not sure I like this,' Dawson demurred.

'I don't suppose he will, either,' Gerry said, unhitching her shoulder bag, her portable office-cum-chemist's according to Bill, the self and same weapon with which she had successfully clobbered the serial killer, Aubrey Sandys, in the final stages of the Matinee Idol Murders.

'This thing weighs a ton, and I should know. I may well end up deformed – one shoulder higher than the other, but swung by the straps, like a mace and chain, it makes a fine offensive weapon. So what are we waiting for? Broad daylight? The return of the tide? An invitation to breakfast?'

'Gerry's right,' Bill conceded. 'The sooner we're out of here, the better. What do you say, Frank?'

Dawson said resignedly, 'All right then. Let's give it a whirl, shall we? After all, what have we got to lose – apart from our lives?'

Gerry interposed eagerly, her writer's imagination in full flow, 'Once Harker's been dealt with, what's to prevent us heading out to sea in Glencochlin's motor launch? That would take the oil out of his diesel engine for starters.'

And so the trio, at Gerry's instigation, embarked on a mission which, if it failed, might well mean death for the three of them.

Dawson had to hand it to Gerry, a brave, intelligent young woman with the heart of a lion, a quirky sense of humour and a devastating way of facing danger head on, not running away from it in sticky situations such as this. He'd been rendered speechless when she'd said, matter of factly, that rounding the headland should be a doddle with the tide on the ebb and unhampered by shopping bags. He was filled with admiration for her enterprising spirit of adventure and utter refusal to be subdued or intimidated by the power crazed Glencochlins of this world.

'You mentioned a possible abduction,'

171

Brambell said, over coffee and sandwiches that afternoon in Stornoway. 'Can you tell me more about it?'

'Afraid not,' Moncrieff replied. 'Mrs Bentine – Gerry – said she'd overheard a heated conversation between the laird and a foreign sounding lady in a turret room of the castle, who she came across later in the boathouse under somewhat bizarre circumstances.'

'How "bizarre"?' Brambell queried, listening intently as Moncrieff explained. Then, 'A countess, you say? In some kind of danger?'

'She must have been since she pleaded with Gerry to help her,' Moncrieff said vaguely, uncertain of his ground, 'then, apparently, Mrs Harker appeared to take charge of the woman, hinting at her being doolally, an escapee from the nearest nut house, and bemoaning the fact of her catching her death of cold – wandering about in the rain.'

Murdoch interposed eagerly, 'But the lady's fur coat was bone dry, not wet. So she cudna have been out in the rain, as Mrs Bentine pointed out tae us. She figured the countess had made her way from the turret room to the boathouse by an internal passage of some kind.'

'I see,' Brambell frowned slightly, 'so how come the abduction theory?'

'Well, sir,' Murdoch continued, 'Mrs Bentine saw the motor launch set out to sea with the countess on the back seat. She was only not sitting up, proper like, but half lying down, and looking as if she'd been drugged, with that young ruffian, Ian Harker, in charge of her, an' Glencochlin at the wheel.'

'All right, Murdoch, that's enough,' Moncrieff said irritably. 'There's no proof whatever that the woman was abducted. The likelihood is that she was in need of a breath of sea air to clear her head. We have no evidence whatever to suggest foul play. No-one has reported her missing. No body has been found. We're dealing in facts here, not fantasy.'

'Sorry, sir.' Murdoch looked crestfallen at the reprimand. 'But I thought that Mrs Bentine had reported her missing.'

One up for Murdoch, Brambell thought. About to say so, he quickly changed his mind, remembering that this case was, strictly speaking, none of his business. And yet he could not help pondering the implications of the countess's desperate plea for help, directed at Gerry that day in the boathouse, the quarrel Gerry had overheard between Glencochlin and the countess in the turret room, the rough guardianship of the Harkers, and the significance of a secret passageway, possibly a network of such passageways, within the walls of Glencochlin Castle.

Astutely, he considered the possibility that the quarrel between the countess and Glencochlin had led to her imprisonment in that turret room. What was the likelihood that she had made her escape by means of that secret passage leading to the boathouse, hence her lucid plea for help and Mrs Harker's tarradiddle about the poor woman being out of her mind, which Gerry had not for one moment believed to be true. Trust Gerry for that, he thought fondly. No pulling the wool over those clear sighted eyes of hers.

He guessed, moreover, that his normally easy going colleague had enough on his plate with two murders to solve, let alone an unconfirmed case of abduction to add to his work load. This Brambell well understood. Moncrieff was working in the dark, to some extent, a stranger in a strange place, lacking a properly equipped incident room, with few, if any, substantive clues to go on so far as the murders of Sam MacNally and Sergeant Kirk were concerned. Nor did Moncrieff fully understand his concern for the welfare of Gerry and Bill Bentine whose lives may well be in danger.

The more Brambell thought about it, the more convinced he was that Gerry and Bill were in extreme danger. Call it a gut feeling, but he knew he was right. The problem was, what the hell to do about it?

He knew, of course, from his long years of experience as a policeman, a senior ranking detective, an upholder of the Law, that evidence was needed to bring criminals to justice, evidence got at by questioning – weighing replies, evasions, inconsistencies, alibis, lies; face to face confrontation with the suspect, his own ability to separate truth from lies – hence his need to question Fergus Glencochlin regarding the whereabouts of Gerry and Bill Bentine. An interview based on a missing persons report received recently from a member of the public at Scotland Yard.

Never one to prevaricate, and as a matter of courtesy to his fellow detectives, he said, when they had finished their sandwiches, 'Now it is my intention to pay Glencochlin a visit, to question him about his association with the Bentines and to establish their present whereabouts if I might impose upon you to give me a lift to Glencochlin Castle.' He hastened to add, not wanting to tread on toes, 'This, of course, is in no way connected with your enquiries into the murders of MacNally and Sergeant Kirk, or the death of Mrs Penny Douglas, in which I have no intention of interfering. Is that perfectly clear?'

'Crystal clear,' Moncrieff replied quietly. 'You must do what you came here to do. Murdoch and I are at your service. Should you need back up, help of any kind, you can count on us. Now we'd best drive you to

Glencochlin Castle, so let's get a move on, shall we?'

'Sir,' Murdoch responded eagerly, as the three of them made their way to the police car parked in the market square.

Brambell recoiled somewhat at the sight of Glencochlin Castle, poised like a bird of ill omen on its rocky promontory overlooking a waste of grey, windcapped water reminiscent of the witches' cauldron in *Macbeth*.

Ye gods, he thought, Abandon Hope All Ye Who Enter Here. The place was an eyesore, a ruin, surely not the home of a man of some considerable wealth who should be ashamed of allowing his property to fall into such a state of disrepair. The place stank of decay – and evil.

By no stretch of his imagination could Brambell envisage Gerry and Bill staying under Glencochlin's roof a moment longer than necessary. Which begged the question, where were they now? The reason why he felt it expedient to confront the laird face to face. Not that he relished the thought of that confrontation, or of crossing the threshold of a replica of a Pinewood Studio's version of Castle Dracula.

Murdoch had stopped the car on the promenade's perimeter to allow Brambell an unfettered view of the building before deciding on his plan of action. To determine whether or not he wished to enter the lion's den alone, for instance, for a prescribed length of time, or be accompanied by Murdoch or Moncrieff, as back up. Not both, in case a getaway car was needed in a hurry, he explained tautly.

Moncrieff said scathingly, 'This is twenty-first century Scotland, not a 1940's gangster movie. A getaway car indeed.'

But the plan made sense to Brambell, realizing as he did the importance of a witness to his meeting with Glencochlin; a verbatim account of the interview; the questions asked, the laird's response to those questions, duly recorded by Murdoch.

Pulling rank, he said briskly, 'Right, Murdoch, you come with me. Moncrieff, you wait here. This shouldn't take long, an hour at the most. Now, Murdoch, ready if you are, so let's get going, shall we?'

'Sir,' Murdoch replied enthusiastically, getting out of the car and searching his pockets to make certain he had with him his notepad and biro, as he and Brambell made their way across the promenade to the front entrance of Glencochlin Castle.

The bell was answered by Mrs Harker, grim faced and taciturn, who, having glanced briefly at their warrant cards, muttered, 'I'll tell the laird you're here.'

Feeling like a spare bridegroom at a

wedding, Brambell inched his way into the hall, closely followed by Murdoch, and stood there, awaiting the arrival of Glencochlin. His gut feeling of disquiet was at odds with his usual savoir faire and he was inordinately glad of young Murdoch's presence, help and moral support in what may well prove to be a decidedly sticky interview if, as he suspected, the laird refused to answer questions pertaining to the present whereabouts of Gerry and Bill Bentine. In which case, the sooner he overcame his nervous apprehension and took control of the situation, the better. He was, after all, a high ranking Scotland Yard detective, not some callow youth on his first assignment.

Even so, his first glimpse of Glencochlin, coming towards him across the hall from, presumably, his private apartments in the east wing of the castle, dressed all in black, smiling charmingly, a hand extended in greeting, came as a shock to Brambell who had anticipated the exact opposite, certainly not a handshake and a warmly uttered, 'Well, Inspector Brambell, how may I help you? Please do tell me to what I owe this visit from Scotland Yard.'

It was dislike at first sight so far as Brambell was concerned. Leaving aside his evil reputation, the man's physical appearance deeply repulsed the DCI, whose flesh had crawled at the touch of the laird's handclasp, knowing instinctively that the man was play-acting: why else the Count Dracula get up? The dyed black hair brushed back from his high domed forehead, the wolfish smile in contrast to the calculating coldness of his eyes, the short black shoulder cape he wore above his black polo-neck sweater; his tightly fitting black trousers, tucked, gaucho style into his highly polished black leather boots. Above all, his air of superiority and bravado, as if confronting not a high ranking officer of the law, but some stupid old git with the brains of a louse.

Well, Brambell thought grimly, he'd soon see about that. 'I am here to question you regarding the present whereabouts of Bill and Geraldine Bentine. In private.' He said brusquely, 'Presumably you would prefer not to conduct the interview here in the hall?'

'Very well then,' Glencochlin conceded un-graciously. 'If you insist, we'll talk in the drawing room.' Leading the way, 'Not that I have the remotest idea what became of them when they left here after breakfast, this morning.'

Entering the drawing room in the wake of Glencochlin, Brambell noted the piled up ashes in the grate, the plethora of booze bottles on the sideboard, some half emptied, some untouched, which alongside various unwashed glasses scattered about the room, suggested some late night celebration. And a dearth of servants to clear up the mess afterwards – to clear the grate of ashes, the sideboard of bottles, the tables of sticky, tell-tale glasses – which led Brambell to wonder why Mrs Harker, not her husband, had answered the doorbell. Had Harker, along with Bill and Gerry, also gone missing?

Taking command of the situation, Brambell seated himself in an armchair near the fireplace, attended by Murdoch, who remained standing; notebook and biro at the ready. Having requested Glencochlin to be seated in an armchair opposite, Brambell launched his attack on the laird. 'Tell me,' he said conversationally, 'what became of the countess?'

Startled by the unexpected question, Glencochlin hesitated a fraction of a second too long, then, 'You have me at a loss, I'm afraid, Inspector. I know of no such person, how therefore could I possibly know what became of her?'

'Fair enough,' Brambell conceded pleasantly, accepting the lie, showing no sign of disbelief and changing the subject, a tactic of his often used to devastating effect in former interviews to undermine a suspect's self-confidence, then just as quickly to restore it by means of a series of easily answerable questions to lull them into a false sense of security, based on the belief that they were dealing with a fool, easily hoodwinked into accepting every lie they uttered as the gospel truth. Until, carried away by a foolhardy feeling of superiority, they realized, too late, that their recklessness had led to their own betrayal, that they were not dealing with a fool, after all.

Glancing about the room, taking in the unswept hearth, the unwashed glasses, the litter of bottles on the sideboard, Brambell said blandly, 'It must have been quite a party.'

Glencochlin laughed. 'It was, believe me. A farewell party to remember.' Entirely at ease now, having denied all knowledge of the countess to the satisfaction of the old fool seated in the chair opposite, Glencochlin continued, 'My house guests should be well on their way now to their various destinations, including the Bentines, Bill and Gerry, who left here after breakfast, presumably to continue their honeymoon in peace and quiet.'

'Did they say where to?'

'No, and I didn't ask. I did, however, give them the key to a cottage of mine should they wish to avail themselves of my offer. Gerry, you see, had expressed a desire to spend time in a shepherd's bothy.' He added jovially, 'Not that the cottage, apart from its layout, retains much evidence of its origins. Far from it, since the addition of a fitted

kitchen, hot and cold running water, a bathroom and the roof space utilized to provide
a spacious bedroom accessible by means of a
staircase from the lounge.'

'Sounds ideal,' Brambell murmured encouragingly. 'Planning permission no problem, I assume?'

'None whatever,' Glencochlin riposted
sharply. 'As the owner of the property and in
my role as a presiding magistrate in this neck
of the woods, I would scarcely have applied
to myself for planning permission, now
would I?'

'I suppose not,' Brambell agreed equably,
assuming his 'country doctor' persona, completely at odds with his razor sharp intellect
hidden beneath his trademark brown trilby
hat, which had remained firmly clamped to
his head from the moment he'd entered
Glencochlin Castle. 'The fact is, I'm a bit
out of my depth here, as you can imagine.
My sole purpose in being here is to establish
the present whereabouts of Mr and Mrs Bill
Bentine, reported as missing by a friend of
theirs, at Scotland Yard, a claim warranting
further investigation as I'm certain you'll
understand.'

'Yes, of course old chap. Not to worry.
They are perfectly safe, I assure you.' Rising
to his feet, assuming the interview to be
over, 'Well, mustn't delay you longer than
necessary, Inspector.'

'Chief Inspector,' Brambell reminded him gently. 'Detective Chief Inspector to be precise. Be kind enough to remember that in future, Laird Glencochlin. Nor do I appreciate being referred to as "old chap". Is that perfectly clear? Now, with your permission, I'd like a word with your servants, the Harker family if my memory serves me correctly. Mr and Mrs Harker and their grandson, Ian.' He added pleasantly, 'Since you are already on your feet, Laird Glencochlin, perhaps you'd be kind enough to send for them?'

On the defensive, badly shaken by the sudden turn of events, the realization that Brambell was not the old fool he'd imagined him to be, Glencochlin burst forth, aggressively, 'Now see here, Chief Inspector, I fail to see the reason for your request. I shall certainly not send for my servants to undergo interrogation at your behest. Why should I? They have all been under a great deal of pressure of late, Mrs Harker, in particular, with the cooking and catering to see to, the provision of food for my house party guests; bed making, dusting and cleaning, ably assisted by her husband and grandson, admittedly. Nevertheless, they are all physically and mentally exhausted, in no fit state to answer questions pertaining to the whereabouts of the Bentines, who, I venture to say, they scarcely remember at all.'

'Ah,' Brambell responded intently, albeit regretfully, 'but they may just remember the countess. Because she *was* here, wasn't she? And I intend to find out what became of her, just as I intend to find out what has become of Gerry and Bill Bentine. The truth, the whole truth, and nothing but the truth. I shall find out eventually, Glencochlin, with or without your co-operation. So will you summon your servants, or shall I?'

Thirteen

'Come in, Mrs Harker. Please sit down.'

Cynthia Harker entered the room unwillingly, mistrustful of Brambell's motives in sending for her and her family, wondering how she would account for her husband's and grandson's absence without giving the game away.

Looking at the grim faced, uncommunicative woman, heavily built and lacking in warmth or the remotest hint of feminine charm, Brambell realized that his softly, softly approach would be wasted on her, and so he went in at the deep end. 'My colleague and I are here to establish the present whereabouts of three missing persons,' he said briskly, 'all of whom were members of Laird Glencochlin's house party; namely Mr and Mrs Bill Bentine and a countess whose identity has not so far been established, but with whom, according to evidence, you came into close contact during her stay here. True or false?'

'I'm paid to do the cookin' and keep the house clean,' Mrs Harker said dourly, 'not tae rub shoulders wi' the guests. An' if yer thinkin' them mucky glasses need clearin', I were told tae leave 'em till later. I've only one pair of hands, think on.'

'Quite so, but that doesn't answer my question,' Brambell persisted. 'I have it on good authority that the countess was staying here, and that you appeared to be in charge of her.' He paused then, 'Come now, Mrs Harker, were you or weren't you?'

'No, I weren't!' Cynthia Harker spat forth indignantly. 'I'm a cook, not a bloody nurse-maid. I were told to keep an eye on her, that's all, her being not right in the 'ead; to tek her grub upstairs tae her room, which I did. What's wrong wi' that?'

'And so, on several occasions, you did "rub shoulders" with the guests? At least one of them?' Brambell reminded her.

'She weren't a guest,' Mrs Harker replied stubbornly. 'She'd turned up, out of the blue, wantin' somewhere to stay for the time

185

bein'. That's all I know.'

Brambell sighed deeply. No use flogging a dead horse, in his experience, having come up against the likes of Mrs Harker more times than he'd had hot canteen dinners. Regarding her mutinously pursed mouth, flushed face and fish-like stare, he said, 'Very well then, I'd best have a word with your husband and grandson.'

'You can't,' Cynthia stated flatly.

'Oh? Why not?'

'Cos they ain't here. That's why not!'

'Then where are they?'

'In Stornoway.'

Brambell had heard of drawing hen's teeth, but this was ridiculous.

Murdoch spoke up at that moment. 'In case you didn't know, Mrs Harker,' he said severely, 'wasting police time is a punishable offence, so you'd be well advised to speak up, unless, of course, you would rather accompany us to the Stornoway Police Station right away. It's entirely up to you to decide.' He added grimly, 'If you know your husband and grandson's present whereabouts, then tell us – or suffer the consequences of your silence.'

'Oh very well then, if you really must know,' Mrs Harker capitulated aggressively, 'my husband's in hospital. Our grandson drove him there in the early hours of this morning. Now are you satisfied?' Her voice shook suddenly, revealing a warmer side to her nature, that of a wife and grandmother deeply concerned for her family's welfare.

A kindly, compassionate man by nature, Brambell asked sympathetically, 'What exactly is wrong with your husband?'

'How the hell should *I* know?' Cynthia retorted violently, sick and tired of the questioning, resuming her carapace of self righteous indignation. 'You're the detective, so why don't you go to the hospital and find out?'

'All in good time,' Brambell assured her. 'Meanwhile, I'd like to take a look at the turret room, if you'd be kind enough to lead the way.' He added courteously, yet firmly, 'I am right in thinking, am I not, that the countess occupied the turret room during her brief interlude at Glencochlin Castle?'

'Well yes,' Mrs Harker admitted sullenly, her mind in turmoil, 'but the room's empty now. Not that she brought much with her in the first place, just an overnight bag which she took with her when she left.'

'You saw her leave?' Brambell asked intently. 'By what means?'

'No, I didn't see her leave. I were busy in the kitchen at the time, preparin' lunch for the master's house party guests: soup an' shepherd's pie. Talk about work. Then Harker came tae tell me he an' Ian were needed in the boathouse; summat about the

187

woman in the turret room bein' tekken elsewhere. "Oh aye," I said, "an' what about me? What about the washin' up?" I were that mad. All right for some, I thought, swannin' off an' leavin' me with everything to see to.'

Brambell nodded sagaciously. Getting up, he said, 'Now for the turret room. Ready if you are, Mrs Harker.'

Lumbering to her feet, 'Huh, a waste of time if you asks me. I've told you, there's nowt to see up there,' she grumbled, 'an' it's a hell of a climb.'

She was right about that, Brambell thought ten minutes later, puffing and panting up the last flight of stairs, preceded by Mrs Harker and followed by Murdoch, thinking that it was, perhaps, high time he took more exercise; joined a keep fit club on his return to London: cut down his intake of food, laid off sandwiches and started on salads. Salads? Perish the thought.

'Well, this is it!' Cynthia opened a hefty wooden door and stood back to allow Brambell and Murdoch access to the turret room. Thank God, he thought. One more flight of stairs and he'd have needed an oxygen mask.

Glancing about him, the sheer ugliness of the chamber struck him; the threadbare floor covering, cheapjack furniture, gimcrack ornaments, the two-bar electric fire in the narrow fireplace. Above all, the ghastly tapestries covering the wall opposite the inhospitable-looking twin beds, in one of which the countess must have spent at least two wakeful nights contemplating the uncertain future, desperately seeking a means of escape from her captivity.

Brambell entertained no doubt that the poor woman had been held here against her will. He had noticed, entering the room, that the key was on the outside, a detail overlooked by Mrs Harker when she had cleared the room of the countess's personal belongings.

Standing on the threshold, she said defiantly, 'Well, I did tell you there was nowt to see up here, didn't I? Now, perhaps, you'll believe me!'

'Certainly nothing to the untrained eye,' Brambell conceded coolly, 'but I take nothing at face value.' Stepping forward, to the housekeeper's dismay, ably assisted by DS Murdoch, he began a detailed examination of the tapestries: twitching them aside, running his fingers down the concealed panelling beneath them, in search of the secret passageway by which the countess had made her way to the boathouse in a desperate bid for freedom.

'Here,' Mrs Harker burst forth, 'the master'll hev summat tae say about heving them tapestries pulled about like that. I shall tell him, never fear, then you'll be in for it. The laird don't take things lyin' down, so you'd best leave well enough alone an' mek yersel' scarce.'

'Not until I've found what I'm looking for. Just hang on to this, Murdoch,' handing him a wodge of tapestry to reveal a button set in a strip of lighter coloured woodwork than the original panelling.

'Bingo!' Brambell's voice betrayed his satisfaction at having chanced upon the entrance to the countess's escape route. 'Well done, sir,' Murdoch piped up, clinging to the handful of threadbare tapestry, filled with admiration for his superior officer's intellect. He added, 'Are you going to press the button?'

'Not yet. That will come later.' Turning to face Cynthia Harker, he said grimly, 'You were the countess's jailer, were you not? You locked her here in this room. You say you brought her food. What else did you bring with you? Drugs? A hypodermic syringe to ensure her silence? And yet she managed to outwit not only you but the man responsible for her abduction, possibly even her murder.'

'No!' Mrs Harker responded, in a voice hoarse with fear. 'I felt sorry for the woman. I brought her food and medicine. I swear to God I meant her no harm. It's all lies. As for locking her in, I did no such thing. An' you can't prove otherwise.'

Regarding the woman coldly, contemptuously, Brambell said, 'I wouldn't be too sure of that. It is my belief that you were an accomplice in the detainment and abduction of the countess against her will. Soon, a clearer picture will emerge when I have interviewed your husband and grandson and the person responsible for the woman's imprisonment.'

Deriving no pleasure from the bringing of criminals to book, however deserving, Brambell phoned the Harris police station to request a SOC team to examine the turret room. He detained Mrs Harker for further questioning before turning his attention to visiting the local hospital to interview her husband and grandson.

Weighing up the situation on Brambell and Murdoch's return to the car, Moncrieff said astutely, 'Take my advice, Foxy, call it a day. Let's get back to Mrs Cameron's, down a couple of stiff whiskies, eat supper, down a few more whiskies, then have an early night. Makes sense, doesn't it?'

Brambell thought differently. 'Sorry, old friend,' he said, 'but I need to see Harker now, not tomorrow. Call it a hunch, if you like, but I have the feeling that he might just be able to throw some light on Gerry and Bill's disappearance. Time is of the essence. And since we're near Stornoway in any case—'

'All right, Foxy, you win,' Moncrieff

acceded resignedly, 'now where's the bloody hospital?'

Ian Harker, unshaven, wearing faded jeans, a crew neck sweater, wellingtons, and sporting a gold ring in his left ear, rose to his feet when Brambell and Murdoch entered the side ward where his grandfather lay, propped up with pillows, his head heavily bandaged. 'Who the hell are you?' he demanded hostilely. 'Bloody police,' he spat forth, 'I might have known. Have ye nowt better tae do than tae pester a poor ole man wi' a sore head?'

'Gently, son, gently,' Brambell advised him mildly, 'we are here to establish how he came by his sore head, that's all. Perhaps you can enlighten us?'

'He were attacked, that's what,' Ian riposted excitedly, 'beaten about the 'ead wiv an 'eavy object, for no reason.'

'And where and when did the attack take place?'

'In the boathouse at Glencochlin Castle in the early hours of this morning.'

'And what was he doing in the boathouse?'

Ian looked startled. Of limited intelligence, aware of having said too much, he replied sullenly, ' 'Ow the 'ell should I know?'

Brambell sighed deeply. Sick and tired of the Harker clan in general, and their nefarious activities, the time had come, he reckoned, to stop pussyfooting about and go for the jugular. He said grimly, 'Your grandmother is presently in custody, helping the police with their enquiries. Perhaps you'd care to join her? If not, my best advice to you, my lad, is to stop farcing about and answer my question. What, precisely, was your grandfather doing in the boathouse in the early hours of this morning?'

'*Gran*, in *custody*?' Ian looked shocked. '*Why*? She ain't done nowt wrong!'

'In which case, she has nothing to fear, and neither have you if you speak the truth, and be quick about it. Otherwise you'll find yourself in nick faster than you can say knife! Understood?'

A groan emerged from the heavily bandaged head at that moment as Harker opened his eyes and asked, bemusedly, 'Where am I? What's goin' on?'

As if he didn't know, Brambell thought sceptically, recognizing a scam when he saw one. Harker was playing the 'Old Soldier', of that he was certain. But why? Why the pretence? What was he trying to hide? Or was his sudden return to 'consciousness' merely a ploy to warn Ian to keep his mouth shut?

He said, keeping his counsel, 'Ah, Mr Harker, a timely recovery. Now you can speak for yourself. Tell me, what *were* you doing in your employer's boathouse last night?'

'Keepin' watch,' Harker said dourly. 'He'd got it into his head someone was after 'is boat. Right upset 'e were an' all. Told me tae keep a sharp look out, an' gied me 'is shot-gun.'

'Good grief! And what happened?' Brambell had seated himself on a chair near the bed. Ian and Murdoch remained standing. 'Were you told to shoot? Think, man. It's very important.'

'Not in so many words.' Harker was flum-moxed now, out of his depth, torn between loyalty to his master and fear of the police presence in his room.

'And did you, in fact, fire that gun?' Brambell demanded icily, every inch the Scotland Yard official; the full weight of the law behind him, his 'country doctor' persona discarded and forgotten for the time being. His narrowed eyes were fixed unblinkingly on Harker, who stared back at him as if mesmerized by that cold, official stare.

'Well yes, I did,' Harker confessed con-fusedly. 'When the attack came out of the blue, I fired a warning shot to scare off the intruders. Then I blacked out, an' that's the gospel truth. Next thing I knew, I were 'ere in't orspital, hevving me 'ead bandaged.'

'Intruders?' Brambell persisted, 'How many intruders?'

' 'Ow the 'ell should *I* know?' Harker retorted angrily. 'It were pitch black, an' I were barely conscious, 'aving been hit on the 'ead with what felt like a ton of bricks. That's all I know. All I can tell yer, an' if yer daint believe me, hard bloody cheese!' He added, closing his eyes, 'Now, clear off, the lot of yer, an' leave me be. Me 'ead's 'urtin' summat shockin', an' I needs a pee.'

'Come on, Murdoch, we'd best be on our way,' Brambell said wearily.

Suddenly, the thought of downing a few whiskies, eating a good hot supper, followed by a few more whiskies, then an early night, seemed infinitely appealing to the DCI – the perfect end to a far from perfect day. He simply hoped that their landlady knew her onions when it came to cooking.

Later, faced with a succulent steak and kidney pie, mashed potatoes, lashings of thick onion gravy, a bread and butter pudding and custard, he breathed a deep sigh of relief, and inwardly rejoiced when, after supper, Moncrieff unscrewed the lid of another bottle of Glenfiddich. So who needed an early night?

In the event, at three o'clock in the morning, Brambell hadn't closed his eyes. The drinks session had ended at half past midnight, since when he had lain in his narrow bed, unable to sleep. The events of yesterday were racing through his mind like an express train; the laird's furious reaction to his housekeeper's removal from Glencochlin Castle to help with police enquiries, his outrage on being told that the turret room had been locked awaiting the arrival of a SOC team to search for clues relevant to the disappearance of its recent occupant, his white heat anger at the discovery of the secret passage hidden behind a tapestry in that sinister apartment.

'How dare you invade my home and privacy in such a cavalier fashion?' he raged at Brambell, pacing the drawing room like a madman. 'By what right have you placed Mrs Harker under arrest?'

'Mrs Harker is not under arrest – as yet,' Brambell reminded him, speaking quietly but firmly. 'Also, as a law enforcement officer, it is my duty to pursue every line of enquiry relevant to whatever case I happen to be working on. But you know that as well as I do.' He paused. 'This is a puzzling and complicated enquiry, far from straight forward. The SOC team will fingerprint the turret room, including the key – found on the outside of the door – and the panelling to establish the truth of the matter. When that happens, the questioning will intensify, I assure you. Statements will be checked, including your own, Mr Glencochlin. Do I make myself clear?'

Talking things over with his colleagues last night had cleared Brambell's mind to some extent, and the whisky had imparted a sense of well-being. Now, thumping his pillows to accommodate his aching head, he thought of the day ahead of him with some degree of trepidation, beginning to wonder if he was getting past it: too old for the job, incapable of solving the case of a missing person, identity unknown, and finding out what had become of Bill and Gerry at one and the same time. He was faced with tissues of lies and prevarications from the laird and his weird assortment of servants, a hard mattress, pillows, slipper satin eiderdown, nylon sheets, the ticking of his bedside clock, and his urgent need to pay a visit to the bathroom.

'Sleep well?' Moncrieff greeted him warmly when, at eight o'clock, the trio seated themselves at the breakfast table to partake of porridge, bacon, eggs and sausages, toast, marmalade, and strong cups of tea.

'Yes, fine,' Brambell responded cheefully, unwilling to admit that he had scarcely slept at all, and pushing the sausages to the side of his plate untasted, feeling unable to look at them for the time being, in his unsettled state of mind, pouring himself a second cup of tea and coating, with butter and marmalade, his third slice of toast.

'So what's on the agenda today, sir?' Murdoch enquired respectfully. 'A return visit to the hospital to interview Mr Harker, or a visit to the nick to interview his missis?'

'I shall need the SOC report first,' Brambell said thoughtfully. 'No use working in the dark.' Not that he relished the prospect of a return visit to Glencochlin Castle, but he needed to know precisely what he was up against before proceeding further with his enquiry. Hopefully, Glencochlin had submitted to having his fingerprints taken, though he doubted it. Knowing the laird, more than likely he'd refuse to co-operate, start flinging his weight about and making a general bloody nuisance of himself. And yet the laird's fingerprints were vital in the discovery of who, precisely, had had their fingers on that panel button recently.

Mrs Harker's fingerprints would have been taken at the local nick as a matter of course, the day before. Not that she had spent the night in a prison cell but, at Brambell's discretion, in a room at a nearby boarding house, locked from the outside, with Constable Mitchell on watch in the hall. Cynthia's husband's and their grandson's would also have to be taken, at the hospital if necessary.

Harker had been armed. So what had become of his weapon? Food for thought. Brambell pondered deeply.

Fourteen

At Glencochlin Castle, Sergeant Lansdale, head of the SOC team, reported that the laird had flatly refused to have his finger-prints taken, claiming immunity from the law by reason of his exalted position as a landowner and magistrate, the arrogant so and so. This came as no surprise to Brambell, who nevertheless had experienced something akin to a jolt when, ringing the doorbell, the door had been answered by Ian Harker.

'What are you doing here?' Brambell had asked.

'I works here, don't I?' Harker had sullenly responded. 'The maister sent for me, an' I'm paid tae do as I'm told, what's wrang wi' that?'

'Then be kind enough to send for him as quickly as possible. I want a word with him.'

Ian smirked. 'You'll be lucky. 'E ain't 'ere. He's hopped it. Buggered off in 'is Bugatti.'

'Ye gods! Murdoch, find Sergeant Lansdale,' Brambell exploded.

'He's on the stairs now, sir. On about the

199

laird refusing to have his prints taken. Not best pleased by the sound of things; calling him all the names under the sun.'

With good reason, Brambell thought, cutting across Lansdale's diatribe concerning arrogant bastards who thought they were God.

'All right, Lansdale, you've made your point. Now, apparently, he's done a runner, and he must be found, the sooner the better. I want every escape route closed, every vessel searched, the mainland notified to keep a sharp lookout, helicopters sent up to search every acre of moorland between here and the Butt of Lewis. This man is dangerous, possibly armed, more than likely a murderer, a drug dealer, a master criminal engaged in people trafficking as a sideline.'

In a voice sharpened by tension, clearly and succinctly the old warrior barked out explicit orders to his assembled colleagues; in total command of the situation, and they knew it. This, after all, was the legendary Brambell of Scotland Yard. A force to be reckoned with.

In an upper chamber of Glencochlin's private apartments in the east wing of the castle, three prisoners, bound hand and foot to uncomfortable upright chairs in the darkened room, realizing the near impossibility of escape from their present dilemma, talked over the events of the night before. The shadowy figure who had clobbered Harker before Gerry had fairly had time to do so with her shoulder bag: the shot fired from Harker's rifle which had alerted the laird and Ian Harker to the boathouse in a matter of minutes, their discovery and arrest, at gunpoint, leading to their incarceration in this turret room to await whatever form of execution Glencochlin had planned for them.

Death by drowning or starvation? Gerry wondered. Perish the thought. But they weren't dead yet. Far from it. Their hands and feet were bound, but their fingers and toecaps were free. Not that Bill's right toecap might be up to hopping right now, but she, Gerry, would worry about that later. She and Frank Dawson must do the hopping for him.

'Quick, Frank,' she said urgently, 'let's pretend these chairs are pogo sticks; hop them together, back to back. You untie my hands, I'll untie yours, then we'll untie Bill's.'

'Not bloody likely,' Bill responded tartly, 'I'll do my own hopping, ta very much!'

'Right, then. All together now. One, two, three – hop!'

Untying the ropes about their wrists was no doddle, they discovered, as their fingertips were numb from lack of circulation. Neither had hopping the chairs together been a piece of cake, the chairs being solid, heavyweight and unwieldy, more like tree trunks than pogo sticks, but at least they were back to back, doing something positive to attempt their escape. Moreover, Gerry had spied her shoulder bag in a far corner of the room, where it had been slung, unceremoniously, by the 'Troll', Glencochlin's henchman, Ian Harker, following their enforced introduction to their prison cell. If only she could lay hands on her secret weapon, Gerry thought avidly, clumsily picking away at Bill's shackles, as he was picking away at Dawson's, Dawson at hers.

Suddenly, blissfully, Gerry's bonds gave way. Her hands were free. Losing no time, quickly she began untying her feet, then Bill's and Dawson's, finally their wrists. Then, picking up her shoulder bag, feeling its comforting weight in her hands, walking unsteadily to the window; looking down at the castle forecourt, seeing a procession of uniformed figures heading towards a police van parked there. Hefting her bag and swinging it wildly to gain momentum, she launched it unerringly through the turret room window, along with showers of broken glass, lumps of lead and a network of cobwebs to mark its explosive exit to the ground below, missing by inches the head of Sergeant Lansdale.

'Bloody hell! What was *that*?'

'Looks like a handbag tae me,' Constable

Mackie opined, inching forward for a closer inspection.

'A *handbag*. Where'd it come from?' Lansdale demanded, deeply shaken, brushing cobwebs from his uniform jacket and looking up at the sky as if expecting to spot a low flying glider, possibly even a UFO.

'You OK, Sarge?' Other members of the SOC team had gathered round to find out what was going on, to kick aside broken glass and to look up at the east wing of Glencochlin Castle.

'There's a woman up yonder in the turret!' Constable MacKenzie exclaimed suddenly. 'Wavin' her arms, tryin' tae attract our attention! Mebbe she chucked that handbag?' He added, 'What's tae do, Sarge? Take a closer look?'

'No. We have our orders. It's Glencochlin we're after. We'll leave this handbag business for Brambell tae sort out. You'd best find him, Mackie, put him in the picture and be quick about it! I have a score tae settle wi' his lairdship.' He smiled grimly, 'I'll hev his fingerprints taken right enough if I catch up wi' him.'

Brambell would have known Gerry's portable office-cum-chemist's anywhere. It was as much a part of her as her little red Mini. Tears filled his eyes. He had found her. At long last, he had found his missing link to job satisfaction. Working with Gerry during the Theatre Murders, he'd been amazed by her courage, resourcefulness and down to earth common sense, allied to her indomitable optimism and quirky sense of humour, that 'feel good' factor which had done wonders for his morale during what had proved to be a particularly complex and unpleasant murder enquiry.

But what was he thinking about? Gerry was up there in the east wing of Glencochlin Castle, in dire need of help. She had sent him a message via that shoulder bag of hers; a cry for assistance by the only means available to her.

Thinking quickly, he realized that she and Bill must be imprisoned in a room similar to that occupied by the countess. Remembering all those stairs and the laird's preoccupation with security, a lot of breath and muscle power may well be needed if it came to breaking down doors, he reckoned. 'You'd best fetch Moncrieff,' he commanded Murdoch, 'and a sledgehammer, if he has one handy.'

'Sir.' Now the game really was afoot, Murdoch thought ecstatically, hurrying to the car to alert Moncrieff, tickled pink by Brambell's quiet sense of humour. A sledgehammer indeed. On the other hand, a set of handcuffs might come in handy if Ian Harker turned nasty. Nasty to begin with, he wouldn't need much turning, Murdoch surmised, relishing the thought of dotting the young villain one in the eye if he resisted arrest, accidentally, of course.

But there was no sign of Harker when Brambell, Moncrieff and Murdoch entered the house, Brambell with Gerry's bag dangling from his shoulder, Moncrieff armed with a monkey-wrench, Murdoch with a set of handcuffs in his pocket.

Harker could be lying in wait for them in the east wing, Brambell realized, armed and dangerous, but somehow he didn't think so. More than likely the young ruffian, fearing that the long arm of the law would seize him by the scruff of the neck, had scarpered to save his own miserable skin.

Crossing the threshold of Glencochlin Castle reminded Brambell of the mystery of the *Marie Celeste,* an abandoned ship which even the rats had deserted. As the rats Glencochlin and Ian Harker had abandoned the castle, leaving the prisoners to their own devices, to suffer hunger and thirst, to starve to death for all they cared, which they might well have done had not his brave, resourceful Gerry drawn attention to their plight by means of her well-aimed shoulder bag.

The key of the east wing door was, thankfully, in its lock, avoiding the necessity of breaking into the laird's private apartments. Apartments as bizarre as Glencochlin himself, Brambell realized, catching sight of weird tapestries depicting Bacchanalian revels, satyrs and naked women engaged in activities that would make a maiden aunt blush. There were tribal masks on the staircase walls, ugly leering faces, bespeaking sinister rituals – human sacrifices, cruelty, the spillage of blood – collected presumably by a man preoccupied with folklore and witchcraft.

Solid oak doors appeared at intervals, none of which was locked. Presumably the laird, in a devil of a hurry to escape justice, had thrown caution to the wind when it came to security.

Moncrieff, Brambell realized, was champing at the bit to make a detailed examination of all the rooms, especially the laird's inner sanctum where, given a modicum of good luck, he would come across proof positive of Glencochlin's involvement in the murders of Sam MacNally, Penny Douglas and Sergeant Kirk, the abduction and possible murder of the countess. Maybe even his drugs dealing and people smuggling rackets, but not until Brambell had made certain that Gerry and Bill were safe and well and out of danger.

Grateful for his colleague's help and support, his sense of justice and fair play, pausing a while to draw breath, Brambell continued his ascent, fearful of what he might find there, the Bentines in dire need of medical treatment more than likely. They would be weak from hunger and thirst if they had been imprisoned without food or water to sustain them.

Feeling a bit like Sir Edmund Hillary about to scale the summit of Mount Everest on the occasion of the Queen's Coronation, heart pounding, Brambell saw, to his infinite relief, having achieved his objective of the turret room landing, that the stout oak door had been locked from the outside, the key in the door, obviating the necessity of entry to the prison by brute force. Even so, in his present state of nervous tension and fatigue, his shaking fingers failed, at first, to turn the key in its lock until, imbued with a sudden burst of energy – commensurate with his drawing in deep breaths of air to fill his lungs and to still the thudding of his heart against his ribs – he heard the satisfying grate of the key in its rusty lock and pushed open the door, commenting drily, as he did so, 'What we really needed here was not a monkey wrench but an oil-can.'

Seconds later, Moncrieff and Murdoch witnessed, from the threshold of the turret room, a reunion to gladden the heart. Gerry tumbled into Brambell's arms, and Bill limped forward to shake hands warmly with the rescuers, at the same time introducing their companion as, 'Our friend Frank Dawson, of Interpol, aka Max Telemann.'

Moncrieff's eyebrows shot up. 'Interpol?' he echoed excitedly. 'My dear sir, a pleasure I assure you. How soon can we talk?' Delighted at this breakthrough; a glimmer of light on the horizon, a probable solution to his problems once he had gained access to Glencochlin's inner sanctum. He would put the laird behind bars for the next thirty years or so with a bona-fide Interpol agent to help him in his search for the evidence, he thought ecstatically.

Brambell said decisively, 'Talk can come later. Right now, we must get Gerry, Bill and Frank away from here, give them something to eat and drink and find them somewhere to stay. Any ideas?'

'Yes, sure.' Moncrieff remembered the small hotel near the Stornoway police station, and a fish and chips café in the main square. Bowing to the inevitable, he knew that Brambell had his priorities right, as usual. The search of Glencochlin's private apartments must wait until the hostages had been fed and watered and given hot baths and accommodation. Meanwhile, he must hold his horses, despite his eagerness to get on with his job, *à toute vitesse*.

And so, reluctantly, he led the procession across the forecourt to his car, and when the six of them were packed in like sardines in a can, he drove them to the fish and chips cafe. On their arrival, he detailed Murdoch to book rooms for Gerry, Bill, and Frank Dawson, at the hotel near the police station.

Fish had never tasted so good before, Gerry thought, tucking in to her meal, neither had freedom. For a while back there in that ghastly secret passage, she had felt entombed, the way she had often felt in London Underground trains between stations. Then had come the boathouse incident, the details of which she could not clearly remember, apart from a hurriedly devised plan to clobber the cadaver with her shoulder bag which had never come to fruition. Someone else had got to him first, someone already secreted in the boathouse? She couldn't be sure. Everything had happened so fast. Harker had slumped forward, a shot had been fired, then had come the sound of footsteps, lights had been switched on, and she, Bill and Frank had found themselves facing the business end of Glencochlin's revolver and a hefty iron bar held threateningly by his henchman, Ian Harker. At which point Gerry had wondered if it was he who had landed a blow to the back of his father's bonce. But there had been more to worry about than who had cracked old Harker's nut. Staying alive taking top priority at the time.

Glencochlin had seemed particularly edgy, she'd thought on their way to his turret room; rattled to put it mildly, grim faced, lacking his spurious veneer of charm, as if something had happened to get under that rhinoceros hide of his. Something or someone? She'd winced with pain when her wrists and ankles were tied together tightly by the Troll, feeling the thin cord biting deeply into her flesh, drawing blood. Hating the sight of his leering face, his obvious delight in inflicting pain on her, the sour smell of his breath emanating from his mouthful of rotten teeth, yet stubbornly refusing to cry out as he tightened the cord about her ankles and hovered, momentarily, above her, smiling down at her, at which point, closing her eyes and turning her head aside, she had uttered *'Phew.'*

The past days had seemed tinged with unreality, especially their reunion with DCI Brambell, Gerry reflected, as she and Bill got ready for bed that night – a double bed with warm blankets, inviting pillows and a puffy pink eiderdown, in which they had spent the past two nights, a haven of luxury after Glencochlin's so-called hospitality.

'Just think, love, we'll be on our way home tomorrow,' Gerry murmured blissfully, snuggling up to Bill, that thought uppermost in her mind. *Home.* The Eyrie, a return to normality, her attic workroom, her type-writer, her little red Mini; Bill's return to his office in Red Lion Square; meeting up again with their friends Maggie and Barney Bowler at their hamburger joint on Old Kent Road. Not that she relished the thought of reliving, even verbally, the details of a honeymoon venture from which she and Bill were lucky to have emerged still alive and unharmed.

On the other hand, had it not been for Maggie Bowler's visit to Scotland Yard to alert DCI Brambell to their disappearance, they might well have ended up as dead as mutton.

The questioning that she, Bill and Frank Dawson had undergone by Brambell and Moncrieff, had convinced Gerry that she and Bill knew too much about the goings-on at the castle to be allowed to live; especially since they had formed a strong liaison with Dawson, now revealed as an undercover agent.

No wonder the laird, fearful for his own liberty, with the law at his heels – facing charges of drug dealing, people trafficking and murder – had disappeared into the wild blue yonder, Gerry surmised. Then, turning her thoughts to the welcome prospect of going home, she rejoiced in her heart that this nightmare would finally be over and done with once and for all.

A return visit to the castle had been necessary to pick up their belongings and to retrace their movements during the time they'd spent there as unwilling guests beneath its crumbling roof, providing every scrap of evidence possible against Glencochlin and his cohorts.

Harker and his wife, the former released from his hospital bed, were now both in custody helping the police with their enquiries. There had been no sign whatever of their grandson Ian or Glencochlin, despite the determined efforts of Lansdale and his team to discover their whereabouts. So where the hell were they?

To Gerry and Bill's infinite relief, their car had been discovered, in good order, in the laird's garage to the rear of the castle; they would drive, in the early hours of next morning, to catch the first ferry to the mainland. Later on, Brambell and Frank Dawson would fly to London via helicopter, to Scotland Yard. There, aided and abetted by Interpol, plans would be drawn up for the detention and interrogation of those associates of Glencochlin now known to have attended the so-called house party of his, during which they had been allocated their forthcoming evil assignments; namely Tony Cannelli, Gloria and Arnold Crowther and Brian Douglas. Frank Dawson had been present, in his Max Telemann disguise, when those assignments were detailed and handed out to his fellow criminals by the master criminal himself – Fergus Glencochlin.

Meanwhile, Moncrieff and Murdoch would stay on at Grace Cameron's cottage to continue their investigations into the murders of Sam MacNally and Sergeant Kirk, and the disappearance of the countess, to further interrogate Jock and Mrs Harker, and to direct operations leading to the discovery and arrest of Glencochlin and his henchman Ian Harker. They could not have simply disappeared from the island as if by magic, and without trace, to Moncrieff's way of thinking. They must be *somewhere*. But *where*?

In the dim and distant past, a potential benefactor of his native soil, Lord Leverhulme, had begun building a road with a view to linking isolated hamlets the breadth of Lewis to one another. A worthy project until, his money having run out halfway, he had been obliged to abandon his brainchild unfinished, a sad disappointment for a man of his calibre.

Now, when the road ran out, Ian Harker bumped the landrover he was driving violently across rough terrain towards a deeply excavated, tree grown quarry, containing the burnt out remains of a vintage Bugatti, until recently the pride and joy of its owner, Fergus Glencochlin.

The laird, Ian knew, would be in hiding, awaiting the arrival of the landrover. He also knew that time was of the essence. But all was ready, as planned, for their escape to freedom by means of a fishing vessel at anchor in a bay beneath a rocky promontory, south of the Butt of Lewis. Once there, the landrover would be parked near the cliff edge, the brake released, and it would roll over the tussocky grass verge to its final resting place on the boulders beneath. Then, shouldering their gear, overnight bags containing money, bogus passports, binoculars, food and a revolver, they would make their way to the cove to board the boat anchored off shore in anticipation of their coming.

There would be little or no conversation, Glencochlin had warned him. The skipper of the coble, a taciturn man, a speaker of Gaelic, had been well paid for his services and his silence. Everything had been planned beforehand. They would cross to the mainland under cover of darkness, and the passage would take some time to accomplish, but there'd be plenty of hot strong coffee to drink. Gaelic coffee laced with rum, whisky or cognac, Ian had thought happily, looking forward to the adventure, relishing the prospect of the freedom ahead of him, far removed from his overbearing grandparents' narrowmindedness.

But Ian Harker was destined never to taste

freedom. Glencochlin had another plan in mind for him. Having served his purpose in putting paid to Sam MacNally and Sergeant Kirk, and in helping to dispose of the land-rover, the man was now expendable, the laird realized, a threat to his own security should he fall foul of the law. No way could he run that risk. Young Harker knew far too much about recent events at the castle; the abduction of the countess, Olga Redezky, for instance, and what had become of her, also the murder of Penelope Douglas and the identity of her killer. These were good and sufficient reasons for the 'accident' the laird had planned for him before they reached the mainland plying the young fool with, not Gaelic coffee, but whisky.

Early the next morning, aboard the ferry bound for freedom – ultimately towards England, home and safety – Bill's arm clasped firmly about her waist, watching, from the upper deck of the vessel, the casting off of cables and hearing the encouraging throb of the engines as the ferry nosed away from its shorelines towards the sea, Gerry thanked her lucky stars that she and Bill had emerged from their disastrous honeymoon venture, still alive and breathing. More in love with each other than ever, despite her wilfulness in wanting an 'unusual' honeymoon. Well, it had certainly been that, with bells on.

Now, all she wanted was normality. To forget Glencochlin Castle and the bizarre events that had taken place there. Particularly of its owner who, for whatever reasons, had wanted her dead.

Thankfully, Gerry thought, all that was in the past now.

PART TWO

Fifteen

They had stayed overnight in Edinburgh, but both Gerry and Bill were anxious to go home, back to the Hampstead Eyrie. They'd had enough of strange surroundings, draughty rooms, crumbling walls, bizarre goings on, mayhem and murder. What they needed now was the comfort and security of their own four walls, log fires, hot baths, home cooked food, a much longed for return to normality. To establish a daily routine as a married couple, so far denied them, Gerry realized, remembering that after the wedding, with a houseful of guests to see to, they hadn't even slept together in a proper double bed. She had occupied her single bed in her attic workroom, while Bill had made do with a settee, a sleeping bag, a couple of pillows and a blanket.

Now, as Bill nosed the hatchback through the rush-hour London traffic towards Hampstead, Gerry experienced an uprush of joy at the sights and sounds of her native city. Lumbering London buses, familiar buildings, lamplights reflected in pavements wet from a recent downpour of rain: hurrying crowds of people heading towards the Underground stations, added to her elation of homecoming.

Maggie Bowler would have been to the Eyrie earlier on to switch on the immersion heater, fires and the electric blanket in the master bedroom, also to replenish the refrigerator and deep-freeze, to bring with her milk and fresh bread and quick-fix microwave meals, bless her. Dear Maggie, who had been close to tears when Gerry had phoned her from Edinburgh the night before, to tell her that she and Bill would be homeward bound early the next morning.

'Right,' Maggie had said, choking back her tears of joy at the glad tidings, 'just you leave everything to me. I'll mek good use of that bunch of keys you left me, but I'll not interfere. Well, you know what I mean? You an' Bill are bound to be tired out after your long journey, in need of peace and quiet, wantin' to be alone together. I daresay wantin' summat to eat, hot baths an' an early night. Am I right? An' are you gonna sleep in the room Bill's ma an' step-pa slept in when they was here?' A perceptive human being, Gerry thought happily, as the Eyrie came into view.

Standing with her back to the front door,

gazing about her, Gerry breathed in the atmosphere of home, noticed, with delight, the red turkey stair-carpet and shining brass rods and the polished half moon hall table on which Maggie had placed a jardiniere of red roses and a Welcome Home card beside piles of neatly stacked letters and junk mail. Bills too, Gerry surmised, to be dealt with later, but not now. Not until she had made a tour of inspection of her domain, beginning with the downstairs rooms, to feast her eyes on her treasured belongings, to take a peek into the refrigerator, and a gander at the garden prior to stepping back indoors to swish the curtains against the encroaching darkness of the world outside. Suppressing a slight shudder as she did so, remembering how close she and Bill had come to losing their lives in a place far removed from the bustling city of London, from England, and above all, from home.

When Bill entered the kitchen, having hefted their luggage upstairs to the master bedroom on the first floor, catching sight of Gerry's woebegone expression, the almost imperceptible shaking of her limbs, he gathered her into his arms and murmured encouragingly, 'Not to worry, darling, we're safe now. Quite safe. So how about a bite to eat? A cheese and pickle butty and a nice cup of tea to be going on with?'

'Oh yes, please Bill,' she replied gratefully,

snuggling into the warm circle of his embrace, wanting to believe, with all her heart, that what he said was true – that they really were quite safe now.

Upstairs next morning, seated at her battered typewriter, she was feeling much better, more relaxed after a good night's sleep in the arms of her beloved. Having waved Bill off to work with a substantial English breakfast inside him, done the washing up, made the bed, and paid a visit to the garage to make a fuss of her little red Mini, what now? she wondered, missing Bill's presence in the house. Begin a new book? Drive down to the village supermarket to shop? For what exactly? More food, when the refrigerator was already full to overflowing?

It was then that she remembered that pile of unopened letters on the hall table, and went downstairs to investigate. The junk mail, she dumped unceremoniously in the swing-bin near the kitchen sink. No, she did not want double-glazing; buy one, get one free settees: nor did she wish to join a book, clothing or video club, to become a Christmas Club agent or, even worse, a party-plan salesperson flogging saucy underwear and sex-aids to frustrated housewives, on a commission basis. Perish the thought.

Next came various requests from women's luncheon club secretaries, wanting her as a guest speaker which, again, perish the thought. Luncheon clubs, smart women in fancy hats, put the fear of God into Gerry.

Putting those letters to one side, seated at the kitchen table, a cup of coffee and a packet of chocolate digestive biscuits to hand, opening the rest of her mail, her heart warmed to a letter from DCI Brambell, thanking her and Bill for their help in what he termed 'The Glencochlin affair'; wishing them a happy homecoming, and inviting them to a celebratory dinner at his home a week come Sunday. He and his wife would be delighted to see them, and their fellow guests would include his former sidekick, Bert Briggs and his wife. The letter was signed, 'All best wishes, Foxton C. Brambell'. So Brambell's baptismal name was Foxton? Being Gerry, she couldn't help wondering what the C stood for.

Next on the agenda came a letter from America, from her former friend and neighbour, Maurice Berenger, whose ex-wife, Lisl, was presently serving a ten-year prison sentence for her involvement in the Antiques Murders.

Poor dear Maurice, Gerry thought compassionately, one of the kindest men she had ever known, a crime novelist par excellence, whom she revered as a kind of father-figure, alongside Barney Bowler.

Reading between the lines of Maurice's

missive, Gerry guessed that, despite the success of his latest crime novel, *The Manhattan Murders*, he had still not come to terms with the loss of Lisl from his life, nor ever would, just as she would never come to terms with the loss of Bill Bentine from hers. Love was like that, all or nothing.

The third letter she opened sent shivers of apprehension down Gerry's spine. Typewritten, in capital letters, she read, THE DAY OF RECKONING IS YET TO COME. I'LL WHISTLE AND YOU'LL COME TO ME, MY LASS.

No doubt about the sender of that letter, Gerry realized, it *had* to be from Fergus Glencochlin. Who else?

So what to do about it? Being Gerry, she knew, beyond a shadow of doubt, that the laird meant what he said, that sooner or later they would meet again, and when that happened she would be called upon to engage in a life or death contest with a lunatic.

When Bill arrived home from work that evening, he discovered his wife in the kitchen, harnessed with a pinafore, hair awry with the steam issuing from bubbling pans of vegetables on the cooker, the table set with a red and white checked cloth, cutlery, condiments and wine glasses.

Sniffing the air appreciatively, he said, 'Hey, something smells good. So what's on the menu? Fish pie?'

'As if!' Treating him to a withering glance, 'Not on your Nellie. We're having roast beef, roast taters, Yorkshire puddn's, carrots, cauliflower, leeks an' frozen peas, if you really must know.'

'Just as well I brought this, then,' he chuckled, plonking a bottle of claret on the table, 'and these,' handing her a bunch of red carnations, 'for the woman I love.'

'Oh Bill,' she murmured, as his lips met hers. 'I love you too. More than you'll ever know,' determined to make the best of whatever time they had left together, not to tell him about the scarcely veiled death threat she'd received from Glencochlin, shoring up her courage, her mental and physical resources to meet that challenge when it happened.

After dinner, which Bill had pronounced to be 'simply delicious', together in the drawing room, Gerry showed him the letters she'd received from Maurice Berenger and DCI Brambell, and told him she'd arranged a Sunday visit by Maggie and Barney for lunch and a good old chinwag.

'Great,' Bill commented happily, 'let's give 'em duck and peas,' recalling an incident during the Antiques Murders when, on learning that Gerry's life was in danger, he had driven from Wiltshire in a devil of a hurry, leaving his hostess's table so abruptly that peas had flown in every direction, before he'd even tasted the roast duck. Since then duck and peas had become an 'in' joke between himself and his wife. Not that they'd been married at the time, but they were now, thank the lord, and despite the traumatic events which had overshadowed their honeymoon, never for one moment did he regret having married a woman with whom life would never be dull or orthodox, but fraught with the unexpected, danger, but also, more importantly, with fun, love and laughter.

'Oh yes, let's,' Gerry concurred, harking back to the subject of Sunday lunch, 'with lots of sage and onion stuffing. And let's eat in the dining room, shall we? They'll love that. Let me think, let's go shopping together on Saturday, shall we? We'll pick up a nice, plump little duck from the butcher's, then go on to the supermarket for the Paxo stuffing, fresh vegetables, smoked salmon for starters, Black Forest gateaux for afters, a bottle or so of booze, a box of chocolates for Maggie, a box of cigars for Barney.'

Never would Gerry's kindness of heart and her outgoing generosity cease to amaze him, Bill thought, finishing his whisky nightcap and reminding her that tomorrow was another day, that, right now, it was time for bed.

Long after Bill had fallen asleep, Gerry lay

awake thinking about the cryptic message from Glencochlin, wondering what he meant by, 'I'll whistle and you'll come to me'. Come, where to? And when? She'd assumed that, as a wanted man, having left the castle so abruptly, he'd be well away by now, on his way to Australia, America, the Bahamas, Italy or Austria. But the letter had been posted here, in England, from Manchester, the day before, according to the postmark, which meant, frighteningly, that the laird could be here in London right now, watching the house at this very moment.

The thought occurred to her that she should, perhaps, have been in touch with Scotland Yard the moment she'd read that letter. Withholding vital information had been a mistake, she knew that now. Glancing at the bedside clock, the hands of which stood at twenty minutes past eleven, getting out of bed, putting on her dressing gown and slippers, she hurried down to the hall, picked up the phone and dialled Brambell's home number. Awaiting a reply, looking up, she saw Bill on the stairs.

Frowning, he asked bemusedly, 'What the hell's going on?'

Breathlessly, she handed him the letter. 'I received this today,' she said, ashen faced. 'I'm sorry, Bill, I should have told you. I can't think why I didn't, except that I didn't want to spoil your homecoming. Please, don't be angry.'

'Angry? My darling girl, of course I'm not angry.' Beside her, his arms about her, 'So who are you ringing?' But he had already guessed who. Detective Chief Inspector Brambell – who else?

At half past midnight, the three of them, Bill, Gerry and Brambell were seated at the kitchen table, drinking the coffee Bill had made to aid their discussion of the letter, which lay open before them, including its envelope. Gerry was shivering, Bill noticed, suffering from shock, he shouldn't wonder, after all she'd been through lately – now this; a cruel reminder of danger, just when she'd begun to feel safe once more.

Thank God for the stalwart, comforting presence of DCI Brambell, he thought, pouring more coffee. Brambell had arrived on their doorstep wearing his battered brown felt trilby and a disreputable raincoat – the striped collar of his pyjamas protruding from the V neck of a hastily donned Fair-Isle sweater, reminiscent of a country doctor called out on an urgent, late night call.

Excusing himself, Bill hurried upstairs to fetch a blanket to wrap round his wife's shoulders, to warm her.

'Thanks, love,' she murmured gratefully, close to tears, 'but all this is my fault. What I deserve is not kindness but a good swift kick in the ... pants for being so stupid.' About to say 'arse', she'd changed her mind at the last minute.

Knowing exactly what she'd been about to say, Bill, smiling inwardly, handed her a fresh cup of coffee laced with a stiff slug of brandy. 'Here, get this down you, and stop talking nonsense,' he said easily, 'it'll do you more good than a kick in the pants, believe me.'

Brambell chuckled, Gerry looked startled, then laughed. Bill bent down to kiss her. Brambell said, 'The laird appears to have given us the slip. Don't ask me how. This is the first lead we've had since he beat the retreat from his ... lair, for want of a better description.' Pushing back his hat to scratch his forehead, 'How he got as far as Manchester without being spotted beats me, but I shouldn't worry too much if I were you, Gerry, I doubt he'll have the nerve to show up here. Chances are he'll be making for Manchester Airport, heavily disguised as a clergyman or whatever, the cunning devil.'

'What do you think he meant by the day of reckoning is yet to come, and I'll whistle and you'll come to me?' Bill asked. 'Reckoning for what exactly?'

'Perhaps he doesn't like the cut of my jib,' Gerry supplied dolefully. 'Well, I'm no oil-painting, am I?'

'Oh I don't know, I've seen worse,' Bill

laughed, 'and you scrub up quite nicely.'

Brambell said, 'It's my belief that you saw or heard something you weren't meant to, some vital piece of information that you've forgotten about or paid no attention to at the time. Think about it, Gerry, and let me know the moment you come up with something, however unimportant it may seem.' He smiled encouragingly. Then, glancing at his watch, 'Hmm, I'd best be off now. Mind if I take these with me?' gingerly picking up the letter and envelope which he folded carefully into his wallet. 'Fingerprints, you see? Hopefully, forensics will discover some clue to the identity of the sender. We can but try.'

'Thank you so much for coming,' Gerry said quietly, sincerely. 'I'm feeling tons better now, just sorry that I've kept you up so late. Forgive me?'

Brambell said warmly, 'There's nothing to forgive. And, for what it's worth, there's nothing wrong with the cut of your jib. From where I'm standing, it looks just fine to me.'

'I'll second that,' Bill said tenderly, a protective arm about Gerry's shoulders. 'Well, goodnight Inspector. Looking forward to seeing you again next week.'

'Why not call me Chas, short for Charles?' Brambell murmured, somewhat shyly. 'Or Foxy, if you'd prefer. Only not in public, if you don't mind.'

'We wouldn't dream of it,' Gerry said

firmly. 'Charles has a nice ring to it. Let's stick to that, shall we?'

The duck was 'quacking' in the oven, the air was fragrant with the scent of sage and onion stuffing, roasting potatoes, and other vegetables. The dining-room table was set with a lace-edged cloth, shining cutlery and sparkling crystal glasses. Bill had gone to fetch Maggie and Barney from the Old Kent Road, and would be back any minute, bringing with him the two people whom Gerry regarded as surrogate parents, closer and infinitely more dear to her than her real parents had ever been.

Lowering the oven temperature, she hurried upstairs to comb her hair, powder her nose and apply a soupçon of lipstick, when suddenly her blood ran cold. *Someone was playing a tune on a penny whistle.*

Seconds later, she heard voices downstairs in the hall, the sound of laughter, the closing of the front door, Bill calling her name. 'Gerry, love, where are you? We're back. Maggie and Barney are here.'

Eyes wide with fright, she stumbled downstairs, gripping the banister for support.

'Good grief! What's the matter? What's happened?' Heart in mouth, Bill strode towards her.

'He's here! Glencochlin. I heard the sound of a whistle.'

Maggie piped up, 'It'll be that church parade. We passed 'em in the street just now: scouts an' cubs stepping it out like good 'uns, banners flyin', an' that little lad out front playin' a recorder. The pore kid were heving all on to play an' march at the same time, so he stopped playin' when his puff ran out.'

Relief flooded through Gerry.

'Come and sit down, love. You've had a shock, but everything's fine now. What you need is a drop of brandy,' said Bill gently.

'No. What I need is to give Maggie and Barney a hug. I haven't even said hello to them yet. I'm sorry,' embracing warmly first Maggie then Barney, 'what ever must you think of me, making a fool of myself the way I did?'

'It's all right, love,' Maggie assured her, 'Bill told us about that letter "Glen Campbell" sent you. Huh, if *I'd* heard that whistle, I'd hev fainted dead away, an' that's a fact.' She added archly, 'An' I wouldn't have said no to a slug of brandy.'

Taking the hint, Bill said resignedly, as he led them to the kitchen. 'Brandy all round then? I'm feeling a bit iffy myself, come to think of it, and I'm sure that Barney is, too. Am I right?'

'I wouldn't say no,' Barney admitted. 'Jest a small 'un, mind you.'

*　*　*

And so the luncheon party had got off to a good start after all, to Gerry's relief. True, the duck was a tad overdone, the veggies not exactly aldente, the gravy a bit lumpy, but who cared?

Maggie's warm, endearing personality had lifted Gerry's spirits, put into perspective her fright on hearing that 'penny whistle', and stiffened her resolve to pull herself together and stop acting like a drama queen in an old Hollywood movie.

Hearing Glencochlin referred to as Glen Campbell, had somehow cut down to size that towering man in black image she recalled so vividly from that first day she'd seen him awaiting the ferry crossing from the mainland. He had seemed to her, even then, the embodiment of evil. And so he had proved to be, and yet, realistically, his wickedness had now caught up with him. A known criminal, a wanted man, his capture could not be long delayed, Gerry figured, not with the likes of Inspector Brambell, Moncrieff, Murdoch and Frank Dawson hot on his trail.

Meanwhile it was good to feel safe and secure in the company of her old, loyal and trusted friends, Maggie and Barney Bowler. Above all, in the unfailing love and devotion of her beloved Bill Bentine, to whom she owed a return to her normal, ebullient self. The sooner the better.

Sixteen

Charles and Jenny Brambell's home in a tree-lined avenue near Earl's Court exuded an atmosphere of warmth, charm, and good home cooking. The kind of pipe and slippers aura conducive to conversation, relaxation or contemplation, attributes necessary to the wellbeing of a hardworking DCI of the Metropolitan Police Force, Gerry thought, as she and Bill crossed the threshold to a rapturous welcome from Brambell and his wife.

Bert Briggs and Polly were ensconced in the drawing room, sipping sherry and relaxing near the warmth of a brightly glowing coal fire, when Charles accompanied Gerry and Bill into the room. Immediately, Bert sprang to his feet to shake Bill's hand and to plant a kiss of welcome on Gerry's cheek, closely followed by Polly, a devoted fan of Gerry's, scarcely able to believe her luck in being on first name terms with a famous author.

Not that there was anything stuck up about her, Polly reflected as Gerry asked how the kids were doing at school. Really wanting to know, not just being kind, Polly realized, coming over shy all of a sudden, and blushing to the roots of her dark brown hair.

Meanwhile, Gerry's husband was talking animatedly to Bert, and DCI Brambell had slipped away, unnoticed, to lend his wife a hand in the kitchen. A special meal Jenny, a splendid cook, had dreamed up for this celebratory dinner in honour of Gerry and Bill.

At eight o'clock Charles re-entered the room to announce that dinner was ready, if they would care to follow him to the dining room. 'Oh, how perfectly lovely!' Gerry exclaimed, catching sight of the beautifully appointed table with its centrepiece of rowan berries and white rosebuds in a shallow cut-crystal bowl, brightly burning red candles and red damask napkins. Gerry was deeply aware of all the hard work and careful planning necessary to the creation of so spectacular an end product, not to mention the immaculate appearance of Jenny Brambell, who came in from the kitchen, smiling, with not a hair out of place, to supervise the seating arrangements. Meanwhile Charles, at the bow-fronted Georgian sideboard, uncorked chardonnay to accompany the first course of smoked salmon. A fine, full bodied claret would come next to complement the boeuf Bourguignonne. A clever woman, his wife,

Brambell thought, not to complicate life with last minute flurries in the kitchen to strain vegetables and thicken gravy giving her the time and opportunity to enjoy the company of their guests, knowing that the kitchen was pin neat, the pots and pans washed and put away, and the raspberry pavlova serving time in the fridge before its appearance on the dining table. The table was set for seven people, not six, Gerry noticed, idly wondering who was missing. Her surprise and delight knew no bounds when she found out – the door opened and Frank Dawson came into the room, apologizing for his tardiness, explaining that his flight from Italy had been delayed.

Rising to his feet, Charles said warmly, 'Not to worry, laddie. By the way, I don't think you've met Inspector Briggs of the Hampstead division and his wife Polly? Bert, Polly, this is Frank Dawson, of Interpol, a house guest of ours during his stay in London, and a much respected colleague, I might add, aiding enquiries into the Glencochlin affair.' Smiling mischievously, 'A handy man to have around in a tight corner. Ask Bill and Gerry if you don't believe me.'

Bert and Bill had also risen from their seats to shake hands with the newcomer. Bill to slap him firmly on the shoulder, Bert to acknowledge the introduction with a murmured, 'A great honour to meet you, sir.'

'You too, Bert. I've heard a lot about you and your charming wife from Jenny and Charles here.' Then, to Polly's surprise and pleasure, lifting her hand, he pressed it fleetingly to his lips, whereupon, blushing, she gasped, 'Well, I never.'

Having awarded Jenny a similar token of respect, he turned his attention to Gerry. 'Now it's your turn,' he said, tongue in cheek.

'Yeah, well, you can stuff that hand-kissing lark, Frank Dawson,' she retorted, getting up to throw her arms about him, 'what I need from you is a hug and a proper kiss. Oh, it's so good to see you again.'

Bill chuckled. 'Go right ahead. Don't mind me.' It was great to see Gerry happy once more, restored to her former self in the company of friends, the nightmare caused by the letter she'd received from Glencochlin over and done with. With the net closing in about him, surely the laird could not escape, for much longer, the long arm of the law, and his capture and restraint behind prison bars, when the police finally caught up with him?

The meal continued merrily as Charles, in his element, liberally replenished their glasses and finally, when the pavlova had made its debut from the refrigerator, popping the cork of a bottle of Bollinger, proposing a toast 'To Gerry and Bill, whose homecoming has gladdened the hearts of all here present. We wish you well. Health and happiness in your future together. May it be long, your happiness unending.'

Nudging Bill in the ribs with her elbow, 'Well, don't just sit there, say summat,' Gerry murmured, 'anything, only make it snappy.'

'Right then, I shall,' Bill conceded. Rising to his feet smiling, he began, 'In reply to the toast, all that I can truthfully say is this. Gerry and I would not be here tonight had it not been for you, Charles, Frank Dawson, and one other person, Maggie Bowler, who alerted Scotland Yard to the fact that we had gone missing. And so, a reciprocal toast, if I may. Here's to the kind of friendship and love bestowed on us, without which we might well not have had a future together at all.'

Later, over coffee in the lamplit drawing room, in the circle of chairs drawn up near the lit fireplace, conversation moved inevitably from topics such as street-parking problems, the World Cup, the recently held Olympic Games, TV chefs and their shortcomings, over-usage of garlic and bad language, to police matters in particular. How could it be otherwise, Bill thought resignedly, with a DCI, an Inspector and an Interpol agent in the same room at the same time.

Casting an anxious glance in Gerry's direction, he dreaded a recurrence of her recent depression at the reaping up of painful memories connected with Glencochlin Castle and its owner.

'Don't worry, love,' Gerry murmured, as though reading his mind, leaning forward to press his hand resting on the arm of her chair, 'I'm not about to take another nosedive. I really want to know what's going on, don't you?'

There had been no trace of the laird since he had given them the slip after the boathouse shooting incident. His Bugatti, or what was left of it, had been discovered in a disused quarry near the remains of Lord Leverhulme's long abandoned roadway project. The wreck of his landrover had been found beneath the headland a few miles east of the quarry. Moreover, a body washed up on a mainland beach near Am Baig had been identified, by Inspector Moncrieff, as that of Ian Harker, Brambell said quietly.

'Ian Harker!' Gerry exclaimed. *Dead?* But *how?* How did he die?'

Frowning slightly, Charles replied, 'Difficult to be precise. There were no signs of physical violence on the body, but the post mortem revealed an inordinate quantity of alcohol in his bloodstream. The consensus is that Harker, aboard some vessel or other, in a state of intoxication, fell overboard and drowned.'

'What about his grandparents?' Gerry asked, feeling sorry for anyone who had lost a close family member.

'They're under arrest,' Charles explained, 'on charges of conspiracy in the nefarious goings on at the castle. Moncrieff's examination of Glencochlin's papers and computer turned up some mighty interesting information; positive proof of their part in the restraint and abduction of Countess Olga Redezky, drug dealing, the murders of Penny Douglas, Sam MacNally and Sergeant Kirk.

'We now know that it was the male Harkers who, on Glencochlin's specific instructions, put paid to MacNally and Sergeant Kirk. And so—', Brambell sighed deeply, 'had not young Ian had the misfortune to meet his death by drowning, he would now, most certainly, be facing a life behind bars. What we don't know is the name of the vessel, its owner, or who helped young Harker overboard, having plied the poor devil with so much booze that he wouldn't have had a clue what was happening until he hit the water. Though I think I can hazard a guess.

'Glencochlin must have hired that vessel with a view to making good his escape to the mainland. Then, realizing that Harker had outlived his usefulness, he administered the coup-de-grace, ensuring that no marks of violence would appear on the body, when it was found, to suggest foul play; a case of cold-blooded murder.'

Gerry shivered slightly despite the warmth of the fire. The quiet, lamplit room suddenly seemed filled with the evil, malevolent presence of Glencochlin.

'And despite all our efforts so far, we still haven't a clue as to the whereabouts of his lairdship,' Charles admitted ruefully. 'Moncrieff told me he was a slippery customer, but *this*! Huh, it's like trying to catch a jellied eel in a barrel of oil.'

Frank Dawson smiled, then said coolly, 'At least my Italian trip yielded results. Although our mutual friend, Tony Cannelli, was damn near as hard to land as—'

'The Ile de France?' Gerry supplied eagerly, recalling the lyrics of an old Astaire and Rogers song of long ago.

'*Gerry!*' Bill reproached her gently.

'*Huh?* Oh, sorry. I tend to get carried away at times. Go on, Frank. As you were about to say?'

'I think we've had enough of police business for one evening,' Jenny said firmly. 'I'm sure that Gerry and Bill don't need reminding of murder and suchlike after all they've been through. This is, after all, meant to be a homecoming celebration not a wake.'

'Quite right, m'dear,' Charles conceded mildly. He laughed, 'Gerry's not the only one who gets carried away at times. I do it all the time. It goes with the job. Once a policeman, always a policeman.'

'Tell me about it,' Jenny chuckled, 'but not *now*.'

'What's the Ile de France?' Polly piped up. 'I don't think I've ever heard of it before.'

Gleefully, Gerry explained, 'It's from a song called "A Fine Romance", sung by Ginger Rogers and Fred Astaire.'

'I've never heard of them neither,' Polly confessed. 'Are they in the charts?'

And so the party had ended on a light hearted note after all, to Jenny and also Bill's infinite relief.

Bidding her goodnight, he murmured, 'Thanks, Jenny. You're a very perceptive lady.'

'I didn't want Gerry to be upset, that's all. Charles told me about that letter she'd received, and about that dreadful man who's supposed to have sent it. What that girl needs is a bit of fun for a change. A second honeymoon?'

Homeward bound, Bill said, 'Gerry love, what would you say to a trip to Gay Paree?'

'*Ooh la-la!* What else? Apart from *why*?'

'Does there have to be a reason? I just figured you might enjoy a break: theatre trips, sight-seeing, shopping, French cuisine and so on.'

'Next spring, you mean?'

'No, next weekend,' Bill explained patiently, sensing Gerry's lack of enthusiasm. 'I thought you'd be over the moon.'

'I will be, next spring, but not now. We've just come home and I'd like to stay put for a while, making like a housewife, putting your slippers to warm, ironing your vests—'

'I don't wear vests!'

'Socks, then. You go through socks like a knife through butter.'

'Socks don't need ironing.'

'They will when I've washed them.'

'All right, Gerry. I get the message. You don't want to go to Paris. Fair enough. If you prefer to stay at home and iron socks, that's entirely up to you. Or—' he suggested hopefully, 'you could make a start on a new novel.'

'No, I don't think so. I – I'm not in the mood.' Gerry shivered slightly, as if a proverbial goose had walked over her grave. 'Sorry, darling, I can't explain. It's just a feeling I have of wanting to stay safe and warm for the time being, in the company of friends! people I know well and trust, if that makes sense?'

'Oh Gerry, my love, of course it does,' Bill responded warmly, realizing that she needed time to come to terms with, and to put behind her, their honeymoon fiasco. 'If it's domesticity you want, that is what you'll have, with my blessing. Let's entertain more, shall we? How about Sunday evening supper parties? Nothing formal, just lots of home-made grub, plenty of booze and so on?'

'Oh yes, Bill,' Gerry said happily, leaning towards him, 'that's exactly what I want. I knew you'd understand. You always do. No wonder I love you so much.'

'Right. No need to strangle me with my seat-belt. Well, here we are, home and dry. Let's get indoors, shall we, poke up the drawing room fire, have a couple of night-caps, plan our Sunday night supper parties, then go to bed and have a good night's sleep?'

Smiling mysteriously, 'Why bother with the fire and the nightcaps?' Gerry asked innocently, 'Why not get down to our good night's sleep right away?'

What a good idea, Bill thought, switching off the hall lights and following Gerry upstairs to bed.

Next morning, when Bill had gone to his office, Gerry rang Jenny to thank her for the party, also extending an invitation to supper the following Sunday. 'Bring Frank if pos-sible,' she added. 'We have a lot of catching up to do.'

This accomplished, she went upstairs to her attic studio for what she thought of as a session in her 'Think Tank', wanting to get the chaotic events of the past weeks clear in her mind. Until that happened, no way could she even contemplate starting a new book. Now, seated at her beloved Olivetti typewriter, and rolling into it a sheet of A4 paper, she embarked on a kind of DIY self-analysis exercise, beginning at the point when she and Bill had set forth on their belated honeymoon trip to the Outer Hebrides.

Difficult to recall now her reasons for choosing that destination in the first place. She'd simply harboured a romantic notion of wanting to be alone with Bill in a spot far removed from the rush and bustle of everyday life. She had imagined a stone-built cottage near a burn, heather clad hills, campfires beneath a heavenly sky filled with stars. Instead they'd ended up imprisoned in a crumbling castle, deeply involved in mayhem and murder, at the mercy of madman. But *why*? This was the burning question which had puzzled Gerry all along, to which there appeared to be no satisfactory answer. But there must *be* an answer, and it was up to her to find it.

Not as simple as all that, she realized. She must sieve every memory, recall each and every confrontation with Fergus Glencochlin. No easy task, damn near impossible in her present state of disorientation. All the more reason to concentrate on her self-analysis, to impose mental self discipline; the kind necessary for a writer of bestselling crime novels, a career dear to her heart, and one impossible to pursue until she had come to terms with the past.

Seventeen

Gerry had invited Maggie and Barney to the Sunday night party. 'No, ta very much,' she replied, when Bill had teasingly suggested making it a hotpot and champagne do, 'I'll stick to things on sticks, quiches and vol-au-vents. There's too many bones in hotpot. As for champagne, forget it. We'll make do with wine, tea and coffee.'

Bill grinned happily, pleased that Gerry had taken seriously his suggestion of entertaining their friends more frequently. Moreover, he had reason to believe that she had begun writing again, though he couldn't be entirely certain of that. He hoped that a return to her typewriter would, in the fullness of time, herald another Virginia Vale novel to ensure her return as a bestselling author of crime fiction. Her publishers were becoming anxious. So, to be honest, was he.

Nothing whatever to do with money – far from it. It had everything to do with Gerry's former dedication to her craft which had seemed, suddenly, to have deserted her.

Frankly, he had never regarded Gerry as a cook-housekeeper before. But then, expecting the unexpected of her should have become second nature to him by now, he realized. At the rate she was going, her next book might well be *A Bride's Guide to Entertaining*, the time and trouble she was taking over the Sunday night soiree was extraordinary, wanting everything just right, making endless shopping lists, though thankfully including frozen pastry for the quiches and vol-au-vents – uncertain of her dexterity when it came to rubbing fat into flour.

Not that Bill minded shopping, to which he'd become inured since their return from Scotland. Acting as her 'guardian angel', he had literally 'brought home the bacon' from Waitrose, on his way home from work, while she got on with her writing or, more likely, tracked down real life murderers in her spare time. This bothered him a great deal, knowing that Gerry, with a total disregard of her own safety, had often run the risk of sacrificing her life to bring killers to justice. That she had done so was to her credit. Her bravery and courage had been remarkable. Now, above all things, he wanted a living lover, not a defunct heroine. Marriage to

Gerry had proved a revelation for him. He'd never imagined that such happiness was possible. She had given herself to him joyously, unstintingly, filling his days with love and laughter, despite their honeymoon fiasco. To lose her now would be unbearable. But he had no intention of losing or mislaying her ever again. Not if he could help it.

On Sunday evening they welcomed their guests indoors and led them towards the drawing room with its brightly burning log fire. 'Please, do sit down and make yourselves at home,' Bill said warmly. 'Now, what would you like to drink? Wine, whisky, sherry?'

Gerry came in from the dining room at that moment – pink cheeked with excitement – after putting the finishing touches to the buffet. Obviously delighted, she bestowed hugs and kisses all round, pleased as Punch that Frank Dawson had put in an appearance, saying, 'I wasn't sure if you'd still be here.' She found it impossible to imagine that this tall, handsome young man had so successfully impersonated an octogenarian at Glencochlin's house party, and Gerry wanted to know more, intrigued by the cool nerve of the man to have even contemplated so brazen a deception, knowing the risks involved if he was discovered trying to infiltrate enemy territory.

Would he have disappeared without trace, as the countess had done? Gerry wondered. Bad luck, pure and simple, she reckoned, that the house party had dragged on too long for him to maintain his credibility. The unexpected death of Penny Douglas had prevented a speedy conclusion to that gathering of master criminals beneath the roof of Glencochlin Castle. Master criminals plus two innocents, Gerry thought wryly, herself and Bill.

'Eh, you've done us proud, love,' Maggie said, feasting her eyes on the buffet. 'All home-made by the look of it.'

'Well no. I cheated on the pastry,' Gerry confessed, 'and I did buy a coupla tins of chicken supreme to fill the "wolly-wants".'

'An' why not?' Maggie nodded approvingly, 'If Delia Smith can do it, so can we. What do you say, Mrs Brambell?'

'I agree wholeheartedly, Mrs Bowler,' Jenny replied, aware of Maggie's reluctance to take liberties so far as first names were concerned, even though they had met briefly before at Gerry and Bill's wedding. She added, 'My name's Jenny, by the way.'

Mrs Bowler beamed. 'Mine's Maggie.'

'I know,' Jenny said, smiling, 'I was privileged to drink your health in champagne last weekend.'

'*Eh?* Well, I never. Whatever for?' Maggie

appeared gob-smacked.

'I'll explain later. Right now, I can't wait to get stuck into one of those "wolly-wants" and a slice of that delicious looking smoked salmon and asparagus quiche.'

'Me neither,' Maggie confided happily, 'nor them there sossidge rolls an' roast beef sangwidges.' Helping herself, 'Honest, Jenny,' she added, pulling a wry face, 'if you only knew how sick an' fed up I am of hamburgers an' chips. My hubby an' me own a hamburger caff in the Old Kent Road, you see? An' if it ain't hamburgers, it's bacon butties. I ask you!'

'I know,' Jenny reminded her gently, 'my hubby's been a frequent visitor of yours in the past, and I know why. He couldn't get enough of your hamburgers and bacon butties.'

Now the men were queuing up to decimate the buffet, to Gerry's delight, who helped them lavishly to the fruits of her labour, wishing she'd invited more people to partake of the hospitality provided by herself and Bill, loving every minute of this brainchild of his, with even more gatherings to look forward to.

When supper was over and done with, the guests, replete and happy, had returned to the drawing room to relax and exchange conversation in a conducive atmosphere.

Thoughts, ideas and beliefs were discussed to the accompaniment of the wine Bill had provided to ensure a happy conclusion to the soiree. Gerry turned to Frank and asked him if he'd ever been an actor.

'Good grief no,' he chuckled, 'what on earth gave you that idea?'

'Your performance as Max Telemann,' she told him. 'You were so convincing, it just occurred to me that you might have been to RADA.'

'Oh that?' He shrugged dismissively, nursing a cut glass tumbler containing whisky and soda. 'A one-off, I'm thankful to say. Not my idea, wearing all that makeup and the time spent studying Telemann through a two-way mirror to master his facial expressions, his movements and his manner of speaking. Not a barrel of fun, especially that prosthetic nose and the false teeth.' He shuddered slightly, then laughed.

'A top up, Frank?' Bill suggested, crossing to the tantalus. Frank shook his head, 'Thanks, but better not, I have an early start in the morning, and I'll need my wits about me.'

'Going far?' Gerry asked brightly. 'Italy?'

'Not this time. Closer to home.'

'Flying?' She persisted, deeply interested.

'I sincerely hope so,' he prevaricated, setting down his drink unfinished, 'which reminds me, it's time I was heading for home. Sorry to leave so soon.' He smiled charmingly, 'Not to worry, Charles, I'll take a taxi.' Turning to Gerry, 'I've had a great evening. Thank you so much. You too, Bill. And it's been wonderful meeting you, Maggie and Barney. Not for the last time, I hope. I'm a great fan of hamburgers, by the way.'

Maggie blushed becomingly. 'Drop in any time,' she said chirpily, 'you'll be more than welcome to a freebie double-decker an' chips, won't he, Barney?'

'I'll say,' Barney replied heartily, wringing Frank's hand. 'It's been a great pleasure meeting you too, sir. Now, get a good night's sleep, and the best of luck for tomorrow.'

The party finally broke up around midnight. Afterwards, alone with Bill in the kitchen, putting away the uneaten food and stacking plates, cutlery, cups, saucers and glasses on the draining board, Gerry asked wistfully, 'Was it my fault that Frank left so early? I didn't mean to pump him, I just wanted to know more about him, his work, his impersonation of Max Telemann. Oh lord, Bill, when will I ever learn to keep my mouth shut?'

'Hopefully never,' Bill murmured tenderly. 'Oh, come on, love, let's leave the washing up till morning, shall we? You're tired, so am I.' Leading her upstairs to bed, he added cheerfully, 'At least we know what we'll be having for supper tomorrow evening:

quiche, warmed up vol-au-vents, and chips.'

Next morning, when Bill had helped her
with the washing up, eaten the bacon and
scrambled eggs she had cooked for him, and
departed to his office in Red Lion Square,
Gerry went upstairs to her typewriter to
continue her self analysis project; recalling,
albeit painfully, her first sighting of Glencochlin, standing apart from his fellow passengers, a bizarre, outlandish figure, sinister
to her way of thinking, and she had been
right. Bill, on the other hand, had dismissed
him as an eccentric old johnny with a
penchant for folklore, witchcraft and old
murder mysteries.

Later had come their meeting with the ill-
fated Sam MacNally and her acute disappointment when she'd clapped eyes on,
not an isolated stone built cottage, but a
modern bungalow on a dusty main road. A
bungalow she had loathed at first sight, with
good reason, remembering the tempera-
mental Rayburn in the kitchen, the paucity
of household equipment, the functional,
uncomfortable furniture, and the shock
horror of an early morning visit from a
police sergeant and his sidekick to question
them about the brutal murder of old Samuel
MacNally.

She now knew that Jock Harker, Glencochlin's cadaverous manservant and his

ruffian grandson Ian had been responsible for the murder of MacNally and that of Police Sergeant Kirk. So where exactly was this delving into the past getting her? Gerry wondered, taking a break for a cup of coffee and a cheese sandwich. Probably nowhere apart from the pleasure she derived from the feel of her typewriter keys beneath her fingers. Moreover, she had scarcely begun her 'memoirs' or figured out more complex situations than those already touched upon.

A thought occurred. Was it remotely possible that Sergeant Kirk had passed on to Glencochlin Bill's random remark of her being in cahoots with Scotland Yard as a consultant in crime? Could that chance remark have triggered the laird's antipathy towards her? Had he seen her as a copper's nark, a kind of latter day Mata Hari, employed by Scotland Yard to spy on him? Ludicrous, of course, but a strong possibility.

Returning to her typewriter, she made a note to that effect. Then, pursuing her train of thought, she recalled that evening at the bungalow when Bill had opened the front door to admit a tall man in black. The man Gerry had noticed on the quayside the day of their departure from Mrs MacNab's boarding house. The man who had reminded her fearfully of Count Dracula.

Harking back, Gerry remembered that it

was she who had accepted the laird's invitation to join his house party: wanting to know what he was up to and determined to find out. A bad decision on her part? Difficult to say. Possibly so, with the power of hindsight, and yet, imbued with the ability to turn back the clock, would she have refused Glencochlin's invitation? The answer was no, she would not, despite her misgivings when, arriving at Glencochlin Castle, she had blurted to Bill, 'Gawd's truth, it looks like a film set for a Gothic horror movie!'

Later on that day, in the overheated drawing room, had come the curious incident of Glencochlin's baleful expression as he'd handed her a glass of gin and tonic. A look of hatred so intense that she had physically recoiled from him, lending credence to her Mata Hari theory. Was she beginning to get somewhere at last?

Food for thought, at which point, feeling peckish, she had nipped down to the kitchen for a slice of quiche and a leftover vol-au-vent.

'Well, darling, what kind of day have you had?' Bill asked eagerly on his return home that evening. 'What have you been up to?' He had brought home with him a bottle of wine, a bunch of flowers and a still warm, ready-cooked chicken.

'What's this in aid of?' Gerry asked suspiciously, unwrapping the chicken. 'Gone off the idea of quiche and chips, have you?'

'Let's just say that I fancied something more substantial,' Bill explained, 'to supplement the leftovers. If there are any left, that is.'

How well Bill knew her, Gerry thought blissfully, turning up her face to be kissed, and planning mashed potatoes, frozen vegetables, and sage and onion stuffing to enhance a meal preceded by warmed up vol-au-vents and concluding with Sunday evening's leftover chocolate cake and cream.

Over supper, pouring more wine, Bill said, 'You haven't answered my question. What kind of day have you had? Come on, Gerry love, spill the beans. I know there's something you're not telling me.'

'Oh, very well then.' Gerry sighed deeply, 'I'm writing my "memoirs".'

'*Memoirs?*' Bill looked thunderstruck. '*Why*, for Pete's sake?'

'Well, not memoirs exactly,' Gerry confessed. 'I just decided to get to the bottom of the Glencochlin affair, to find out why he had it in for me all along. Now I think I know why. He had me sussed out as a Scotland Yard agent. In other words a "mince-pie"!' Reverting momentarily to her native Cockney rhyming slang.

'A spy, you mean? Oh, surely not. But that's ridiculous.'

'No, it isn't! Sorry Bill, I should have told you sooner. Forgive me?'

'Don't talk so daft. I'm your husband, not your inquisitor. This concerns me too, remember? I want to help, not to hinder you. Let's write those memoirs of yours together from now on, shall we?'

'Thanks, Bill. You really wouldn't mind?'

'As long as it doesn't involve typing, that's all.'

'You mean a kind of duet for four hands on the same keyboard?' Gerry asked mischievously. 'Now why didn't *I* think of that?'

'Knowing you, I'm surprised you didn't,' he replied, tongue-in-cheek. 'So what do you want me to do, apart from the washing up?'

Getting up to clear away the supper pots from the kitchen table, pleased that he'd possessed the nous to bring home with him that ready-cooked chicken in view of the inroads his beloved had made on the leftover food from Sunday, 'Just point me in the right direction. Tell me what to do, and I'll do it. Can't say fairer than that now, can I?'

'I suppose not,' Gerry sighed deeply, picking up a tea-towel, 'but you don't really approve my raking up of the past, do you? Be honest, Bill. You think me paranoid, don't you, in wanting to come to terms with the happenings at Glencochlin Castle? Frankly, love, that letter I received from Glencochlin put the fear of God into me. Or rather the fear of the devil. It's no joke, believe me, being on the receiving end of so much malice.'

'Oh Gerry, my love,' Bill murmured contritely, holding her close in his arms, leaving the washing up to its own devices and leading her through to the drawing room. 'Sit down, darling. Try to relax. I'm here for you always, remember? Now, you do the talking, I'll do the listening.'

Her first question startled him somewhat. Gerry said, unexpectedly, 'About Penny Douglas. Is there anything you haven't told me about your lunchtime conversation with her, preceding her murder?'

'I don't think so.' Bill frowned. 'I wasn't really listening, and it wasn't a conversation as such, more of a monologue on her part. Sorry, but it was terribly boring, mainly about money and possessions, that gold cross and chain she was wearing which she had picked up "for a mere song at Tiffany". The "mere song" being twenty thousand dollars.'

'Yes, I remember you told me that much,' Gerry said, 'and about the apartment overlooking Central Park. What I couldn't figure out was who killed her? Who had a strong enough motive – apart from the obvious person?'

'You mean Glencochlin?'

'No, not Glencochlin. Her husband, Brian

Douglas!'

'*Brian?* You must be joking. He surely wouldn't have killed his wife.'

'That's what I thought at first, now I'm not so certain. Think about it, Bill. There was Penny, talking nineteen to the dozen, babbling on about their new found wealth to a complete stranger; the laird taking it all in, harbouring doubts about her ability to keep her mouth closed about more important matters. I think that's when he made up his mind to ensure her silence.' She paused dramatically.

'In which case,' Bill protested flatly, 'Glencochlin, not Brian must have put paid to her. I'm sorry, love, why on earth should Brian have killed the woman he loved? We both saw, with our own eyes, the state he was in when her body was discovered. The poor devil was crying like a baby, for heaven's sake, when he carried her to the boathouse.'

'I know,' Gerry shivered, 'and it was Glencochlin's insistence on Penny's death being accidental when it was obviously murder that led me to the belief that, strictly speaking, it had been neither one nor the other, but an execution! Sorry, Bill, I know it seems bizarre, but it's my belief that Glencochlin coerced Brian Douglas into killing his wife to prove his loyalty to the cause or suffer the consequences, his own execution more than likely. Well, that's it in a nutshell. I could be wrong, but I don't think so.'

Uttering a groan, covering his face with his hands, 'That poor devil Brian,' he muttered, 'and that bloody murderous swine who made him do what he did. My God, it sickens me to even think about that arrogant bastard, Glencochlin, and that benighted house party of his. Given the chance, I'd strangle the bugger with my bare hands.' He added bleakly, 'Just as well I'm not a swearing man by nature, otherwise I'd really tell you what I have in mind for him.'

'OK, love,' Gerry said mildly, handing him a glass of brandy, 'I get the picture. Now, get this down you before you blow a gasket,' beginning to wish she had never embarked on all this digging and delving into the past in the first place. And yet, how could she possibly achieve peace of mind until she had discovered the whereabouts of the countess, for instance? She couldn't, and that was that. No matter how unpalatable the truth might be to swallow, swallow it she must, as she had done the execution of Penny Douglas, to aid her return to normal life.

She knew that her execution theory had shocked Bill, but the more she thought about it the more sense it made, remembering Brian's infrequent appearances following the death of his wife, almost as if Glencochlin had deliberately kept him out of sight of his fellow guests, a shadow of his former self, a shambling wreck of a man, remote and uncommunicative, seemingly bowed down by a burden of grief too hard for him to bear. A guilt-ridden man? An executioner?

Would any other member of the house party have been aware of the truth? Gerry wondered. Unlikely, in her view, recalling the heavy atmosphere of the dining room that day when, to break the unnatural silence, she had felt it expedient to propose a toast to the dead woman: 'To Penny, God bless her,' wanting the distraught husband to know that he was not alone in his grief, not imagining for one moment, on that fraught occasion, that he might have been responsible for her death.

But she was getting ahead of herself, Gerry realized, jumping the gun. Alone in the Eyrie, seated at her typewriter, having cooked Bill a substantial breakfast and waved him farewell on the doorstep, wracking her brain, needing to get things clear in her mind, she remembered her confrontation with Glencochlin regarding her dissatisfaction at being allocated a cold damp turret room which fell far short of her expectations, Glencochlin's grudging acceptance of her complaint, preceding their removal to that twin-bedded apartment with its adjoining bathroom, in which she and Bill had been destined to spend their honeymoon together – he with a badly sprained ankle, she doing her Florence Nightingale act.

Later had come the conversation she had overheard when she had gone up to the turret room stairs to retrieve the belongings Bill had dropped due to his accident; a heated argument between the laird and a foreign sounding woman – whose pitiful cry for help at the boathouse, and her inability to answer that cri-de-coeur, had weighed heavily on Gerry's conscience ever since.

If she only knew for certain what had become of the woman. Was she alive or dead? A futile question, Gerry realized. At least she now knew her name; Countess Redezky, and knew that she had been held prisoner in that turret room before being bundled into Glencochlin's motor launch to face whatever fate he had decreed for her. Death by drowning, more than likely, her body weighted with stones and flung overboard.

Sick at heart, wishing she had never begun her so called memoirs in the first place, Gerry went downstairs to put on her anorak and boots. In dire need of fresh air and freedom, she headed towards Hampstead Heath, walking briskly to clear her mind of cobwebs, the detritus of past events which threatened to overwhelm, rather than to enhance, her clarity of vision so far as the sinister happenings at Glencochlin Castle were concerned.

Deep in thought, she remembered recent cases she'd been involved in. The sheer horror of the Antiques Murders, that underground network of caves and caverns, in one of which she had chanced upon the crucified skeleton of a woman chained up alive and left there to die of starvation. Then had come the Theatre Murders, during which she had been abducted by a madman whose attempt on her own life had followed a series of brutal killings to which he had finally confessed without a trace of regret. In fact with a sense of pride in what he'd regarded as his achievements.

And so, presumably, madness was inherent in all murderers, but Glencochlin's surpassed any Gerry had touched upon before. He seemed to her the embodiment of evil, a malignant force which carried all before it. God alone knew how many lives had been ruined by his insatiable greed for power; how many men, women and children had been sold into slavery or prostitution, had died of drug addiction, Aids, starvation or suffocation; desperate people packed into container lorries like sardines in a can, without access to food, water or fresh air. Poor devils who had given all they possessed in the vain hope of a better life for their families; employment, in some unattainable El Dorado of the mind.

Seldom, if ever, had Gerry thought so

deeply, so profoundly before. Suddenly, standing stock still, chilled by the icy wind blowing across the Heath, she realized the futility of raking over the past instead of doing something positive about the future.

Making up her mind in an instant, retracing her steps to the Eyrie, opening the garage and entering her beloved red Mini, imbued with renewed vigour and a strong sense of purpose, she headed towards New Scotland Yard to seek the help and advice of her friend and mentor, Detective Chief Inspector Brambell.

Eighteen

'What's brought this on?' Bill asked bemusedly, coming home to find Gerry getting on, not with her memoirs but a new Virginia Vale novel.

'Put it this way,' she explained, 'I saw the light on the road to—'

'Damascus?' Bill interrupted eagerly.

'No, not Damascus, Scotland Yard, as a matter of fact. So just wipe that idiotic grin off your face, and listen.'

'I'm all ears!'

'Hmmm, well, you could try Sellotape, I suppose,' she riposted tartly, tongue-in-cheek. 'But seriously, love, it simply occurred to me that those memoirs of mine were a waste of time when I'd be far better occupied starting a new novel.'

'So why the visit to Scotland Yard?' Bill asked. 'Or shall I hazard a guess? To expound your execution theory to DCI Brambell. Am I right? If so, what was his reaction?'

'Disbelief, at first,' she confessed, 'but I felt he had a right to know. I'm sorry, Bill, the last thing I wanted was to land Brian in hot water, but if my suspicions are true, it is important he is found.'

'Yes, darling, of course,' Bill admitted resignedly. 'In any case, the ball's in Scotland Yard's court now, it's entirely up to them to decide whether or not to arrest Brian for further questioning, the poor devil.'

'A poor devil engaged in drug running and people smuggling,' Gerry reminded him regretfully, 'loyal to the cause, a handy tool at the mercy of a master manipulator like Glencochlin: by no means an evil man, just greedy for the good things in life which only money can buy, or so he believed.' She shivered slightly, 'Or perhaps he believes differently now that Penny is dead and gone? Frankly, in Brian's shoes right now, I'd call Glencochlin's bluff, give myself up, pull the plug on the laird, and suffer the consequences.'

'I know, love,' Bill said gently, 'so would I, so would any right thinking person.' He added tenderly, 'Now, take my advice, put the past behind you and concentrate on the future.' Taking a calculated risk, 'What's for supper, by the way? More importantly, what's the title of your new book?'

'*Virginia Vale's Highland Fling*,' Gerry responded primly. 'As for supper, I bought a steak and kidney pie on my way home from Scotland Yard. So just nip down and bung it in the oven whilst I finish the first chapter. OK?'

Very much OK so far as Bill was concerned. The happiest of men now that Gerry was back at her typewriter, he went down to the kitchen to bung the pie in the oven and to peel a panful of potatoes, whistling 'Scotland the Brave' as he did so. A different scenario than Scotland might have been preferable, he thought, scraping carrots and shaving the whiskers from a parsnip, but Gerry being back on track again was all that really mattered, and soon, if she kept up the momentum, he'd be in a position to offer her latest brainchild to her publishers and begin dealing on her behalf. After Christmas, he reckoned, startled to realize how close they had come to the festive season. In a matter of weeks they'd all be thinking in terms of holly and mistletoe, wrapping paper and presents, food and fairylights.

They'd invite Maggie and Barney to stay, of course. Christmas wouldn't be Christmas without them, he reflected mistily, recalling the Christmas Eve when he'd asked Gerry to marry him, and she'd said, disbelievingly, 'Who, *me*?'

Never had he regretted that proposal. Now on this, their first Christmas as husband and wife, he envisaged a celebration, an oasis of warmth and happiness to dispel all thoughts of their honeymoon fiasco from her mind; warm fires in every room, fairy-lit Christmas trees, a holly-wreathed front door; lots of good food and friendship. Above all, friendship, and love.

Seldom had Gerry's writing gone so swimmingly before. Making up for lost time and the temporary writer's block she had suffered on her return home, words fairly tumbled from her fingers on to the keyboard.

Virginia Vale, Gerry's glamorous supersleuth was in fine fettle, living the life of Riley aboard a wealthy admirer's yacht until, during a violent storm, the vessel had struck a rock, when Virginia, her stalwart uppercrust boyfriend Gervaise Lanfear, and six other members of the shipboard party had been flung overboard by the force of the collision and obliged to swim for the shore.

A cracking good beginning to what promised to be a nail-bitingly good thriller, Bill realized, reading the first chapter and wanting to read more, lost in admiration of the page-turning quality of Gerry's writing plus the power of her imagination; her chilling description of a storm at sea and the thoughts and feelings of a handful of people struggling for survival in a heaving waste of icy, wind lashed water. Gerry, who to Bill's certain knowledge had never been aboard an ocean-going yacht, much less in a storm at sea, and couldn't swim an inch if her life depended on it. And the body count hadn't even begun yet.

Asked which of the survivors would be the first for 'the chop', Gerry replied haughtily that she hadn't thought that far ahead. He'd have to wait and see, so the sooner he made himself scarce, the better. How could she concentrate with him breathing down her neck? And so on. After all, there was a time and place for everything, and this wasn't it, so he'd best go down to the kitchen to see to the supper, hadn't he? At the same time, smiling and blowing him a kiss, adding, 'It's pork chops tonight, by the way. Thanks for reminding me. I'd almost forgotten until you mentioned "the chop". There are two of them in the fridge, and some Bramley apples for the sauce.'

'Of all the maddening, impossible women,

you take the biscuit,' he replied equably. 'At least you bought me a pork chop of my own, otherwise I'd have probably ended up gnawing on a bone.'

'Oh, I dunno,' Gerry laughed, 'you could have had an apple.'

The old camaraderie, the rapport between them remained intact, Bill realized, going down to see to the chops, the magical laughter which had always been part and parcel of their relationship: the wise cracks reminiscent of Jerry Lewis and Dean Martin, George Burns and Gracie Allan, or Morecambe and Wise which had suffered an eclipse, until Gerry had returned to her writing.

In the week preceding Christmas, Gerry had met Bill in Regent Street to choose presents for the Bowlers, the Brambells, Bert and Polly Briggs and their offspring, the two Charlies at the garage, Dorothea Lazlo and her staff. Presents galore to stack under the drawing room Christmas tree, having decided upon a Boxing Day buffet to which their friends, including Bert and Polly's children and Dorothea's dog, Bruno, had been invited to partake of Gerry's quiches and 'sossidge' rolls.

In her element, and with the first six chapters of her novel completed, Gerry had gone to town on her baking, adding mince pies to her repertoire and fancy snowmen biscuits for the kids. Meanwhile, Bill had done the shopping, bringing home with him food enough to feed an army: a sirloin of beef, a couple of nice plump little ducks, a York ham; smoked and fresh salmon; pine-apples, grapes and peaches, frozen and fresh vegetables; Black Forest gateaux, lashings of cream, and masses of flowers: roses, carna-tions, bowls of cyclamen, lilies of the valley, and hyacinths.

Determined to make this a Christmas to remember, on his final, Christmas Eve visit to the Hampstead supermarket to purchase fresh bread, eggs and bacon to be on the safe side he added to his trolley a couple of turkey breasts, several fat, scented candles, and a bottle of Coca-Cola.

At the check-out, he suddenly caught sight of a tall, grey haired man, stoop shouldered, poorly dressed in a shabby raincoat and sporting a straggling grey beard and mous-tache, just ahead of him in the queue, searching his pockets for change to pay for a newspaper and a box of matches which he laid on the counter with trembling fingers, dirt encrusted, with ragged fingernails. A man who, despite his tramplike appearance, reminded Bill of Fergus Glencochlin.

Deeply disturbed, having paid for his own purchases, Bill hurried out of the super-market to the carpark, anxious to catch another glimpse of the man who could not have gone far, judging by his shuffling gait as he'd headed towards the exit doors.

But there was no sign of him anywhere. The man had seemingly simply disappeared into thin air. And yet, from afar, Bill could have sworn he'd heard the sound of a penny whistle. Suddenly his blood ran cold. If, as he suspected, the tramp he'd seen at the check-out was Glencochlin, the sooner he contacted Scotland Yard the better.

Entering his hatchback and picking up his mobile, prodding in the number he knew like the back of his hand, and wasting no time when Brambell's voice came on line, 'Bill Bentine here,' he said tautly, 'I believe I know the whereabouts of Fergus Glencochlin. He's here, in Hampstead, disguised as a tramp. I'm in the supermarket car park – down the road from the Eyrie.'

'Right, Bill. Stay put! I'm on my way.'

Thank God for the Brambells of this world, Bill thought gratefully. No unnecessary questions, no prevarication, just quick decisive thinking and action.

Brambell arrived, accompanied by a DS Robin Holdsworth, Bert Briggs's replacement, and two uniformed constables.

'Sorry I lost sight of the man,' Bill said, 'and I could be mistaken. There was just a momentary flash of recognition; something about the man's eyes. Then I heard the

271

sound of a whistle.'

Brambell nodded briefly, 'We'll split up. You, Holdsworth, Harmon and Fielding, mosey down the road a way, keeping your eyes skinned. Our man might well have taken to open country, but he might be on foot, and have not gone far. Bill and I will head towards Hampstead Village. Make sure the car radio's switched on in case you need back-up, and call me on my mobile, if necessary. Got it?'

'Sir,' Holdsworth responded smartly: a bright-eyed, eager young man who obviously thought the sun shone out of his superior officer, the legendary 'Brambell of The Yard'.

'There's a lay-by a mile or so down the road,' Bill said, when he and Charles were settled in the hatchback, 'with a greasy spoon caff and a long distance lorry drivers' carpark. Chances are the tramp might have popped in for a cup of coffee or a mug of soup.'

'Right then, we'll have a look,' Brambell replied briskly, settling his battered headgear more firmly on his head. 'Tip me the wink if you catch sight of him.'

Catching sight of anyone was easier said than done, Bill realized, in an atmosphere fuggy with cigarette smoke, steam from the fish-fryer, and the tightly jammed together tables at which sat knights of the road tucking into all day breakfasts, hamburgers and fish and chips. When his vision had cleared somewhat, raking the room with his eyes, he muttered hoarsely, 'He's over there, at that table near the window.'

'Fair enough, son,' Brambell responded quietly, 'let's have a word in his ear then, shall we?'

The tramp looked up sharply as they approached his table, on which lay his newspaper, matches, a twenty pack of king size cigarettes, a half empty mug of coffee, and a dog-eared notebook alongside a pencil stub in dire need of a sharpener.

'Mind if I join you?' Brambell asked pleasantly. Not awaiting a reply, he pulled forward a vacant chair, sat down, produced his warrant card, and said mildly, assuming his country doctor persona, 'Now sir, your name and address and proof of identity, if you don't mind.'

The tramp snorted derisively, 'If you mean me platignum credit card, me coronet an' me invitation to the Queen's next birthday bash at Buck 'Ouse, I left 'em in t' weskit pocket of me evenin' suit, so yer'll have ti whistle for 'em.'

'Interesting you should say that,' Brambell said intently. 'Fond of whistling, are you?'

'Huh?' The man's jaw sagged. 'Wot are you on about? Wot *is* all this? Why all the questions? Wot am I supposed to hev done? Why pick on me? Oh, I get it! Harassment, that's wot it is. Some ould biddy gets mugged an' I'm in the frame as a likely suspect.' The man's demeanour changed entirely, so, unaccountably, did his manner of speech and his appearance. 'Well thanks, Inspector, you've just confirmed my belief that the down and outs of this world don't stand an earthly when it comes to justice. A fitting conclusion to the subject I happen to be pursuing at the moment. Frankly, Inspector, you've made my day! Now, arrest me, why don't you? Drag me to the nearest cop shop and charge me – with what exactly? Causing a disturbance? A breach of the peace? Being drunk and disorderly? Or simply because I look like a vagrant?'

Bill said hoarsely, 'I'm responsible. Blame me, not Inspector Brambell. It was a case of mistaken identity. I'm sorry. What more can I say?'

The man smiled faintly, 'So who did you mistake me for? James Galway or the Pied Piper of Hamelin?' Getting up from the table, 'Am I free to leave now? If so, I have work to do, a report to finish to a deadline. My name is Gervaise, by the way. Frederick Gervaise. I'm an investigative reporter with the *Independent* at the moment. Well, gentlemen, with your permission, I'll bid you good-day.' He made his way to the door where he paused momentarily to look back, then with a smile and a wave of the hand, he was gone.

'Well, what did you make of that, Bill?' Brambell asked, on their way to the hatchback. 'Do you think he'll mention me by name in that report he's writing?'

Suddenly part of the conversation with Gervaise struck Bill as being strange. 'No, I shouldn't think so,' Bill replied upset, 'for the good and sufficient reason that there won't be one. Don't you see, Charles, we've been hoodwinked? It wasn't a case of mistaken identity. That man *was* Glencochlin. God, what an all-fired fool I've been! Can you forgive me?'

Mentally kicking himself, 'Forgive *you*?' Brambell muttered. 'What the hell was I thinking about not to have checked his credentials? But he can't have gone far! I'll alert Robin, get him to backtrack, to meet us here *immediately.*'

Bill sighed, 'Knowing Glencochlin, he'll be well away by now. Driving a fast car, I shouldn't wonder.'

Rubbing his forehead perplexedly, 'God, what a shambles,' Brambell uttered despairingly. 'So what put you on to him in the first place? What did he say or do to make you so certain of his identity?'

'When he picked up on that "fond of whistling, are you?" remark of yours, and he replied, later on in the conversation, "So who did you mistake me for? James Galway or the Pied Piper of Hamelin?". But how could he have known that the whistle you referred to was that of a musical instrument, not a mere puckering of the lips, a so-called "wolf whistle"? If I hadn't been so dim-witted, so slow, so bloody useless, I'd have said so at the time, and he might have been behind bars now. I'll never forgive myself. *Never!*'

'Come on, laddie,' Brambell said kindly, 'he had me fooled too, remember? I, not you, am to blame for what happened.' He sighed deeply. 'I'll tender my resignation, if necessary. Perhaps it's high time I retired, considering the pig's ear I've made of this assignment.'

Deeply shocked, 'You'll do no such thing!' Bill exploded. 'So far as I'm concerned, all that happened in that bloody awful wayside caff, was my failure to identify the tramp I'd seen earlier in the supermarket. End of story.'

He continued hoarsely, 'Think about it, Charles. Think about Gerry's reaction if she knew of Glencochlin's presence in the vicinity. The poor girl's just gone back to her writing once more, and she's looking forward to Christmas, so please, *please*!'

'Fair enough, Bill,' Brambell conceded thoughtfully, 'for Gerry's sake, not mine, you understand?'

'Thanks, Charles,' Bill replied tautly. 'Now

I'd best be getting back to her right away, before she posts me as a missing person.' He added conspiratorially, 'Not to worry, I'll tell her I was held up at the check-out longer than expected, so I shan't be lying through my teeth exactly, shall I? Just bending the truth a little to make certain she has a carefree Christmas.'

And so his wish had been granted. Christmas had been a joy from start to finish, despite Bill's nervousness over the supermarket affair and the constant worry of knowing that Glencochlin was close at hand, playing cat and mouse with the police. An ever present threat to his own and Gerry's safety and peace of mind. He dreaded the laird turning up at the Eyrie one day when Gerry was in the house alone. In which case, he considered carefully, dare he risk not warning her of that possibility? But not now. Not yet. Not at a time of rejoicing, peace on earth, goodwill to men. Not until Christmas was over. No way could he bear to shatter her happiness, to see fear, not laughter in her eyes.

And when he did tell her, as he must, he would do so gently, holding her close. But not now, not tonight, not on Christmas Eve with its glowing log fires, bauble bedecked Christmas trees, flower filled rooms; awaiting the arrival of Maggie and Barney Bowler whose presence in the house would add lustre by their sheer enjoyment of the festive season, their warm, outgoing natures, lack of pretence, Cockney accents and above all their deep affection for Gerry whom they regarded as their own flesh and blood, the daughter they'd always longed for and never had, just as she regarded them as her adoptive parents.

When the doorbell rang at ten o'clock, opening the door to welcome them, 'Merry Christmas, Bill love,' Maggie sang out. 'Guess what? It's snowing.'

Nineteen

Christmas dinner had been a fun affair, after which they'd opened their presents near the drawing room fire, Maggie oohing and aahing with delight when she unwrapped a flagon of Chanel No. 5, matching soap and dusting powder nestling cosily in a handsome satin lined coffret.

'Eh, ah've niver 'ad Channel No. 5 before,' she gasped. 'Ah'll smell like the Queen of Sheba.'

There were more surprises in store for the

gob-smacked Maggie, a lace-trimmed night-gown, matching negligee, quilted slippers, Belgian chocolates, and a holiday for two at a hotel in Benidorm, the following spring. 'But we've niver been abroad before!' Maggie had protested initially. 'Niver closed the caff afore.'

'High time us did, then,' Barney had advised her. 'It'll be like a second 'ony-moon.'

'Ha,' Maggie treated him to a withering glance, 'we niver had a fust, as I recall, unless you mean that day trip to Southend after pledging us plights.'

Leaving Maggie and Barney to their good natured banter, 'This is for you, Gerry darling,' Bill said quietly, handing her a morocco leather box containing a diamond eternity ring, 'with all my love.'

Gerry's face glowed. 'It's *beautiful*! And to think all I've bought for you is socks.' She laughed suddenly, 'Apart from this,' handing him a box in which lay a gold Rolex watch.

The Boxing Day luncheon party had been a huge success. Maggie had been in her element helping Gerry to set the buffet table with all the food she'd prepared beforehand. Whilst Bill, in the kitchen, aided and abetted by Barney, had seen to the booze: polishing wine glasses and tumblers in readiness to receive their guests' favourite tipple: sherry, beer, champagne or gin and tonic; Coca-Cola for the kids, not forgetting a bowl of water for Dorothea Lazlo's dog, Bruno.

' 'Ow many fowk, all told?' Barney asked, arranging cans and bottles on a work surface, thinking he could just fancy a glass of lager.

'Oh, let me think. There'll be Jenny and Charles Brambell, hopefully Frank Dawson, Polly and Bert Briggs and their kids, Billy and Grace, the two Charlies from the garage, Dorothea Lazlo, her manservant, his wife and daughter, that adds up to thirteen, plus you and Maggie, myself and Gerry. Seventeen in all. Why do you ask?'

'I just wondered, that's all. There's enough booze 'ere ti launch a battleship, enough grub in yonder ti feed an army.'

Bill grinned happily, 'Well, you know Gerry. She never does things by halves.'

'That she don't,' Barney responded warmly, remembering the box of Havana cigars, the plaid dressing gown, fur-lined slippers, the silk pyjamas and the bottle of malt whisky he'd unwrapped yesterday, not to mention the tickets to Benidorm as a joint present to himself and Maggie. 'That lass'd give her heart away to a – tramp – if one turned up on her doorstep.'

Suppressing a shudder, at that moment Bill knew, beyond a shadow of doubt, that he must confide his fears concerning Glencochlin's present whereabouts to Maggie and Barney, as soon as possible, but not right now, with the doorbell ringing to announce the arrival of the first of their guests. Polly and Bert Briggs and their children, clad like Eskimos, entered the hall, laughing and brushing snow from their shoulders, to an ecstatic welcome from their hostess.

'Isn't this great?' Polly chortled. 'A white Christmas! The kids have had a ball building a snowman. These are for you,' she added, handing Gerry a bag of brightly wrapped presents, 'nothing much I'm afraid, just little things the kids chose, paid for and wrapped themselves: Smarties, chocolate drops, biros and pencil sharpeners.'

'Don't tell, Mummy,' Grace piped up, 'you'll spoil the surprise.'

Billy said, 'Is that lady bringing her dog?'

'I expect so,' Gerry replied. 'I certainly hope so.'

'What's his name?' Billy wanted to know.

'Bruno.'

'What make of dog is he?'

'A lurcher. Leastways I think so,' Gerry supplied.

'Why? Can't he stand up properly?'

Bill, who had joined the Briggses and Gerry in the hall, chuckled quietly. Ruffling the little lad's hair, he said, 'Bruno should be here soon, then you can have a word in his ear. P'raps he has dizzy spells, his legs being on the long side.'

'G'arn,' Billy pulled a face, 'dogs don't have dizzy spells.'

At that moment, the doorbell rang, heralding the arrival of Dorothea Lazlo, her devoted manservant, his wife and daughter, and Bruno. Dorothea Lazlo, a world famous artist with whom Gerry and Bill had become deeply involved during the Theatre Murders, whose husband, Elliot Lazlo, had received a prison sentence for his part in aiding and abetting, albeit unwillingly, a convicted serial killer.

Kissing Dorothea warmly and shaking hands with her servants, Tom and Sarah Forbes and their daughter Kitty, Bill turned his attention to Bruno, kneeling to feel the laving of the dog's tongue on his face and hands, recalling momentarily the trauma of the Theatre Murders, and wondering what had become of Elliot Lazlo. Had he come out of clink and returned to Bagdale Manor, or was he still finishing his perversion of justice sentence? Hopefully the latter. A nasty piece of work, Elliot Lazlo.

Billy piped up, standing at Bill's elbow and staring wistfully at Bruno, 'Can I stroke him?'

Dorothea laughed, 'Of course you can, young man. Bruno loves being made a fuss of, and I can see that he's taken a shine to you, so why not take care of him on my behalf? I'd be so grateful. If you want to, that is.'

Billy smiled from ear to ear. Bill said, 'In which case, why not take him to the kitchen? There's a bone in the refrigerator. Ask "Uncle" Barney, he'll show you where.'

And so the luncheon party had got off to a flying start to Bill's infinite relief and Gerry's utter delight, as the full complement of guests arrived to partake of their hospitality: the two Charlies, the Brambells and Frank Dawson.

After lunch, during which Bill and Barney had acted as wine waiters and Maggie had helped to serve the food and clear the table, Bert Briggs had taken his kids into the garden, accompanied by Tom Forbes and the two Charlies to play ball games with Bruno. Meanwhile, Gerry had taken Polly, Sarah Forbes, Kitty and Jenny on a conducted tour of the Eyrie, while Maggie kept Dorothea company in the drawing room, and Frank and Charles had joined Bill and Barney in the kitchen to help with the washing up.

'There's news, Bill,' Brambell said quietly, 'of Brian Douglas.'

'What kind of news?' Bill asked intently. 'Good or bad?'

'A bit of both. I gather,' Brambell sighed deeply, 'At least he's being co-operative.

Naturally he's under arrest for his wife's murder and his complicity in people and drug smuggling, none of which he has denied. The good news is that he is prepared to blow the whistle on Glencochlin's un-American activities, name names etcetera, to the infinite relief of Uncle Sam's Coast-guards. The bad news is that he'll spend time behind bars for the murder of his wife, and rightly so in my opinion. It was, after all, a particularly nasty, cold-blooded killing, albeit one committed under duress.'

Knowing that Polly Briggs, in particular, was fairly bursting to take a gander at her studio on the top floor – the workplace of a bona-fide authoress, no less – Gerry had suggested a tour of inspection as a means of satisfying the girl's curiosity in a roundabout way. Well aware of Polly's romantic delusion that writers were somehow set apart from 'ordinary' people, Gerry hoped that she would not be too disappointed when she clapped eyes on her ancient Olivetti typewriter, her common or garden desk, divan bed in a corner of the room, her spring-busted sofa, modest bookshelves and the stack of dog-eared folders on the bottom shelf containing copies of manuscripts dating back to her first ever brainchild, *Virginia Vale Investigates*.

She need not have worried. Polly entered the room as she might have done Charles

Dickens's immaculately preserved study at Gad's Hill, her face aglow, as if she was treading hallowed ground, not a threadbare Axminster which Gerry had bought for a song in her bed-sit days and had never got around to replacing.

'So this is where it all happens?' Polly breathed ecstatically.

'Well, yeah,' Gerry admitted, thinking back to the night she'd very nearly been murdered in her divan bed in this very room.

Dorothea Lazlo, whose health had deteriorated since the trauma of the Theatre Murders, was happy to sit quietly in the drawing room with Maggie Bowler for company, although the two women would have appeared ill-matched to a casual observer. Dorothea, tall, slender, elegantly dressed and still remarkably beautiful despite her frailty, resembled, in artistic terms, a portrait by Fra Filippo Lippi of an elderly Madonna. Maggie, on the other hand, might well have featured in a painting by Renoir or Augustus John, who preferred well-upholstered models.

Maggie, who had met Dorothea before, at Gerry and Bill's wedding reception, was saying how grand it was to have them safely back home again after that disastrous honeymoon of theirs in the wilds of Scotland.

'They might have been goners,' she said

dramatically, 'if I 'adn't 'ad the nous ti report them missing. Went to Scotland Yard, I did, for a word wiv Inspector Brambell, knowin' 'e'd do summat about it, which 'e did, Gawd bless 'im!'

Dorothea frowned bemusedly, 'I had no idea. You mean they got lost on the moors?'

'No, much worse than that. They was conducted an' kept prisoners in some rummy ould castle owned by a bloke wiv a weird soundin' name – Glencoffin or somesuch. A right bad 'un by all accounts, into smugglin', murder an' God only knows what else. Devil worship, I shouldn't wonder, judgin' by Gerry's description of 'is 'ouse an' the way he was dressed all in black, wi' a cloak, for all the world like that there Count Dracula.'

She continued avidly, ''E scarpered when he knew the police was on to 'im, leavin' Bill an' Gerry an' that nice Frank Dawson locked up wiv nowt to eat or drink, the rotten swine. The police ain't caught up wiv 'im yet, but it's my belief 'e ain't far away, in London more than like since poor Gerry 'ad a nasty note from 'im, wot yer might call a threatening letter which put the fear of God inter the lass. Summat about 'im whistlin' for 'er when 'e were good an' ready. Trubble is, London's a big place an' he could be anywhere.'

Half rising to her feet, a stricken look on her face, 'I must speak to Inspector Brambell at once,' Dorothea muttered hoarsely. 'Do you know where he is? Please, it's very important.'

''E's in the kitchen. Just you sit down, Mrs Lazlo, I'll go an' fetch 'im,' Maggie responded, hurrying from the room in search of the Inspector: wondering what the hell was happening, if she had done or said something to upset Mrs Lazlo. If so, she couldn't think what. Happen she'd find out sooner or later. Meanwhile, she'd best alert Mrs Lazlo's manservant to his mistress's 'funny turn' in the event that she might want to go home after her conversation with Inspector Brambell.

'What's up, love?' Barney asked when they, Bill and Frank Dawson were alone in the kitchen. When Maggie had explained, Bill said bleakly, 'There's something you should know, something I haven't told you. The fact is, I saw Glencochlin in the Hampstead supermarket on Christmas Eve. That he got away is my fault entirely. I won't go into that now. I didn't tell Gerry for obvious reasons, not wanting to spoil her Christmas. I *shall* tell her, of course. Meanwhile, I'd rather we kept this between ourselves. I figured she'd be safe for the time being. Today of all days, with you Frank, Bert Briggs and Charles Brambell under our roof. Glencochlin may be reckless, but he's not a fool. Hardly likely he'll start playing his damn penny whistle until the house is clear of policemen.'

Frank said quietly, 'I'm willing to stay on, if that would help.'

'Us an' all,' Maggie declared stoutly, 'ain't that so, Barney?'

'You can bet your life.'

Bill could have wept. He said shakily. 'You don't know how much this means to me.'

Dorothea had sunk back in her chair when Brambell entered the room.

'My dear Dorothea,' he said concernedly, 'are you ill? Shall I send for a doctor?'

'No, I'm not ill. Please sit down, Charles, I have something important to tell you.' Drawing in a deep breath, she added, 'I think I know the whereabouts of Fergus Glencochlin.'

The last thing Brambell had expected to hear, he looked at Dorothea in amazement. *'You know Glencochlin?'* he asked disbelievingly.

'Not personally, but I knew *of* him through my first husband, Aubrey Sandys.' She shuddered slightly, recalling a painful period in her life which she would far rather forget. 'As you know, Charles, Sandys was a member of the acting profession in his early days, by no means a potential Gielgud or Olivier, what one might call a struggling actor. We were living hand-to-mouth at the time until, one day, he came home, blind drunk, boasting that his luck had changed, having met up with a man who had given him a fairly large sum of money, and had offered him considerably more, depending on his absolute discretion pertaining to the "chance of a lifetime" proposition he had in mind.

'The name of that man was Fergus Glencochlin,' Dorothea continued hoarsely. 'I realized, of course, that this could not be an honourable proposition. Why else the secrecy involved? I begged my husband to have nothing more to do with Glencochlin, to no avail until, late one night he came home the worse for wear. I guessed he'd been drinking heavily, but there was more to it than that. I had never seen him so angry or upset before. I later discovered that he had been to Glencochlin's flat to discuss that proposition of his, to find that the bird had flown.

'According to the night porter, the tenant of the penthouse had packed up and left earlier that evening, leaving no forwarding address. Nothing unusual in that. His lordship, as the porter referred to him, often went away on the spur of the moment, reappearing as abruptly as he'd departed. No skin off *his* nose. What the tenants did was none of his business. They came and went as they pleased.

'To cut a long story short, when Maggie

Bowler told me that Glencochlin might well be hereabout, it occurred to me that he could be at that penthouse apartment of his in Tower Gardens. What do you think?'

Heaving a sigh of relief, 'That you have probably saved a lame-brained detective from an early retirement,' Charles replied. 'Thank you, my dear.'

When the Briggses, Charlie and Charlotte Dickens, Dorothea and the Forbses had departed, the Brambells, the Bowlers, Frank Dawson, Bill and Gerry gathered in the drawing room for a final cuppa, made and served by Gerry who entered the room with the tray, cups and saucers, to ask, 'Now, is anyone going to tell me what's going on?'

Glances were exchanged. He might have known that Gerry would pick up on the atmosphere, Bill thought, knowing the time to come clean about Glencochlin had arrived and it was up to him to tell her. Getting up to relieve her of the tray, he said resignedly, 'Sit down, love, and I'll explain.'

'No need!' Gerry pulled a wry face, 'Let me guess. This has to do with Glencochlin, hasn't it?'

'I'm afraid so,' Brambell said gravely, taking over from Bill. 'We have reason to believe he's here, in London. Thanks to Dorothea Lazlo, we think we know where!'

'We do?' Bill looked bemused. It was the

first he'd heard of it. 'Then why are we sitting here when we should be out looking for him?'

'Not to worry, the wheels have been set in motion. I've alerted my sergeant who'll be here shortly to pick me up. Jenny love, you take the car, make your way home when you're ready. I'll meet you there – whenever.'

'I'm coming with you,' Bill announced grimly.

'Me too,' Dawson said tersely.

Jenny spoke up, 'Let's *all* go, shall we? Take flasks and sandwiches, hire a charabanc; make a night of it?' She added scathingly, 'If you think for one moment that I'm about to go home, leaving Gerry in the lurch, you'd best think again, Charles Brambell! I'm staying put! There's safety in numbers, and Gerry needs all our help and support right now. What say you, Maggie, and you, Barney?'

'Jenny's right,' Maggie said eagerly. 'Wot I mean is, if that Glencoffin gives you the slip – as 'e 'as a way of doin' – an' comes sniffin' rahnd this 'ouse, blowin' 'is bloody whistle 'e'll be in for a shock, that's all. We'll guard Gerry with us lives. Barney's still 'andy wiv 'is fists, an' I used ter be a lady mud-wrestler, think on.'

So where exactly did she fit into the picture? Gerry wondered. She hadn't had a say in the matter, so far. Curiously, remembering the words: 'I'll whistle and you'll come to me', she knew, deep down, that inevitably, one day, she would be called upon to meet her persecutor, face to face, in a life or death struggle for survival between herself and Glencochlin.

An icy wind was blowing newly fallen snow into drifts and strangely convoluted eddies, somehow in keeping with what Bill had always regarded as a grim area of the City – too close to the Tower of London for his liking. The keening of the wind reminded him acutely of the crying of lost souls undergoing torture, or awaiting execution within the confines of that sinister edifice.

Imbued with a strong feeling of unreality, watching the silent arrival of police vehicles in Tower Gardens; the emergence of uniformed men, including a team of sharpshooters armed with rifles, others with sniffer dogs in leash, getting out of the vehicle driven by DS Holdsworth, and accompanied by Brambell, Frank Dawson and Police Constable Harmon, was the end of the Glencochlin saga really in sight? Bill wondered. If so, why his gut feeling that this was in the nature of a wild goose chase? Shivering with cold and nervous tension, he followed in the wake of the professionals, feeling like a spare bridegroom at a wedding. Neither use nor ornament. For Gerry's sake, he had really needed to be here. On the other hand, might he not have served a more useful purpose in staying with her at the Eyrie, to protect her? In any case, it was too late now to weigh up the pros and cons. Here he was, and here he must stay until the siege of Glencochlin's penthouse apartment had been resolved for better or worse. The latter, he feared, and he was right.

In the early hours of next morning, when the police contingent had finally entered the penthouse, there was no sign of Glencochlin. There was, however, the emaciated figure of a woman, bound hand and foot and gagged with masking tape, huddled on a spare-room bed, more dead than alive. 'Ye gods,' Brambell uttered in disgust. 'Glencochlin's handiwork, no doubt.' Then, 'Send for an ambulance, Holdsworth,' he barked, 'and tell them to get a move on!' Picking up a blanket, tenderly he covered the woman's attenuated body, a gesture of respect which Bill, standing next to him, found infinitely moving; typical of the kind hearted Inspector, although, he suspected, the poor woman was too far gone to appreciate that gesture.

Suddenly Frank Dawson entered the room and, uttering a low cry of anguish, approached the bed and lifted the unconscious woman into the circle of his arms, cradling her in a warm embrace: tears streaming down his face unchecked, 'Maman,' he whispered brokenly, 'thank God I've found you at last!'

'Maman?' Bill queried gently. 'You mean that this lady is your mother?'

Looking up bemusedly, Frank said hoarsely, 'Yes, she *is* my mother, Olga Redezky. Countess Olga Redezky!'

Twenty

Lights were still on at the Eyrie when Brambell, Bill, Holdsworth and Harmon returned, sadly in need of warmth and refreshment.

Trust Gerry to have kept the home fires burning, Bill thought gratefully, to have anticipated their need of hot food and coffee on their arrival, hence the chicken stew in the Aga and the flasks of brandy-laced coffee on the kitchen table.

'I don't think you've met Robin Holdsworth and Paul Harmon,' Bill said wearily, so dog-tired, cold and hungry that he could scarcely speak.

'I have now,' Gerry said cheerfully. 'Sit down, gentlemen, and welcome.' Weighing up the pros and cons in her usual astute fashion, she added, despite her gut feeling that something had gone badly wrong; with a swift glance in Maggie and Barney's direction, the realization that Jenny would be in the hall with her husband, pro-tem, and they would put in their appearance sooner or later, she asked, 'Where's Frank Dawson, by the way?'

'On his way to the Royal London Hospital,' Bill explained briefly as Gerry lifted the chicken stew from the Aga, Maggie poured the steaming hot coffee, and Barney added a soupçon more brandy to the beverage.

'Hospital? But why? Has he been injured?' Gerry's heart sank like a stone.

Brambell and Jenny entered the room at that moment. Charles said quietly, taking command of the situation, 'No need to worry, Gerry love, Frank's fine. Wait for it! The great news is that his mother, Countess Olga Redezky, is still alive! Thank God we found her just in time.'

'The countess?' Gerry's heart lifted as suddenly as it had sunk. 'Still alive? Oh, thank God. Thank God!' Sinking down at the kitchen table and covering her face with her hands, Gerry wept tears of relief.

It was then that Maggie Bowler, engaged in ladling hot chicken stew, her dander up, asked the burning question, 'So, did you or didn't you catch that bugger Glencoffin? No, I thought as much! So 'e's still on the loose, ain't 'e? Mekkin' us lives a misery. Blowin' that bloody penny whistle of 'is wheniver 'e feels like it. Well, it just ain't good enough, if you arsks me!'

'You are right, Maggie, it isn't,' Brambell acknowledged wearily, 'unfortunately the place was empty apart from that poor woman, who may well have died had we not found her when we did. All we can hope is that she will recover, but it's by no means certain that she'll pull through. I'm sorry, Maggie, we did our best – and we'll continue to do so. My dearest wish is to see Glencochlin behind bars, where he belongs.' Grim-faced, he stopped speaking abruptly.

Jenny murmured consolingly, 'None of this is your fault. We're all tired out. Sit down, my dear, you look exhausted. Have some coffee, something to eat. I'm sure that Maggie didn't mean to speak so forcibly.' She cast a reproachful glance at Mrs Bowler who, realizing that her outburst had been mis-construed as a personal attack against a man she deeply admired, said, 'No, I didn't! I wasn't 'avin' a go at you, Inspector. Arsk Barney if you don't believe me. 'E's allus tellin' me this mouth of mine will land me in trubble sooner or later. Now it seems 'e were right, an' I'm sorry!'

Getting up from the table, Gerry said gently, 'That's all right, Maggie. I'll finish dishing out the stew. Meanwhile, you and

Barney had best go upstairs to bed, and try not to worry unduly. Sleep for as long as you've a mind to, and remember that I love you. We all do.'

'I can't think why,' Maggie murmured tearfully as Barney, placing a comforting arm about her, led her from the room.

This had been quite a day, one way and another, Gerry thought wearily when Jenny, Charles, Robin and Paul had departed to their respective homes, and she and Bill were alone together, surveying the wreckage of their so-called luncheon party.

'Oh, come on, love, let's leave all this till tomorrow, shall we?' she sighed, 'I couldn't wash another pot if you paid me! Just take me to bed, hold me close, and...'

'And – *what*?'

'Don't forget to switch off the alarm clock, that's all.'

'As if!' Bill chuckled.

'And just one more thing, if you don't mind. I know it sounds a bit soppy and sentimental, but I'd really like us to pray together for the countess's recovery.'

'Amen to that,' Bill said gently, switching off the alarm. 'You say the words, I'll hold your hands, as I did on our wedding day, remember?'

'Remember? Oh Bill darling, how could I possibly forget the happiest day of my life?'

No one put in an appearance until midday. At least everyone, apart from Gerry, had slept well; who, despite her tiredness, had kept on waking up to worry about the Countess Redezky and Frank Dawson.

Never in her wildest dreams had she imagined a mother and son relationship between them. It seemed so unlikely, so bizarre somehow. She could, however, well imagine Frank's feelings, keeping vigil at his mother's bedside, willing her to regain consciousness, awaiting the merest flicker of an eyelid, the slightest sign of movement indicative of her emergence from her present state of oblivion; some longed for miracle to prove that, somehow, the spark of life would not be extinguished: would not simply flicker and die like a blown out candle.

Her mind made up, when the clearing up had been done Gerry announced her intention to visit the Royal Hospital, as a matter of urgency, to stand by Frank Dawson in his time of need. She was anticipating a negative reaction to her plan but, of course, she might have known better.

'Let's all go, shall us?' Maggie replied prosaically. ''Appen the poor lad'll need a flask of 'ot coffee, a packet of sangwidges, a razor, a cake of soap, a towel an' a toothbrush. Well, stands ti reason, don't it? So don't let's just stand 'ere doin' nowt. The sooner we gets crackin', the better!'

'We'll go in my car,' Bill said, matter of factly, warming Gerry's heart with his smile of complete understanding. And so the party had set off to reassure Frank Dawson that he was not alone in his hour of need. A fact he registered gratefully, with outspread hands and tear-filled eyes when he saw, coming towards him, a contingent of friends, of well-wishers, bringing with them piping hot coffee laced with cognac, chicken and salad sandwiches, fresh fruit, mince pies and a shaving kit.

Blinking away the tears, 'You don't know how good it is to see you,' he said, attempting a smile as Maggie unearthed a china mug, a plate and a serviette from her shopping bag, exhorting him to sit down before he fell down and to get something to eat and drink inside him, fussing over him like a mother hen with one chick. Pouring and handing him a mug of coffee, 'Sup this fust,' she advised him, 'it'll mek you feel better, then tell us abaht yer ma. 'As she come rahnd yet, the pore lady?'

Trust Maggie, Gerry thought, to get her priorities right. Coffee first, questions and answers later; giving Frank time to collect his thoughts and regain his composure before engaging in painful conversation.

Finishing his coffee, he said, 'The doctors

are with her now. I have no idea of the outcome. I just feel so helpless, so useless. Waiting's the worst thing. Waiting and not knowing.'

Gerry murmured compassionately, 'We know, Frank dear. We understand, but you mustn't lose hope. After all, miracles *do* happen. Your being there when your mother needed you, proves that. Think about it, love. Think about one thing leading to another: a Boxing Day luncheon party leading to Dorothea Lazlo's recollection of Glencochlin's London hideaway, leading to discovery of the countess's predicament and your blessed reunion, and her being here, receiving the best of care and attention, with you close at hand, willing her to get better. You've come this far, please don't give up hope now. Promise?'

'Thanks, Gerry, I promise.'

At that moment the door of the countess's room opened, from which emerged two doctors and a ward sister, deep in conversation. Shakily, Frank Dawson rose to his feet, followed instinctively by Gerry, Bill, Maggie and Barney Bowler. The silence was intense. Bill laid a sustaining arm about Frank's shoulders, Gerry clasped hold of Frank's hand which she held tightly in hers, scarcely daring to breathe, heart pounding as the five of them stood together awaiting the doctors' verdict. Did the countess stand a chance of survival, or had her rescue come too late to rekindle that spark of life buried deep within her?

The senior doctor, a slightly built, elderly man, bearing a faint resemblance to Inspector Brambell, broke the silence. Nodding and smiling, he said quietly, 'We have every reason to believe that, in due course, our patient will make a full recovery. She has responded well to our treatment so far. She is, of course, still seriously ill and will remain so for some considerable time, but she is showing signs of consciousness, a faint awareness of her surroundings, which augurs well for her eventual return to normality. At the moment, we would describe her condition as serious, yet stable. I should warn you, however, that our present concern hinges upon her parlous physical condition, her state of near starvation, linked to signs of restraint which suggest that the poor lady had been subjected to imprisonment of some kind, against her will. In my capacity as a senior physician, this requires further investigation. Recourse to the law, if necessary.'

Frank Dawson said quietly, 'I am with Interpol. Rest assured that we are well aware who is responsible for my mother's mistreatment.'

'You are Countess Redezky's son?'

'By a former marriage,' Frank admitted

briefly in reply to the second doctor's question.

Gerry's heart went out to him. He was a proud and private man, and she knew that he was in no fit state to undergo questioning right now. What he needed was sleep, a warm bed, soft pillows, the peace and quietude of a darkened room, someone he trusted to remain here, in the hospital, to stand guard over the countess during his absence.

She said softly, 'Take my advice, love, get a bit of shut-eye. Bill will drive you to the Eyrie. There's a comfy bed awaiting you. Well, you did offer to stay with us, didn't you, until this wretched affair is over and done with?'

'Well yes. But it isn't over and done with yet,' he demurred, 'and no way could I leave my mother alone and unattended, after all she's been through.'

'You won't have to, Frank,' Gerry reassured him, 'for the simple reason that *I'll* be with her, at her bedside, holding her hand, taking the best possible care of her. You have my word on that!' She added wistfully, 'Of course, if you don't trust me.'

Frank said gratefully, 'I'd trust you with my life, Gerry! You and Bill!' Emotionally, worn out with worry and lack of sleep, he recalled the turret room in Glencochlin Castle, from which they had escaped due to her hefting of

302

her shoulder bag through the window to draw attention to their plight.

'Right. Then you'd best get going, hadn't you?' She clung to Bill momentarily, brushing aside Maggie's motherly concern for the state of her stomach, seeing as she hadn't had a bite to eat inside her, apart a slice of toast and marmalade, at midday.

'Not to worry, Maggie darling,' Gerry reassured her, 'there's bound to be a canteen: a coffee machine. I'll be fine, just fine!' She added, sotto-voce, 'I'm relying on you and Barney to take good care of Frank Dawson. You will, won't you, whilst I'm taking care of his mother?'

'I guess so,' Maggie conceded reluctantly, 'but wot if that Glencoffin fellah starts playin' 'is penny whistle in't middle o' the night?'

What indeed? Gerry wondered. But, of course, she knew that sooner or later she would answer that call: come face to face with her persecutor. But not now, not tonight. Quite soon, perhaps, but, God willing, not tonight.

Having showered and shaved, Frank Dawson had sunk into bed, falling fast asleep the moment his head touched the pillow, whereupon Bill, who had shown him to his room and lent him pyjamas and a dressing gown, had switched off the bedside lamp and gone downstairs to ring Charles Brambell. In need of *what* exactly?

303

Reassurance? Advice? He scarcely knew which. All he knew, for certain, was that he must get back to the hospital as soon as possible, to be with Gerry, harbouring a gut feeling that she may well be in danger of some kind. Certainly she would be in need of sustenance, food and drink, of moral support, someone to watch over her. That someone being himself – whom she had once dubbed her 'Guardian Angel'.

Answering his phonecall, Brambell asked astutely, 'What's up, Bill? What's wrong? I've been in touch with the hospital, so I'm au-fait with the countess's condition. The least I could do. The fact is, I've slept most of the day, when I should have been up and doing.' He added wistfully, 'Perhaps it's high time to hand in my resignation, to take an early retirement, to admit that I'm too old for my job.'

'Bollocks to that,' Bill said bluntly. 'For your information, Frank Dawson is now fast asleep in bed. A man much younger than yourself. Meanwhile, Gerry's alone at the Royal London Hospital, so to speak, and I'm worried sick about her. So when you've stopped feeling sorry for yourself, why not stir your stumps and meet me there as soon as possible?'

'Right, Bill. You can rely on me!' Suddenly galvanized into action, donning his raincoat and jamming his battered trilby firmly on his head, forgetful of his tiredness and all thoughts of retirement. When Jenny asked him where he was going, and why, he replied jauntily, 'To work, of course. Where else? Expect me when you see me.'

'But your supper's just about ready, and it's your favourite, beef stew and dumplings!'

'Sorry love,' he said breezily, kissing her cheek, 'gotta go now. I am, after all, a policeman, remember? Not Rip Van Winkle.'

Bill was in the reception area when Brambell arrived. He was clutching a bag containing flasks of hot coffee, packets of foil-wrapped sandwiches, plastic boxes of vol-au-vents, sausage rolls and similar delicacies left over from Boxing Day. In case her beloved Gerry came over faint all of a sudden, from starvation, Maggie had pronounced dramatically, adding to the bag a bottle of smelling salts, a cake of lavender scented soap, spray-on deodorant, a hair brush and comb and a discreetly wrapped parcel containing two pairs of clean knickers and a toilet roll, in the event of her needing to freshen up a little in the early hours of the morning.

'I'm so glad you're here,' Bill said warmly, shaking Brambell's hand. 'Gerry's with the countess at the moment. I figured we could go in together. She has no idea I'm here yet. She'll be as delighted to see you as I am.'

'You too, Bill, I daresay,' Brambell remarked drily.

'Aw, well, I reckon she guessed I'd turn up sooner or later,' Bill said awkwardly. 'Perhaps I'm being over protective, but I couldn't help worrying about her spending the night alone here. Well, not alone exactly, with people coming and going all the time: nurses, doctors, ward orderlies, cleaners and so on – men as well as women.' He shuddered slightly, 'Men in particular. Sorry, Charles, but I can't help feeling that Gerry is in danger of some kind.'

'Let's go and find out then, shall we?' Brambell responded grimly. 'You lead the way, I'll follow.'

A young police constable posted in the corridor outside the countess's sick room, sprang to attention on the appearance of the legendary 'Brambell of the Yard'.

'Anything to report, Constable?'

'No, sir. Nothing at all. Just the usual comings and goings.'

'Any sign of Mrs Bentine?'

'Yes, sir. She went into the room, to sit with the patient. She's been there ever since.'

Brambell tapped on the door before entering the room which, apart from the still figure of the countess on the narrow bed in front of him, was devoid of any other presence excepting his own, and Bill's. The chair beside the bed was empty. Gerry had disappeared.

***

Her assailant had entered the sick room by means of unguarded exit door leading to a service elevator, Gerry vaguely remembered, regaining consciousness. The sound of a throbbing engine and water lapping the sides of a motor launch of some kind. *Of some kind?* But despite her haziness and the cloying smell of chloroform in her nostrils, Gerry knew exactly to whom the launch belonged and why she was here, lying face down on a bunk, tied hand and foot and with a gob-stopper of masking tape covering her mouth.

How Glencochlin had managed to convey her from the hospital to his motor launch, she hadn't the faintest idea, but she could hazard a guess, via an ambulance parked in the hospital's rear yard, pushing a wheelchair, to all intents and purposes a white coated orderly conveying a seriously ill patient to another hospital. In reality, she imagined, to St Katharine Docks, close by Tower Hill, to wheel her aboard his motor launch, now, presumably, heading towards the Outer Hebrides?

Suddenly, unmistakably, she heard the sound of a penny whistle, blown close at hand, clearly audible above and beyond the throb of the engine and the slapping of waves against the sides of the launch: a nameless tune piped by a madman, whose

307

cryptic message, 'I'll whistle and you'll come to me' had once put the fear of God into her, sending her into a tailspin of despair. Following her discovery that Glencochlin, a man she loathed and detested with every fibre of her being, was still out there, somewhere, intent on the destruction of her happiness and peace of mind. As a means of revenge? If so, for what possible reason?

Now, here she was, bound and gagged, totally at the mercy of a deranged serial killer, yet, curiously, she was no longer afraid of him. Glencochlin was, after all, inescapably mad. She, on the other hand, was sane, disadvantaged at this moment in time, but with her mental faculties in good working order. Sooner or later, she figured, Glencochlin would be bound to release her from bondage, and when that happened, it would be entirely up to her to get the better of him. *How*, she hadn't the faintest idea. But she'd think of *something*.

Twenty-One

'They can't have gone far!' Brambell exploded. 'God Almighty, why didn't anyone tell me about that exit door? What a shambles. I'm sorry, Bill. This is *my* fault! Had I had my wits about me I'd have made damn sure of the security arrangements early this morning, instead of lying abed like a lump of wood: bloody useless old fool that I am!'

'I slept late too,' Bill reminded him. 'We all did, for the good and simple reason that we'd been up all night, so why punish yourself?' Checking first to see if the countess was OK, he quickly added, 'Hadn't we best take a look and find out where that exit door leads to?'

Marching across the room, beside himself with worry, Bill slammed open the exit door with a clenched fist and strode out into a corridor adjacent to a service elevator, leading, as he had suspected, to a rear car park on which were stationed several ambulances, so far unmanned, yet geared up to instantly attend the scene of an accident. The crews were closeted together in a canteen-cum-billiard hall close to the exit gates of the compound.

Impulsively Bill strode into the building and called out in a voice harsh with emotion, 'Please, may I have your attention? My wife has been abducted. Her life is in danger. If you have noticed anything unusual, suspicious, for God's sake tell me before it's too late!'

Silence had fallen on the room. All eyes were focused on Bill. The ambulance crews had stopped what they were doing: eating, playing billiards, throwing darts, drinking tea, laughing and talking, to stare at him bemusedly, uncertain what to make of this distraught stranger in their midst.

'All right, Bill. Take it easy. Let me have a word,' Brambell advised him sotto voce, laying a hand on his sleeve. 'Fair enough?'

Bill nodded. Brambell stepped forward. Producing his warrant card, 'I am Detective Chief Inspector Charles Brambell of Scotland Yard,' he announced decisively. 'What you have been told, is true. A Mrs Geraldine Bentine has been abducted from this hospital, and this is a police matter. So think carefully, and if any one of you has seen or noticed anything in the least suspicious within the past hour or so, I want to hear about it now. Is that perfectly clear?'

A muttering ensued, then one man spoke up. 'Well yes, as a matter of fact, I did notice a tall bloke I'd never seen before, an orderly, pushing a woman in a wheelchair across the compound, but I thought nowt of it at the time. Why should I? 'Cept I did wonder who the bloke was an' where he was going. You see, sir, orderlies ain't supposed to take charge of patients. That's our business, strictly speaking. I just figured that if he was a new member of staff, he wouldn't know that!'

'Did you speak to the man?' Brambell enquired anxiously.

'Well yes, sir, as a matter of fact, I did. I told him he'd better hop it back indoors or he'd land himself in trouble.'

'And what was his reply?'

'He said the old girl in the wheelchair was being transferred to another hospital and he was waiting for an ambulance from t'other hospital to pick her up. Spoke ever so polite, he did. Said he was ever so sorry, but he couldn't very well leave the old lady on her own, so he'd best stay with her till the ambulance arrived.'

'Then what happened?' Brambell insisted.

'Then I headed here for a bite to eat and a game of pool, an' thought no more about it. Later on, when I looked out of the window, the orderly and the woman in the wheelchair had gone, so I figured the ambulance had arrived to collect the old woman an' he'd gone back indoors to get on with his work.'

'And your name is?' Brambell pursued relentlessly.

'Dave Gaskell, but honest to God, sir, that's all I know! I ain't involved in no kidnapping.'

'Easy, son. I believe you, but think back. Was there an ambulance parked near the exit gates, apart from your own, I mean?'

Gaskell wrinkled his forehead, 'No sir, there wasn't. But come to think of it, there was a van, a delivery van which didn't ought to have been there.'

'Was there a name on the van?'

'Yes. Now let me think. Oh aye, it was a florist's van with a fancy name on the sides. "Garlands". Yes, that was it! I thought the driver must have gone into the hospital by the back entrance to deliver the flowers. He wouldn't be the first, nor the last, the dozy bugger. He should've used the tradesman's entrance round the corner.'

'Thank you kindly, Mr Gaskell,' Brambell said gratefully, 'you've been most helpful.' Then, signalling to Bill, 'Come on, laddie,' he muttered, 'we have a lead. I'll tell you about it later, but I'm fairly certain now what happened. Gerry was rendered unconscious, brought down here to the ambulance station in a wheelchair, then bundled into a florist's van and taken to some carefully worked out destination familiar to her abductor, Fergus Glencochlin. It *has* to be

Glencochlin!'

'No need to tell me that,' Bill thrust back at him impatiently. 'I wasn't born yesterday! You spoke of a lead. What lead?'

'The florist's van, laddie! A stolen vehicle, I shouldn't wonder, with the name, Garlands, painted on the sides. The sooner we find that van, abandoned now I daresay, having served its purpose, the sooner we'll narrow the search to a certain area. I'm about to alert all available forces to the discovery of that van. Trust me, Bill, I will do everything humanly possible to put paid to Glencochlin once and for all, to find Gerry and bring her back home to you unharmed.'

'I know, Charles,' Bill said mistily. 'Sorry I spoke so impatiently. Forgive me? I'm not thinking very clearly at the moment.'

'Then take my advice, go home, tell Frank Dawson and the Bowlers what has happened, and leave the rest to me. I'll keep you au fait with future developments. Right now, Bill, you're more of a hindrance than a help.' He grinned wryly, 'No offence meant.'

'None taken,' Bill assured him, clasping Brambell's hand. 'All I ask is, please find Gerry and bring her back to me. You see, Charles, my life would seem pointless without her.'

'Well, wot's been goin' on?' Maggie demanded on Bill's return to the Eyrie. 'I thought you was intendin' to stay wiv Gerry, so wot you doin' back 'ere?' Maggie turned away from the Aga to stare at him. 'Is summat up?'

'I'm afraid there is.' Bill sat down at the kitchen table, the picture of misery. 'Sit down, Maggie. You too, Barney. Please listen and try not to get too upset at what I'm about to tell you.' Knowing Maggie's volatile nature and fearing one of her outbursts, he waited until they were seated before dropping his bombshell. 'The fact is, Gerry's gone missing from the hospital.'

'*Gorn missin'?*' Maggie burst forth. 'So wot the 'ell are you doin' 'ere when you should be out lookin' for 'er?'

'Hush, Maggie.' Barney laid a restraining hand on his wife's arm. 'Let the lad have 'is say. If he ain't out lookin' for 'er, he must hev damn good reasons why not!'

'Thanks, Barney,' Bill murmured gratefully. 'I'm here because, quite frankly, I was hindering, not helping DCI Brambell who told me to clear off home, to tell you and Frank Dawson what had happened, and to let the police get on with their work.'

Later, as they all sat round the table, worrying and waiting for news, Maggie said fearfully, 'That bloody Glencoffin blew 'is damn penny whistle. Ah've dreaded this all along. Ah've lain awake nights listenin' for the sound of that blarsted whistle. Now the

314

bastard's got 'er where 'e wants 'er! Tekkin 'er back ter that bloody castle of 'is, I shouldn't wonder! Well, that's where the trubble started, ain't it?'

Bill felt startled, as if he'd received an unexpected kick in the rear; had glimpsed a ray of light at the end of a dark tunnel. Of course, Maggie was right! Why hadn't he thought of it? Glencochlin Castle! The laird's home territory with its maze of secret passageways, long gloomy corridors, twisting staircases, cold empty rooms, and that benighted boathouse of his. The *boathouse*! The *motor launch*!

The police might search London from now till Kingdom Come in the hope of finding Gerry and Glencochlin, Bill realized. Would they think of extending their search as far north as Scotland: begin to gauge the damn cheek, cunning and daring of the man in returning to that Gothic horror castle, from which he had recently made his escape in his vintage Bugatti motor car? Returning to it, perhaps, in that powerful sea-going launch of his?

Springing up from the table, 'Barney,' he said hoarsely, 'please will you go upstairs, wake up Frank Dawson, tell him what's happened? And will you, my dear, wonderful Maggie, make him a bite to eat? Meanwhile, I have an important phone call to make.'

'Huh?' Maggie stared at him in amazement. 'What's come over you all of a sudden?'

'Hope, Maggie,' Bill replied warmly. 'Thanks to you, I believe I know Gerry's present whereabouts. My belief is that she is aboard Glencochlin's motor launch – on her way to the Outer Hebrides!'

'To that rummy ould castle of his?'

'Precisely that, Maggie. It was your idea, remember? And I believe that you have hit the nail squarely on the head, as usual.'

'Well, fancy that!' Maggie glowed momentarily. 'But think on, if that bastard 'arms one 'air of Gerry's 'ead, I'll stuff 'is whistle dahn 'is wind pipe so far 'e'll end up sittin' on it!'

The waves were getting choppy, darkness had fallen, Gerry's mouth felt as dry as stale breadcrumbs and the ropes about her legs and wrists were cutting painfully into her flesh. Moreover her desire to spend a penny had become a matter of urgency uppermost in her mind. Soon, humiliatingly, she would have the misfortune to wet herself. How long, she wondered, before nature took its course and she ended up lying in a pool of her own urine?

Suddenly a dark shape descended the ladder into the cabin, and there was Glencochlin, bending over the bunk, looking down at her, his face illuminated by a hand-held paraffin lamp, revealing his wolfish smile, his expression of unholy joy that he had, at last, gained mastery over her.

'I have brought you food and water,' the laird said silkily, stripping off her masking tape gag and untying her bonds. 'Need I advise you to keep quiet? Escape is impossible! Unless, of course, you feel inclined to commit suicide by jumping overboard?'

'Look, Glencochlin,' Gerry said succinctly, 'all that I feel inclined to do right now is empty my bladder! OK? Well, don't just stand there, tell me where to go. Oh never mind, let me guess.'

He had expected her to show signs of fear, timidity, unsteadiness, a loss of circulation as a result of being tied up, wooziness from the chloroform. He had hoped she would beg for mercy, ask where he was taking her, and why.. She did neither, nor did she appear to be any the worse for his rough treatment of her.

Returning to the cabin, she sat down on the bunk and looked up at him. 'This has given me an idea for my new book,' she said coolly. 'Tell me, have you ever tried your hand at fiction? You should give it a whirl. Of course it requires hard work, concentration and a vivid imagination. Crime fiction in particular. Thinking up nasty ways to commit murder isn't easy, in my case, but I've come across a few humdingers lately, so my new book should go down a bomb with my publishers. What do you think?'

She added wickedly, 'Oh, leaving me so soon? What a pity, just when I felt I was getting to know you better.'

Then he was gone, locking the cabin door behind him leaving her in the dark. Whistling in the dark, pretending to be brave when, quite frankly, she felt scared stiff, was bloody exhausting, Gerry thought. Cold, tired and hungry, pulling up a blanket to drape round her shoulders, huddled on the bunk, she realized the gravity of her present situation. She had no doubt whatsoever that Glencochlin was taking her back to his castle, to put paid to her, she shouldn't wonder, dreading the thought of re-imprisonment within its walls. Alone, this time, and at the mercy of a madman. No Bill, no Frank Dawson to share her captivity, no DCI Brambell to come to her rescue.

She simply prayed that when her end came, she would face it courageously. To do otherwise was unthinkable. She was, after all, a Cockney born and bred. Besides which, she wasn't dead yet. Just dead tired ... Sliding down on the bunk, suddenly, blissfully, she fell fast asleep.

The florist's van had been discovered, abandoned, near St Katharine Docks, close to Tower Hill, near to Glencochlin's flat. It suggested Glencochlin's presence was somewhere in the Greater London area, to Brambell's way of thinking. Until, answering Bill's urgent phone message from the Eyrie, he was updated. 'Whatever gave you that idea?' Brambell demanded brusquely. 'Scotland, you say? *Whose* idea? Maggie Bowler's? She said *what*? Ye gods, Bill, she may well be right! I'll get onto it straight away. The river, of course. Why the hell didn't *I* think of that?' A pause, 'What? I would have sooner or later? Thanks, Bill, kind of you to say so, but I'm not so sure. If Maggie's right and I'm wrong, and I hope to God that she is right, I'll tender my resignation, take up gardening as a hobby, write my memoirs and, well never mind. You get the picture? Frankly, Bill, I'm just a clapped out ould "has been", and I know it!'

Bill said, 'Whether you want me there or not, I'm coming. No way can I stay here doing nothing. I'll drive Frank to the hospital to be with his mother, then make my way to the scene of activity, which is *where*, exactly?'

'The St Katharine Docks area. I should be there in half an hour.' Brambell sighed deeply, 'It's all a bit complicated. The season of the year, the time of night. There'll be officials on duty, of course. Bound to be; Port and Customs officials, not in the best of tempers, I dare say, in no mood for questioning, wishing they were safely at home with their families, and who can blame them?' He added wistfully, 'Tell me, Bill, have you ever been on night duty?'

'Only once,' Bill replied, 'seven nights in a row when my dad was in hospital, to relieve my mother who had been with him all day. He'd suffered a stroke, and he died holding my hand.' He paused momentarily. 'I'm just so glad I was there.'

Gerry awoke hazily to the realization that the launch had reached its destination – the boathouse at Castle Glencochlin – and the laird was standing over her, revolver in hand, telling her to get up and start walking. 'Where to?' she asked warily.

Glencochlin chuckled evilly, 'You'll find out soon enough.' Digging the revolver into her ribs, 'Remember the countess? How you overheard a conversation you were never meant to overhear? How you refused to accept that the death of Penny Douglas was not accidental, but murder? How you have thwarted and frustrated me at every turn, so far, you egotistical, clever-clever, holier than thou, overweight, plug-ugly bitch. You, with your airs and graces, your bravado, your string of bestselling crime novels, your bloody self-rightousness. Well, tell me how you are feeling right now, Mrs Bentine, knowing that your life is in *my* hands from now on?'

★ ★ ★

Never until his dying day, would Frank Dawson ever forget that magical moment when, regaining consciousness, his mother smiled at him and whispered his name.

'There's someone here I'd like you to meet,' he said tenderly. 'Her name is Maggie. She will stay with you for a while.'

The countess smiled faintly, pressed his hand, closed her eyes and drifted off to sleep.

Sitting down beside the bed, Maggie said nervously, 'Will you be gone long?'

'I don't know,' Frank replied quietly, 'impossible to say for certain. Before I leave, thank you for coming, and promise not to tire yourself: in other words, don't wait up for me.'

'Garn,' Maggie assured him. 'Ah'll be fine, jest fine! Barney's in the corridor wiv sangwidges, coffee an' such, an' ah've fixed up wi' Jenny Brambell ti stagger me shifts, ti mek sure yer ma'll be well tekken care of. So hop it! You do yer dooty, an' we'll do ours. OK?'

She added discerningly, 'Wrap up warm. It'll be freezin' up yonder in Bonnie Scotland.'

'How the hell did...' Frank began.

'I know where you was orf to?' Maggie finished the sentence for him. She chuckled softly, 'Well, never you mind. Let's just say I come from a long line of gipsy fortune tellers, an' me great granma, Gipsy Meggie, left me 'er crystallized ball!'

Twenty-Two

'No need to point that – thing at me,' Gerry said coolly, referring to Glencochlin's revolver. 'If you'd meant to shoot me, you'd have done so on the launch and bundled me overboard. But getting rid of me quickly, the way you did Ian Harker, isn't what you want, is it? Let me guess. You want me at your mercy: to hear me begging for mercy, pleading for my life. You'd enjoy that, wouldn't you? Well, it isn't going to happen. I wouldn't give you the satisfaction.'

'Let's wait and see, shall we?' His expression betraying his insanity, 'You may well end up pleading, not for your life, but a bullet through the brain to end your suffering. Now stop bragging and keep walking. I'll tell you when to stop.'

Keeping a stiff upper lip, 'Oh, not that turret room again?' Gerry protested. 'Not that ghastly staircase of yours with all those nymphs, satyrs, wall masks and cannibalistic jiggery pokery?'

She was taking a calculated risk, hoping against hope that if he lost control of his temper, she might well gain the upper hand, send him reeling backwards down the stairs and make a dash for freedom, as her resourceful alter ego, Virginia Vale would have done in a similar situation.

But she was not Virginia Vale, heroine of her bestselling crime novels, and fiction had no bearing whatever on the grim reality of her present dilemma, Gerry realized. No way could she write herself out of the mess she was in right now, in view of Glencochlin's chilling reply, 'No, not the turret room this time, Mrs Bentine, but the basement, or the cellars, if you prefer to think of them as such. You may stop walking now. Push open the door ahead of you and enter your future domain. Take care, the steps are steep and slippery.'

Gerry shuddered inwardly, fighting her dread of confined spaces as best she could: a windowless cell, a hard bunk, damp bedding – with her luck, no bedding at all. The atmosphere stank of dampness and decay. The stone walls encompassing the steps were moss covered, dripping moisture. Glencochlin was behind her, still holding his revolver with one hand, shining a torch with the other, the torchlight revealing a narrow passage leading to what had once been the wine cellars, Gerry assumed, in the long gone days of her captor's forebears when, presumably, the castle would have been a focal point of the community, a source of employment: judging by the extent of its wine cellars, also a place of riotous living. Had the Glencochlin clan all been ne'er do wells? she wondered: engaged in nefarious activities. Perhaps smuggling, for instance, hence all the secret passages and the turret rooms, strategically placed to command uninterrupted views of the sea?

Gerry had come up against smuggling activities before, during the Antiques Murders: had witnessed the unloading of contraband, stolen works of art, and drugs worth a fortune, brought ashore from a vessel anchored in Robin Hood's Bay off the north east coast of Yorkshire, on which occasion she had also been held at gunpoint by her captors. But as frightening as that experience had been, her present situation seemed far worse, infinitely more dangerous, with little or no hope of escape from this underground warren of dark, dank passageways, at the mercy of a mentally deranged, cold blooded killer at whose hands she might well face both mental and physical forms of torture before he finally put paid to her.

With a low, mindless chuckle, 'Ah, here we are at last,' Glencochlin hissed triumphantly, shining his torch on a heavily bolted and barred wooden door, which he flung open to reveal a windowless interior, a bunk bed, a bucket and stool, a rough wooden crate on which reposed an enamel plate containing crusts of stale bread and mouldy cheese, an enamel water jug and mug, and an enamel candlestick with a half burnt out candle and a box of matches. 'As you can see, I have provided you with the necessities of life; food and drink, a bed and bedding, a means of illumination. So think yourself lucky, Mrs Bentine, and you may rest assured that I'll return later to make certain that you are well established in your new accommodation.'

So saying, thrusting Gerry forward into her cell and bolting and barring the door securely behind him, the laird turned back the way they had come, leaving Gerry alone in the dark.

Feeling her way forward, she found the bunk with her kneecaps, swore softly and sat down, clinging to the mental impression of her cell and its contents glimpsed briefly by torchlight when the laird had shoved her across the threshold.

Resisting the temptation to light the candle, she ascertained that there was a bunk – comprising a wafer thin mattress, a couple of equally inadequate blankets and one rock hard pillow – which stank of dampness and decay.

Thanking God for her suitable clothing, Gerry was relieved she'd been wearing a warm thick knit sweater, tweed skirt, anorak, fleece lined boots, a knitted cap, gloves and a muffler at the time of her abduction. She realized, thinking quickly, that her only hope of escape lay in outwitting her captor: that time was of the essence, a case of now or never.

Not that she had much going for her right now. But she was a writer, for God's sake, so she had best think up something damn quick, or suffer the consequences.

At that moment an old half forgotten, infant school song sprang to mind. 'Jesus bids us shine with a pure clear light: like a little candle burning in the night. In this world of darkness so let us shine. You in your small corner and I in mine'.

Wasting no time, Gerry rose quickly to her feet, lit the candle, and stuffed her pillow into the bucket which she perched atop the stool. Then, dragging a blanket from the bunk, she draped it about the shoulders of her 'dummy' to cover both the bucket and the stool.

Next, tying her woolly hat to the pillow with her muffler, she placed the enamel plate of mouldy food next to the dummy, with its back to the door.

Later, her heart thudding against her ribs as she heard the sound of Glencochlin's returning footsteps along the passageway outside her prison, taking off her anorak to drape about the dummy, she placed the candlestick near the enamel plate.

Now for it, she thought, Custer's Last Stand, edging into the darkness of the corner near the door, praying that her ploy would work. She hoped the laird's attention, on entering the cell, would focus on the candle, the dummy, and he would gain the impression of his captive spewing into the bucket: hopefully he would move forward for a closer inspection, at which juncture, with a modicum of good luck, she would slide from her hiding place, through the door which she would slam shut behind her, bar and bolt and get the hell out of Glencochlin Castle as fast as her legs could carry her.

Viewing the dummy, it looked quite realistic she thought. Standing stock still, scarcely daring to breathe, she reminded herself that if she managed, by some miracle, to make her escape from her prison, she would need her wits about her to bar and bolt the door behind her in total blackness. So she'd best have her wits about her.

Now the door was opening and Glencochlin was crossing the threshold, cursing under his breath as he did so, his eyes centred on the curious scene confronting him. His torch briefly illuminated the lock and key on the outside of the door and Gerry committed this to memory, knowing her life depended on turning that key before

Glencochlin realized what she was up to, which wouldn't take long, she figured, steeling herself for the most dangerous mission of her life. A do or die situation, she realized, depending on her own will and judgement to choose the precise moment to make her dash for freedom. Now that moment had come. Was here, was *now*.

'What the hell?' Glencochlin uttered as she brushed past him from her hiding place. Suddenly a shot rang out and Gerry clenched her teeth against the searing pain of a bullet wound in her left shoulder as, moving quickly towards the open door of her prison, she slammed it shut behind her and turned the massive key in its lock. Then she stumbled, in complete darkness, towards the flight of stairs leading to the boathouse: towards freedom. Pray God, towards freedom.

Cold, tired and hungry, aware of the seepage of blood from the bullet wound the laird had inflicted on her, at last, she reached the boathouse and emerged from darkness into the light of the world beyond the confines of her prison cell. Suddenly she heard, with an overwhelming feeling of joy and relief, the rotating blades of a helicopter about to land on the forecourt of Glencochlin Castle, and saw, coming towards her, three of the favourite men in her life – Charles Brambell, Frank Dawson, above all, her beloved Bill.

Lurching forward, arms outstretched to greet them, her strength suddenly gave out and she fought against a tidal wave of blackness that threatened to engulf her. All she clearly remembered before she fainted, was Bill's anguished cry of despair: 'Gerry's been shot! For Christ's sake. We must get her to hospital as quickly as possible!'

She came round to the realization that she was being stretchered aboard the helicopter, being told not to worry, that she was on her way to Stornoway Hospital to receive medical treatment. Bill was beside her, smoothing back her hair, whispering soft words of encouragement: telling her he loved her, advising her tenderly to save her strength, not to talk if she didn't feel up to it. Explanations could wait until later, he reminded her quietly. But Gerry knew otherwise.

Urgently clasping Bill's hand, she said hoarsely, 'About Glencochlin. He's in the wine cellars leading down from the boat-house. I managed to lock him in. Don't ask me how. That's when he winged me. Just a pot shot, that's all. Nothing to worry about. I'll be fine when I've been cleaned up a bit.'

She smiled disarmingly. 'The thing is, I want you to stay here with Charles and Frank. They'll need all the help they can get. Please, Bill, do as I ask. Know what? I've always thought of you, Charles and Frank as the Three Musketeers. One for all, all for one.'

'But I—' Bill protested, 'But what about *you*?' Torn between love and duty, in the event, Bill emerged from the helicopter seconds before it lifted skywards en route to Stornoway.

'What happened, Bill?' Brambell inquired anxiously as the helicopter disappeared from view.

Bill said wryly, 'Gerry happened! Need I say more?'

Frank led the way unerringly through the boathouse to the cellar steps. 'Careful,' he warned, switching on his torch, 'they're a tad slippery. Gerry managed to lock up Glen-cochlin, you say? How the hell did she achieve that, I wonder?'

They were destined soon to find out. The door of the cell stood open, the lock of which had been shot off by a well aimed bullet from the laird's revolver. Their quarry had vanished into thin air.

Crossing the threshold, Frank's torch beam picked up the dummy in the corner, the flickering candle, the plate of mouldy food, Gerry's scarf, hat and anorak, skilfully arranged to lure Glencochlin into the cell prior to her plucky bid for freedom.

'So *that's* how she did it,' Brambell said

gruffly, filled with admiration for Gerry's sheer courage in the face of the seemingly impossible odds stacked against her, slotting together the jigsaw pieces in his mind's eye to form a composite whole. He added gruffly, taking command of the situation, 'Right then, back the way we came. I'm calling in reinforcements. No way will Glencochlin escape justice this time.'

At Stornoway Hospital the doctor in charge of Emergencies told Gerry, 'You're a very lucky lady, Mrs Bentine. The bullet fired at you has caused extensive laceration, bruising and bleeding; it did not, however, enter your shoulder, so there's no bone damage in evidence. We shall of course take X-rays to make certain, and you will need a blood transfusion and morphine injections to deaden the pain.'

He smiled encouragingly. A nice, elderly man, grey haired, bespectacled, a comfortable kind of man, Gerry thought, a bit like DCI Brambell, a trustworthy man. And, truth to tell, she could do with a bit of tender loving care, a pint or two of blood, and a pain killing injection to ease the throbbing misery of her injuries. She wouldn't mind in the least spending time in bed, being cossetted and cared for, being fed three meals a day. Decent meals, not mouldy bread and cheese.

Suddenly, uncharacteristically, she began to cry, recalling the horror of her imprisonment in that cold, dank prison cell, the gut churning tension of her bid for freedom. 'I'm sorry, doctor,' she murmured, clasping his hand.

'Not to worry, m'dear,' he said patiently, 'tears are as necessary as rain, at times. Nothing to be ashamed of; a means of release. Not surprising, after all you've been through.'

A frisson of fear ran through Gerry. How the hell could this man, this doctor, possibly know what she'd been through? Unless he'd put her through it himself?

Daylight was fast fading from a leaden sky, rain was coming down furiously, scurried by a gale force wind blowing in from the sea. Gerry's Three Musketeers, badly in need of rest, shelter and sustenance, had no choice other than to remain within the crumbling confines of the castle overnight.

Frank Dawson, who knew Glencochlin Castle like the back of his hand, had assumed command of the situation. Leading the way to the kitchen, switching on lights, he raided the deep freeze for ready made meals: macaroni cheese, battered fish fillets and oven chips, then lighting the oven to render edible the inedible, he said drily, 'Not exactly haute cuisine but thank heaven for small mercies. We'd have fared badly without electricity and convenience food.'

Opening store cupboards and the refrigerator, Bill knew that Frank's positive attitude towards their present, far from pleasant or desirable incarceration in this draughty edifice was meant to mitigate, to some extent, his deep concern over Gerry's welfare. It was up to him, therefore, to respond to Frank's efforts on his behalf, as cheerfully as possible. Gerry would expect it of him, in her absence. He said brightly, determinedly, 'There's soup enough to float a battleship: tins, packets. Minestrone, mulligatawny, chicken noodle, cauliflower and Stilton. You name it. Plus tins of evaporated milk, jars of Nescafé: boxes of teabags, in the store cupboards.'

'Great. Good! How about the refrigerator?' Frank asked.

'The least said about that, the better!' Pulling a face, Bill closed the door firmly on its contents: rancid butter, bottles of sour milk, stale eggs, mouldy cheeses and chicken pieces, rotting vegetables and a maggoty pork pie.

'Thanks Bill, we catch the drift,' Frank phewed sympathetically, turning his attention to the oven to keep a wary eye on the macaroni cheese, the battered fish portions and the oven chips. 'Are you all right, Charles?' he added concernedly, as he turned away from the cooker.

'Huh?' Looking up from the writing pad on which he was scribbling with a kind of fierce concentration, impervious to his surroundings, 'Yes. I'm fine, thanks. Just working out tomorrow's plan of campaign. Those reinforcements I mentioned. I'm calling in Moncrieff and Murdoch, Sergeant Lansdale and his constables Mackie and MacKenzie, a team of sharpshooters and tracker dogs, as a matter of urgency. They should be here tomorrow.'

Frank said levelly, 'Assuming that Glencochlin is now on the run? But what if he isn't? What if he is holed up here, in the castle? Has he any means of transport apart from his launch? If not, hardly likely he'll go walkabout in this weather!'

'Frank's right,' Bill frowned. 'But he must eat, bathe and sleep, presumably. The man's a monster, but not superhuman.' A thought occurred, startling in its simplicity. 'The launch, of course! He could be well away by now. Hadn't we better find out?'

Frank smiled wickedly. 'No need, old chap! The launch is out of fuel! I took the precaution of draining the tank on our way to the cellar. We made our way through the boathouse, if you recall? Now, methinks, it's time for supper. The macaroni cheese should be done to a turn. So let's eat, shall we?'

'Mind if I join you? After all, that is *my*

food you are about to enjoy. This is *my* house, *my* kitchen.' The voice belonged to Fergus Glencochlin. He was leaning against the door, wearing his 'Count Dracula' get up and holding a revolver.

Frank said calmly, 'Sure thing. Take a pew. We've been expecting you.'

Had they? Bill wondered, keeping his mouth closed, his ears and eyes wide open, his glance falling on the notes Brambell had been writing so earnestly, and had slid over the table to him. His words, underlined, *'We are under surveillance.* Proceed with the utmost caution. Remember he's armed, therefore dangerous. Reinforcements in place, according to plan. The castle infiltrated and surrounded. My team fully alerted and ready for action. One shot fired from his revolver and the sharpshooters will move in on him like lightning to either disarm him or to put a bullet through his brain. All that we can possibly do now is to await the outcome.'

So the wily old fox had led the laird to believe that he'd allowed the grass to grow under his feet, which meant that Glencochlin must have access to closed circuit television and had been watching their every move, listening to every word they uttered, hence his appearance in the kitchen. To do what exactly? Bill asked himself wryly. Would he say 'Eeny, meeny, miny mo' to choose which of the three of them to shoot first? A vague idea occurred: a childhood game called 'Blind Man's Buff' ... A possibility? A shot in the dark? Worth a try? All they needed was *one* shot!

The Three Musketeers exchanged glances, each attempting to read the others' mind. Glencochlin chuckled evilly, 'What's the matter? Cat got your tongues?' Moving forward as he spoke, he approached the table slowly, savouring every moment of their discomfiture, his mastery of the situation, the weight of his revolver levelled against them.

Suddenly, Brambell sprawled forward, clutching his chest, eyes closed; apparently fighting for breath. A masterly performance. When Dawson rose to his feet to administer the kiss of life, Bill raced towards the door to switch off the lights.

'What the hell?' Glencochlin thundered, as the kitchen was plunged into darkness, and Bill called out, 'I'm behind you!'

Completely disorientated, spinning round, cursing violently, raising his revolver, Glencochlin fired a random shot in the dark.

And all they had needed was that one shot.

'Well done, Bill!'

In no mood for adulation, having witnessed the capture of Fergus Glencochlin, now on his way to a life behind bars, the only thing that mattered a damn to Bill was Gerry. A return to normal life, his wife beside him. He was a literary agent, for God's sake, not a hero. In any case, the glory belonged to Charles Brambell and Frank Dawson, not himself.

Twenty-Three

Homecoming had been a sheer delight. Helicopters, as a means of transport, had the train beaten any day of the week, Gerry decided as she gazed down at the familiar landmarks of her beloved London appearing through the mist of a bitterly cold January evening: the dome of St Paul's Cathedral, Tower Bridge, the Houses of Parliament, Old Father Thames rolling down to the sea.

The Musketeers and their D'Artagnan had boarded the helicopter on the forecourt of Stornoway Hospital to a cheery send off from doctors and nurses who had heard tell of the recent dramatic events at Glencochlin Castle, leading to the arrest of its owner on charges of murder, attempted murder, drug dealing and people trafficking. Well, who'd have thought it?

The nurses had clubbed together to buy Gerry a bouquet of spring flowers, daffodils, tulips and narcissi, and a Get Well card, which her personal physician, Doctor Duncan Burns, had presented to her on her somewhat shaky emergence from the elevator to the reception area, tenderly escorted by her tall, good looking husband.

'Think on, lassie, ye'll need tae take guid care of yeself for a wee while yet,' he advised her.

'I know. And I'm sorry I gave you such a hard time over the morphine injections. I'd got it into my head that you were an imposter, you see?'

'Aye, I kenned that when ye told me, in nae uncertain terms, where tae stick ma syringe, rolled off the trolley, an' made a dash for the door.' He chuckled reflectively, 'Had ye tekken the trouble tae ask how I knew what ye'd been through, I'd have explained that the helicopter pilot had given me an inkling.'

Bill said apologetically, 'My wife does tend to get carried away, at times.' He added, tongue in cheek, 'Did she make it to the door, by the way?'

'Nae, laddie!' Duncan burst out laughing. 'She got her feet taffled up in the loose strings of her hospital gown, skidded on a patch of wet lino, an' landed up in the arms of ma Emergency Ward assistant, who bundled her back on the trolley an' gave her a penny lecture on correct hospital procedure.' He continued merrily, 'I have tae say that I shall long treasure the memory of that particular incident. Not tae mention the pleasure I've derived from meeting, and treating this wonderful wife of yours.'

There had been a great deal of clearing up to do after the arrest of Glencochlin: masses of paperwork, reports, statements. questionnaires; precisely detailed orders issued and received. Nothing left to chance regarding correct police procedures in a full scale manhunt involving trained marksmen and dog handlers.

Not that Brambell minded. Realizing the importance of a watertight case against Glencochlin when his case came to trial, he assumed responsibility for each and every statement and questionnaire. Checking and double checking his facts, collecting every shred of evidence relevant to the capture of a master criminal. He recalled every facet of that arrest, the vital shot from the laird's revolver, his team of marksmen appearing to persuade the laird to relinquish his weapon, the laird's capture as he put up his hands and accompanied Brambell to a police vehicle parked on the forecourt of Castle Glencochlin. All this despite Brambell's longing to go home to his wife Jenny, to lashings of hot water, a home cooked meal, a warm, comfortable bed and a good night's sleep.

Now, gazing down on the old City of London wrapped in the haze of a cold winter evening, Brambell knew that the arrest of Glencochlin marked the end of his career, that Jenny was quite right in her belief that it was high time he retired from the job which had been his life, his raison d'etre for the past forty years.

Forty years? Was it really as long as that? And how would he fill the years of his retirement? Perhaps he'd write his memoirs? Grow roses? Give talks to women's luncheon clubs? Become a TV personality? Who knew? Who cared? All he cared about right now was holding Jenny in his arms once more.

As the helicopter hovered over London, Frank Dawson's thoughts centred on his mother, the amazing Countess Olga Redezky, a long standing member of Interpol whose dedication to that organization had imbued in him, from an early age, a strong desire to follow in her footsteps. He had studied hard at school to gain a scholarship to Queen's College, Oxford, where he finally obtained First Class Honours degrees in Modern Languages, French, German and Italian.

Not that she had encouraged him to follow in her footsteps. Law enforcement was not the glamorous occupation that some people imagined it to be. She might as well have saved her breath. His mother, happily married to his father, Don Dawson, at the time, was glamour personified: stunningly beautiful; tall and slender, with long ash-blonde hair, as intelligent as she was beautiful, adored by his father and himself, until came the shattering news that his father, also a member of Interpol, had been fatally wounded in leading a raid on the hideout of a gang of drugs smugglers. His dad had died instantaneously from a bullet, fired at close range, into his heart, which had, effectively, stilled his brave heartbeat forever. Thus hardening the young Frank Dawson's resolve to follow in his parents' footsteps as soon as possible; to join the crusade against lawlessness, as a matter of honour; to avenge the death of his beloved father.

Right now, all he longed for was a return to his mother's bedside, to sit beside her, to assure her, if possible, that the man he held responsible for the death of his father was now under arrest, disarmed, no longer a threat to her safety and peace of mind. The same applied to Gerry, he realized, bearing in mind Glencochlin's mad dislike of the writer.

'Are you all right, Frank?' Gerry asked, thinking how quiet he'd been throughout the journey, how strained and tired he looked.

He smiled, keeping his thoughts to himself. 'Yes, fine. A bit tired, that's all. Not to worry about me, how about you?'

'Nothing that a hot bath, a decent meal and a good night's sleep won't cure. When you've been to visit your mother, come round to the Eyrie. We'll leave sandwiches and coffee for you in the kitchen. Well, I guess this is it? Time to go our separate ways for the time being.' Her eyes filled with tears at the thought of parting company, however briefly, with her Musketeers.

The helicopter had landed on the car park adjacent to Scotland Yard, and the five of them, herself and Bill, Frank, Charles, and the helicopter pilot were standing on the tarmac, shivering slightly in the cool January air, spinning out their goodbyes, reluctant to end what they all regarded as an important, unique episode in their lives.

Charles said brusquely, hiding his emotion, 'High time you went home, young lady. As for you, son,' turning his attention to the pilot, 'come through to the canteen. It's late. Got anywhere to stay the night? No? In which case, forget about the canteen. You're coming home with me.'

'Thanks, Inspector, but strictly speaking I should keep an eye on my machine. There'd be hell to pay if it went missing.'

Brambell chuckled deeply. 'Tell me about it. I'd be the hellion in charge of the case.

Not to worry, I'll detail a couple of constables to keep an eye on it.'

And this was what he was used to, Charles thought happily, issuing orders and having them obeyed without question, so to hell with growing roses, writing his memoirs, and chatting up women's luncheon clubs. Time enough for that on his retirement – at some time in the dim and distant future but not *now*. Not quite yet. Not with Glencochlin's trial looming on the horizon, when he'd be called upon to give evidence as the senior law enforcement officer in charge of the investigation which had finally put the laird where he belonged, behind prison bars.

'Oh Bill, it's so good to be home!' Gerry gazed about her, savouring the experience. 'There were times when I thought I'd never see it again.'

He knew what she meant. He'd felt the same way. So far they hadn't talked about it. There hadn't been time, and now was not a good time, he realized, with Gerry still woozy from her spell in hospital. He said, 'Come on, love, to bed with you. How's your shoulder, by the way?'

'A bit sore,' she admitted, as Bill helped her upstairs to their room, undressed her and lifted her into bed, plumping up the pillows to cradle her damaged shoulder blade, inwardly cursing the man who had inflicted suffering on the woman he loved.

Keeping his thoughts to himself, 'Now, darling,' he said briskly, 'what do you fancy for supper?'

'Boiled eggs and "soldiers", please,' Gerry said blissfully. 'They've been on my mind all day. If the bread's stale, I'll have toasted soldiers. Oh, and what about my flowers?'

Bill grinned, 'I'll put them in water, bring them up so you can look at them.'

'And don't forget Frank's sandwiches and coffee. Have we anything to put in the sandwiches, by the way? And what if the bread's stale?'

'There's a loaf in the freezer,' Bill reminded her. 'It'll soon thaw out. And there's tinned salmon and tuna in the store cupboard.' He added grinning, 'Dinna fash yersel', lassie. I'll do my best tae gie satisfaction.'

He recalled suddenly that night of the Blind Man's Buff; rummaging through the laird's cupboards and that odiferous refrigerator of his which might well have been able to walk out of the kitchen unaided.

On his way downstairs to see to Gerry's supper, he paused awhile to ring the doctor's surgery, to book a home visit next morning, not wanting to run the risk of her injury turning 'sceptic' as she would have put it, in that tongue-in-cheek way of hers. He simply thanked God that they were home at last, free to get on with their lives, to pick up the pieces of that disastrous honeymoon venture which might, so easily, have ended in tragedy for himself and Gerry, as it had done for Penny Douglas, Sam MacNally, Sergeant Kirk, and Ian Harker, all of whom had been brutally murdered by, or at the behest of one man, Fergus Glencochlin.

Never till his dying day would Bill ever forget the expression of malice on Glencochlin's face, the look of sheer hatred, his curled back lips and flow of invective when faced with a team of marksmen, grim faced and purposeful, who had been alerted by the single shot from his own revolver. They had broken cover to convince the laird that to resist arrest was virtually useless, unless he had a death wish by means of a bullet through his brain.

Dramatically, the countdown had begun. Sixty seconds, fifty-nine, fifty-eight, -seven, -six, -five, -four, -three, -two, -one. With less than a second in hand, dropping his revolver, Glencochlin submitted to the inevitability of his arrest and was read his rights, before being led away, in handcuffs, to the prison van destined for a prison cell in Tarbert. Not that he had gone quietly. Far from. He had gone, cursing his captors, snapping and snarling like a caged beast, maintaining his innocence: swearing his revenge on the lot of them sooner or later.

Bill Bentine, who had occasioned the arrest of the laird by simply, forcing him to fire his revolver in that blacked-out kitchen at Castle Glencochlin, was now happy stuffing flowers into water, boiling eggs and making toast soldiers to gratify the simple needs of his beloved.

Meanwhile, holding his mother's hand, Frank said quietly, 'I came as soon as I could. How are you feeling, my darling?'

'Better. Much better. But how about you? You look so tired.' Tracing the outlines of his face with her fingertips, 'How like your father you are. The same eyes, the same smile, the same sense of duty. He was so proud of you, as I am. But what you need, right now, is rest. "Sleep to knit up the ravelled sleeve of care", as William Shakespeare so wisely put it. And so, my son, take my advice, go home, have a hot bath, a shave, a good hot meal, and a good night's sleep. Come back tomorrow.' She smiled up at him, 'Where are you staying, by the way?'

'At Hampstead, with friends of mine, Bill and Gerry Bentine.' But she wasn't listening, she had fallen fast asleep. And so, unclasping his hand from hers, smoothing back her hair, and kissing her cheek, he walked to reception, rang for a taxi, and arrived at the Eyrie to find Bill, in the kitchen, making coffee and sandwiches for him.

'Sorry to intrude,' he apologized. 'I let myself in. Have I come at an awkward moment?'

Stepping forward to shake Frank's hand Bill assured him, 'That you haven't. In the nick of time, as it happens. Don't know about you, but I'm so hungry I could eat a horse. All Gerry wanted was boiled eggs and soldiers. She's asleep now, the poor lass, worn out and in some considerable pain from her shoulder. The doctor will be here tomorrow morning, thank God. Now, how would you fancy a bit of a fry up? Bacon, eggs, sausages and chips?'

He grinned amiably, inordinately glad of Frank's company, a man he had come to regard as a brother, after all they had been through together since he had led himself and Gerry through the secret panel, into the comparative safety of the passageway leading to the boathouse.

'Yes, fine by me,' Frank responded warmly. 'Thanks, Bill. Anything I can do to help?'

'No. Just sit down before you fall down. How is the countess, by the way?'

'Better, much more lucid, but still very weak, physically speaking.' He added bitterly, 'Little wonder, since that bastard, Glencochlin, attempted to starve her to death. Know what I resent most, Bill? That he'll be fed three square meals a day, in prison. Whoever said that the meek shall inherit the earth, must have been short of a marble or two. Who was that, incidentally? William Shakespeare?'

'No,' Bill said, cracking eggs into the frying pan, 'someone in the bible.'

Dishing up the food, Bill said, 'We never did get round to eating that macaroni cheese, did we? After all the trouble you went to in cooking it. Did you know what Brambell was up to?'

'I had an inkling. I didn't know for certain until I saw what he'd written, warning us that we were under surveillance. I hadn't a clue that the marksmen were in the house. They must have moved like shadows. I didn't hear a sound.'

'Nor I, but there was a hell of a racket going on outdoors, what with the wind blowing a gale and the rain coming down in torrents. All very film noir. That castle gave me the creeps, to be honest. What will happen to it now, I wonder?'

'It will remain locked and shuttered, I imagine, till after the trial. It is, after all, the laird's property. It all depends on the verdict – Guilty or Not Guilty,' Frank spoke harshly. 'It is remotely possible that he'll emerge squeaky clean. I've known it happen before, given a clever barrister, lack of substantive evidence, unreliable witnesses, a plea of diminished responsibility.'

Bill looked stricken. 'Surely not! But that's

unthinkable.' Pushing aside his plate, rising to his feet, he said, 'Don't know about you but I could do with something stronger to drink than coffee. When you've finished eating, how about a nightcap?'

In the drawing room, Bill poured whisky and they sat near the fire to nurse their glasses and continue their conversation.

'We know that Glencochlin didn't kill Penny Douglas,' Frank said, staring into the flames of the simulated log fire, 'nor did he murder Sam MacNally or Sergeant Kirk. And there isn't a shred of evidence that he despatched Ian Harker from the deck of that fishing vessel, if that's what it was, since it has never been found.'

'But he did attempt to murder the countess and Gerry, and what about his drugs and people smuggling rackets?' Bill sighed, deeply disturbed that Glencochlin might somehow escape the full weight of the law on mere technicalities.

'Not to worry unduly,' Frank consoled him. 'We still have a few shots left in our locker. Now, if you don't mind. I think I'll hit the hay.'

When he had gone upstairs to his room, picking up the phone, Bill dialled the number of the hamburger joint. Maggie Bowler answered the call. No way could Bill have gone to bed without letting her know that he and Gerry were home once more.

Maggie said huskily, 'Thank God! I'll come round the first thing tomorrow mornin'. 'Appen you'll need an 'elpin' 'and.'

'Happen we will, Maggie,' Bill assured her, knowing he'd feel a lot better when she appeared on the scene to take charge of things in her own inimitable way.

Twenty-Four

Glencochlin had been transferred to London to await trial, alongside members of his gang: Tony Cannelli, Gloria and Arnold Crowther, and the Harkers – what Maggie termed, 'A right boiling of bastards.'

Meanwhile, life had assumed a modicum of normality for Bill and Gerry since their return home, despite the resurfacing of memories and emotions connected with events leading to Glencochlin's arrest, and Gerry's graphic accounts of her abduction from the countess's hospital room, her incarceration in that dark and lonely cell in the depths of Castle Glencochlin, from which she had managed to escape by the skin of her teeth.

'He meant to kill me, Bill,' she'd uttered

350

hoarsely, within the compass of his arms, 'because he told me so, and I believed him. I'd have been as dead as mutton now, if I hadn't dreamed up that dummy scam to lure him into the cell. Honest, Bill, I was scared shi ... witless!'

Bill knew the feeling. He also had been scared witless when, in the kitchen of Castle Glencochlin, he had made a dash to switch off the lights: calling out, 'I'm behind you,' for the specific purpose of coaxing a shot from the laird's revolver, risking the possibility of a bullet through the brain, the heart, or with his luck, a less lethal, more tender part of his anatomy.

He said consolingly, 'Not to worry, darling, we're home and dry now.'

The countess had received permission to leave hospital and Frank had found a private nursing home for her where she would be well looked after until she was well enough to return to her home in Poland: the ancestral home of her late husband, Count Ivan Redezky. Frank had explained, the count was a fine man who had regarded him as his own flesh and blood, the son he'd always longed for and never had until, late on in life, he had met and married Frank's mother, Olga. She had been blissfully happy until the count's death, five years ago, when she had continued her work with Interpol as a means of grief assuagement, leading to her near fatal involvement with Fergus Glencochlin.

'I tried to warn her, but she wouldn't listen,' Frank said briefly. 'She was, of course, deeply involved in the happenings at Castle Glencochlin. Can you imagine my feelings when the laird found out about her? I was there when he broke the news of what he called "a traitor in our midst" who must be got rid of.' Frank suppressed a shudder. 'My own mother, and I was powerless to help her.'

'Will she be called upon to give evidence at the trial?' Gerry asked.

'Yes, I'm afraid so, but I'll be with her. We'll need every scrap of evidence we can come up with.' He paused, frowning, 'If only we could tie his lairdship to the murder of Ian Harker. We've tried, believe me, we have a rough idea who owns the vessel in question. Moncrieff and Murdoch have done sterling work in that area, but to no avail. Moncrieff told me that getting information from a close-knit community of tight-lipped fisher folk is tantamount to prising open an oyster shell with a teaspoon. Questioned, they look blank and reply in their native Gaelic.' He sighed deeply, 'A no-win situation, I regret to say.'

They had been conversing in the drawing room, after supper, a meal prepared and served by Bill; enjoying a nightcap before bedtime. Glancing at his watch, swallowing his last mouthful of malt whisky, and getting up from his chair, Frank said huskily, 'I don't think I've ever thanked you properly for your hospitality, the way you've taken care of me these past few weeks, as if I were a member of the family.'

'You are, Frank,' Gerry said warmly, 'and you always will be.' She smiled, 'How does that poem go? "One man in a thousand, Solomon said, will stick more close than a brother, and it's worthwhile seeking him all your days if you find him before the other." Well, we have found you, thank God. This is your home now, to come and go as you please. No thanks necessary.' She added, in her usual forthright fashion, 'Well don't just stand there, go to bed, if you're going, before I start blubbing.'

She'd been blubbing a lot recently, Gerry realized, coming over emotional for no apparent reason. To do with being shot at, she reckoned.

The trial had been fixed for the second week in April. The media had gone to town on the story of Glencochlin and his involvement in drugs and people trafficking. And the fact that members of his organization, plus his manservant and housekeeper, would also appear in the dock at the Old Bailey, charged with murder, attempted murder, and abduction.

One enterprising newspaper editor had published a photograph of Glencochlin Castle under the banner headline: HOUSE OF HORROR. The story continued, 'It was here, in a crumbling castle perched on a rain and windswept promontory overlooking the sea on the Isle of Lewis, that Fergus Glencochlin masterminded his evil plans to sell human beings – men, women and children – into slavery, prostitution, despair, even death from lack of food, water and oxygen during their transportation, in appallingly inhuman conditions, to what they foresaw as freedom, a new life ahead of them. A promised land of opportunity, sadly unrealized as they fought for breath, for life itself, in sealed containers from which escape was impossible, in which survival was a miracle.'

His paper would be sued, of course, the editor surmised, but what the hell. It wouldn't be the first time, nor likely the last. Publish and be damned, was his motto. His baptismal name was Foo Ling Su. His pseudonym, Fred Ling, and he hated Glencochlin's guts, with good reason, recalling the recent, appalling loss of life on the sands of Morecambe Bay. The lives of his fellow countrymen: winkle pickers, honest, decent men and women, swept away and drowned when the tide had suddenly raced in on them to end even the meagre living they were trying to earn, before death claimed them.

'Not to worry, darling,' Bill said tenderly on the third day of the trial, helping Gerry out of the hatchback prior to their entry into the Old Bailey, understanding her reluctance to come face to face with Glencochlin again. 'Just remember that he can't harm us now. Not any longer.'

'But what if he's found not guilty?' Gerry demurred, feeling sick. 'It could happen, you know! There's no proven case of murder against him, is there?'

'No, but he's almost certain to end up behind bars for the foreseeable future, if you take into consideration his drugs and people trafficking, allied to your own and the countess's evidence of abduction,' Bill reminded her. 'Oh, come on, love, it will soon be over. Just stand in the witness box, tell the truth, the whole truth and nothing but the truth, and you'll be home and dry.'

'That's not what's bothering me,' she replied lugubriously.

'What, then?'

'My feet are killing me.'

'Huh? How come?'

'My boots are on the wrong feet, that's now come,' she hissed. 'I just figured that my old boots would be warm and comfortable. I bunged 'em on without looking! Now my hammer toe is where my bunion should be.'

'And so, Mrs Bentine, am I right in thinking that you earn your living as a writer of crime fiction?' Gerry was undergoing cross-examination, disliking intensely the man doing the questioning. He was a leering individual whose nonchalant stance, carelessly donned apparel, and lopsided wig, gave the impression of a university student in Rag Week, propping up a lamp-post after a session in a nearby public house.

Hot under the collar, Bill prayed that Gerry would answer the man's questions as briefly and concisely as possible: keeping her cool, not letting her tongue run away with her.

'Yes,' she replied woodenly.

'Yes, *what*? Mrs Bentine.'

'Yes, sir?' she enquired innocently.

Nonplussed, the QC continued, 'And am I right in supposing that you possess a vivid imagination?'

'Yes, sir.'

'To the extent of dreaming up your so-called abduction from a busy hospital ward?'

'No, sir.'

The barrister laughed unpleasantly, 'You really expect this court to believe that you went missing without anyone noticing or doing anything to assist you? Well, speak up,

Mrs Bentine. Can you give this court a reasonable explanation how you came to be abducted from a hospital ward under the circumstances aforementioned?'

'Yes, sir. I was in a private room, at the time, not a ward.' She added ingenuously, 'I don't mind waiting, if you need time to check your facts.'

Oh God, Bill thought, she's building up to it. Not that he could fault her demeanour so far, but the explosion was bound to come sooner or later, when she really crossed swords with her inquisitor.

'Very well, then, accepting the fact that you were in a private room, what happened next?'

'I was abducted.'

'So you say, but how can you be sure?'

'When I copped a faceful of chloroform, passed out, and came to aboard a motor launch heading towards the north east coast of Scotland.'

'I see. And what did you do about it?'

'Nothing.'

'*Nothing?* I find that hard to swallow. A feisty lady such as yourself? Did it not occur to you to call out? To try to escape?'

'Yes, sir, of course it did, but my hands and feet were bound, at the time, and I had a gobful of masking tape to contend with, so there wasn't much I could have done about it, was there?'

'You are here to answer questions, not to ask them.' The QC was rattled now, and it showed – to his detriment. Someone in the public gallery called out, 'Aw, come on, man, give the lass a break.'

'Silence in court,' the judge bellowed. The prisoners in the dock remained impassive, apart from Glencochlin whose expression betrayed a kind of impotent fury at his captivity, his deep-seated hatred of Gerry Bentine, above all the ineffectiveness of his barrister in allowing her to get the better of him. Now the jury was on her side, and had been ever since Gerry had asked him if he needed time to check his facts, at which juncture the fool had forfeited his credibility in the eyes of the jurors. Possibly also in the eyes of the judge?

Now the QC, Sir Archibald Trim, fazed yet determined, faced Gerry, and said coldly, 'Did you not claim that, aboard that motor launch, your so-called abductor released you from your bonds and offered you both food and water?'

'Yes, sir, he did,' Gerry admitted truthfully.

'And what was your response to his overture of friendliness?' Trim demanded.

'I told him my bladder was bursting, and I'd wet myself if I didn't spend a penny. Well, you did ask.'

Beginning to wish that he hadn't, Trim continued urbanely, 'And so, did you feel that a degree of intimacy had been established between yourself and your so-called captor?'

'Well no, not really, since he had his revolver pointed at me, at the time,' Gerry replied, 'and had threatened to kill me, which he damn near did, in the long run.'

'Oh come now, Mrs Bentine,' Trim suggested sneeringly, 'isn't that merely another figment of your overwrought imagination?'

Then came the explosion Bill had anticipated. 'No, sir, it bloody well isn't!' Gerry retorted, 'and I can prove it!' She added hoarsely, 'Would the court care to take a look at the bullet wound in my shoulder? As for you, sir, why not stand up straight for once in your life instead of lounging; and fix that lopsided wig of yours? You see, I happen to loathe and detest anything in the least crooked!'

The court erupted. People in the public gallery were cat-calling, laughing, applauding and cheering.

Excusing the witness; the judge retired to his private chambers, after calling a lunch recess above the din of the court room. He partook several cups of hot, strong coffee, before reading a missive, handed to him by the clerk of court, which placed a different aspect entirely on the Law versus Fergus Glencochlin. A witness who had come forward to substantiate the fact that Glencochlin had indeed murdered Ian Harker, having seen, with his own two eyes, the callous way in which the laird, grasping young Harker by the throat and ankles, had thrown him, from the deck of his fishing vessel, into the dark, icy cold waters beneath, to suffer death by drowning.

'I really blew it, didn't I?' Gerry reproached herself bitterly over a luncheon table in a restaurant adjacent to the Old Bailey. She was unable to touch a bite of the food set before her, in the company of Bill, Frank Dawson, and Charles and Jenny Brambell. 'Me and my big mouth!' She said fearfully, 'I may well end up in prison for contempt of court!'

'What? For telling the truth and shaming the devil?' Brambell chuckled deeply, 'Not to worry, m'dear, it won't come to that. Trust me, Gerry love. I have it on good authority that this trial is all over bar the shouting. Glencochlin is about to face a life sentence for the murder of Ian Harker.'

'You mean?' Gerry swallowed hard. 'You mean that DCI Moncrieff actually succeeded in prising open an oyster shell with a teaspoon?'

Frank grinned. 'Kinda looks that way, doesn't it?'

Epilogue

JUSTICE PREVAILS! ran the headline. Fred Ling had gone to town with his story. It continued: 'Events at the Old Bailey took a dramatic turn yesterday when fishing vessel owner, Saul MacDuff, entered the witness box to give evidence of murder against Fergus Glencochlin.'

This was Saturday. Bill had brought early morning tea and the newspaper to bed with him. He said, optimistically, 'Well, it's all over now, thank heaven!'

'No Bill, it isn't,' Gerry said bleakly. 'I keep on going over it in my mind, thinking it was all my fault. If I hadn't been so pig-headed about our honeymoon: wanting something different, communing with nature, camp fires and barbecues and all that nonsense, none of this would have happened. But no, I wanted everything my own way, as usual. And, well, there must have been times when you regretted marrying a selfish, fat, plain little cow like me! Wondering what you'd let yourself in for?'

'Gerry, my love, I knew exactly what I was letting myself in for when I asked you to marry me,' Bill reminded her. 'In case you've forgotten, we'd already been through one hair raising adventure together, the Antiques Murders, remember?'

'Yes, but that was a doddle compared with this.'

'A *doddle*? My darling girl, it was nothing of the kind. You damn near lost your life!'

'I know,' Gerry conceded, 'but I wasn't up against a psychopath then. Glencochlin threatened to kill me, and I knew he would enjoy doing so, taking his time about it, because he told me so, and I believed him.' She shuddered. 'But surely, shouldn't he be, not in prison, but an institution for the criminally insane?'

'That's up to the law to decide,' Bill reassured her, pushing aside the teatray and the newspaper and, holding her more closely, nestling beside her in the warmth of the space beneath the duvet.

'Tell me, darling,' he murmured, 'have you thought of having a baby one of these days?'

'Hmmm?' Drowsily, 'Yes. The second week in August, as a matter of fact.'

Startled, *'Huh?* What do you mean, the second week in August?'

'Whaddayou mean what do I mean? I've just said, haven't I?' Gerry opened her eyes. 'That's when it's due! Honestly, Bill, I wish you'd lie down and relax!'

In a transport of delight, fidgety to put it mildly, sitting bolt upright in bed, 'You mean that I am going to be a father?' Bill responded joyously. 'Why didn't you tell me sooner?'

Gerry smiled mysteriously, she said, contentedly, 'What? And risk your going into orbit sooner than necessary? No way!'

Bill said, 'Darling, you should be resting! Putting your feet up!'

'My feet *are* up!'

'Shouldn't we be telling people?'

'Put an announcement in *The Times*, you mean?'

'I don't know what I mean. Gerry, love, I just want to make you as happy as you've made me.'

'Hmmm,' she said reflectively, tongue in cheek, 'How about a second honeymoon?' Teasingly, 'I've heard that Siberia is quite cool at this time of year!'